THE DEVIL BETWEEN US

AN EPIC HISTORICAL TALE

A Novel by S.C. Wilson

Copyright © 2018 S.C. WILSON
Published by Backabity
Peru IN

All rights reserved. Without limiting the rights under copyright reserved above, no part of this publication may be reproduced, stored in or introduced into a database and retrieval system or transmitted in any form or any means (electronic, mechanical, photocopying, recording or otherwise) without the prior written permission of both the owner of copyright and the above publishers.

This is a work of fiction. Names, characters, businesses, places, events, locales, and incidents are either the products of the author's imagination or used in a fictitious manner. Any resemblance to actual persons, living or dead, or actual events is purely coincidental.

Cover design and formatting by Serendipity Formats
Map illustration by Michael Christopher
Title page image copyright © tmainiero
www.fotosearch.com

ISBN: 978-1-7323601-0-5

JODI MYERS

*This book definitely wouldn't exist without you.
Thank you for the endless hours.
Let's hope that fortune cookie was right.*

CHAPTER ONE

1864

The orange bands of early July sunlight kissed the tips of the towering pines in the foothills of northern California. A slight breeze blew at the base of Mount Perish, the cool air unsympathetic, continually assaulting her tall physique. Undaunted, she disregarded her trembling limbs and chattering teeth, focusing instead on bigger concerns than being chilled to the bone. The ground beneath her was damp and a metallic smell tickled her nose. She recognized it immediately—blood.

She was lean and strong; all muscle from years of hard work. Her short, strawberry-blonde hair looked as if it hadn't been combed in days, and she was dirty from head to toe. Still, the face hidden beneath was quite beautiful.

Struggling to sit up and make sense of her surroundings, she startled a nearby squirrel. The foothills teemed with wildlife, and the movement of this one small creature set off a chain reaction of motion. Branches shook. Loosened leaves danced to the ground as birds took flight and deer scattered.

She brushed away the pine needles embedded in her cheek as she took in the lay of the land. Evergreens lined the countryside; the atmosphere was thick with the scent of pine. Even in the dim light penetrating the dense canopy overhead, she could see the roaring river twisting its way through the trees. The water roared, thunderous in her ears. The rising fog reminded her of steam escaping a boiling kettle.

Her eyes landed on her friend standing sentinel nearby. He stood tall and muscular, light tan in color, with a mane as dark as midnight sky. She whistled softly through clenched teeth. Her faithful companion lifted his head and came to her.

"Good boy," she said, voice weak, barely above a whisper.

The horse lowered his head, allowing her to grab the reins. She staggered to her feet as he lifted his head. Lightheaded from blood loss, she wobbled like a newborn taking its first steps. Her body continued to shiver uncontrollably.

Gently, she raised her shirt to examine her injuries. A bullet hole bled on her right side. She grimaced, gingerly reaching to feel for the exit wound on her back. Her skin was wet and tacky from the steady stream oozing from each hole. It flowed relentlessly; she needed to cauterize them before she bled to death. Fire became her priority.

She stumbled toward some brush, hoping to gather enough wood to start a fire. Her strength waned. She grabbed the closest tree to stop herself from falling. Her attempt failed, and she slid down the rough trunk until her butt hit the ground. She cried out.

Reaching for a stick caused pain to shoot through her body, like a dull knife slicing her in half. She fought against the agony. She had to. The effort and movement increased her blood flow. As her small collection of pine needles and wood grew, so did the bright red flower pattern blooming across her shirt.

The tall evergreens spun before her. Everything became a blur. Dizzy, she lay on the ground.

Eyes closed.

Scared.

Willing the revolving world to stop.

Wheezing sounds now came with every breath, frightening

her even more. Simply maintaining control over her rising panic presented another challenge. She curled into a fetal position, pushing her fist tight against the growing stain on her shirt, hoping to stanch the flow of blood and ease the pain. She had dealt with physical suffering before, but nothing like this.

Her mind flashed on the rattlesnake that bit her when she was twelve. That had been a scratch, a splinter compared to what she felt now. The thought carried her to the events that brought her to this place in the woods. This place where she would surely die.

Dying at twenty-one would be a tragedy, but at least it would be an end to her heartache. She had endured more grief than most ever will, understood all too well how brutal and cruel life could be. She missed her family terribly, and often wondered how things might have been had evil not come into her world that day.

Not long before, she would have welcomed death. Now, everything had changed.

He needed her.

That was all the motivation she needed to survive, in spite of the mortal wound in her side. Flashing images and sounds took her further back in time. She desperately tried to hang on to the memories pouring through her fevered mind like sand slipping between fingers.

And then everything went black.

Unbeknownst to her, salvation had been riding just two-hundred yards away on a well-traveled road connecting two neighboring towns. The pair hurried along as if also concerned about life and death. She was too far hidden in the thick copse of pines to be seen by these passersby. If only she had made it back to the road hours earlier, she would have already been receiving the help she desperately needed. Instead, she had to fight for her own survival.

She heard her horse chomping on his bit, felt his soft nose nudging against her cheek. The sunlight made her squint. Disoriented, she struggled momentarily to recall how she ended up in this place, isolated and alone. She eased into a sitting position, fighting through the pain and against the darkness threatening to engulf her once more.

As her memory returned, so did the severity of her situation. She drew a burst of strength from this urgency, staggered to her feet and rifled through her saddlebag. She hissed in agony when she collapsed back to the ground. A flint rock gripped in her weak fist was the spoil of this small victory.

She removed the knife hanging on her hip. Her hands shook as she repeatedly struck the blade against the flint. Finally, she managed to land a spark on the pine needle tinder. Her blue lips quivered as she carefully blew life into the fire. She hurried. Giving in to unconsciousness was a luxury she could not afford.

After arranging the kindling, crisscrossing small twigs on the flame, a small amount of hope rekindled as the tiny fire sprung to life. She fed it more wood until satisfied with its size. She stared anxiously as it began to burn. A loud, popping spark darted skyward. She flinched.

Knowing better than to put a loaded pistol near fire, she pulled it from her holster and shot at a bush off in the distance. A shot rang out, and then another, followed by the clicking sound of an empty cylinder.

With her foot, she nudged a rock toward the edge of the fire and propped the gunpowder-free weapon on the makeshift support. Flames licked the barrel. Her heart pounded as the end of the barrel glowed red with heat. She wondered if she had the fortitude to do what needed to be done.

She knew she didn't have a choice.

She removed a lead ball from her pouch and put it in her mouth. With her tongue, she guided it between her teeth. She wiggled out of her buckskin coat, wrapped the sleeve around her hand, and reached for the heated gun.

Holding in a deep breath, she bit down hard on the round piece of lead, and jammed the scorching tip of the barrel on the open wound. Her teeth carved grooves in the lead as she clenched them harder.

The pain, stench, and sound of her sizzling skin filled her senses. She fell onto her side, landing with such force the bullet shot from her mouth when her face hit the dirt. She closed her eyes, thankful to release her grip on consciousness at last.

CHAPTER TWO

1853

Sarah Pratt was bent over a washtub, the ache in her back momentarily forgotten as she mulled over the list of supplies she needed to purchase on the trip to Granite Falls later that morning. An all too familiar spasm shot a wave of pain through her body. She gripped the tub, leaving her husband's shirt floating in the sudsy water. Pressing her fists firmly in the small of her back offered little respite.

Stretching, she glanced up at the clear and cloudless October sky. *Should be nice weather for the trip to town,* she thought as she absentmindedly swept away a stray strand of hair which was stuck to the side of her face. Eager to finish the chore, she plunged her hands back into the steaming water.

Just inside the cedar log house behind her, Sarah's eldest daughter, Jamie, poured water from a bucket into a cast iron pot which hung over the fire. She then stood with one hand resting on a cool stone, sunk deep in the mortar of the large fireplace, and the other on her hip as she waited on the water to heat. Jamie glanced repeatedly at the ornate clock sitting atop the hand-hewn mantle—the one possession her mother was protective of.

Along with her mother's gentle nature and soft-spoken ways, Jamie was also gifted with the same wispy, blonde hair. Truth be told, the two looked more like sisters than mother and daughter, and on more than one occasion they had been mistaken as such. Even though she was only sixteen, Jamie Pratt was fast becoming a beautiful woman.

The grin that had been playing at the corners of Jamie's mouth grew into a true smile. The approaching trip to town was the reason for her joy; more specifically, their stop at Carlson's General Store.

Jacob worked there and she liked him—a lot.

Jamie had no misconceptions. She knew the handsome eighteen year old could have his pick of any girl he might want to court, and yet, she had the impression he was fond of her too. At least, she hoped so.

Any time her family made a trip to town, he made it a point to stop what he was doing and spend a few minutes talking to her. She also noticed no matter what they bought, he took the time to walk the purchases out and load them into the wagon. It was unnecessary, but she was grateful for any extra time she got to spend with him. Their exchanges over the last three years were always brief. Even so, these interactions managed to make her blush and tickle her stomach.

Sarah's youngest boy, Toby, was busy mucking out the stalls inside the barn. It was by far one of his least favorite chores, but on that day he didn't seem to mind. He worked quickly as his calloused hands deftly swung the pitchfork, for this was no ordinary day for him. It would be the first time he was allowed to drive the wagon into town for supplies.

At thirteen, Toby was of slight build. Much to his dismay, he still hadn't had a growth spurt. What he considered to be muscles his younger sister teasingly called 'kneecaps on a sparrow'. The remark would send him into a sullen rage, even though he knew it was true. He would sometimes wander off somewhere secluded to sulk about his stature, until his older brother, Daniel, would find him.

Daniel was Sarah's eldest child. By seventeen, he had grown

into a tall, responsible young man. Toby's strongest desire was to be just like him. This wish dominated Toby's thoughts as he continued to swing the pitchfork, ignoring the bits of manure-caked straw sticking to his sweaty arms.

Sarah's youngest, Jessica, walked the well-worn path from the stream to the house as fast as her short legs would carry her. She made her way at a steady pace, her cheeks flushed from effort, as her strawberry-blonde hair bounced against her head. She swore she had already made a hundred trips back and forth, hauling bucket after bucket. Jessica was more than ready to be done with this chore.

During the morning meal, Jessica's father had given her a choice: go to town with her mother, or go fishing by herself. She had jumped up out of her chair, thrilled to have a say for once. It would be the first time in her life that her father trusted her to go anywhere unsupervised. He was finally seeing her as old enough to do things without constant supervision. If she could make it through the day without any problems, her parents would trust her more in the future and she would no longer have to beg for her freedom.

For Jessica, it wasn't always bad being the youngest. At ten, her life was happy and carefree. She felt safe knowing someone was always looking after her. Best of all, in the little girl's world, she was still small enough to sit on her father's lap. She adored those times the most. Some evenings they did nothing more than talk about their day. On others, he would read to her until she fell asleep in his arms.

While being the youngest could be a good thing, today being old enough was the greatest. Before, Toby would have to go with her. She liked having him around, but she was eager to test out her newfound independence.

Jessica spent most of her time with Toby. As soon as their

chores were done, the two would set off on some new adventure. More times than not, their mother would have to holler at them repeatedly to wash up and come in to eat. This would earn them a stern talking to by their father during the meal, but Jessica could tell by the set of his mouth his heart was never truly in his reprimands.

Lately, Toby had begun to distance himself from Jessica. The growing teenager felt too mature to be playing with his little sister as much. He was more interested in spending time with Daniel, whom he idolized and constantly tried to emulate.

Two days ago, Jessica had been sitting up in the large oak tree next to the barn, watching as Toby unknowingly walked right underneath her perch. Before she could say anything, Toby started talking aloud to himself in a voice she had never heard. He was trying to get his voice to sound deep, like Daniel's. To Jessica, he sounded like a broken goose. She covered her mouth in a vain attempt to contain her laughter. Still, she laughed so hard she almost fell out of the tree. She noticed something else last night after supper. Daniel always used his fingers to rub the day-old growth of hair on his chin whenever he was deep in thought. Toby now did the same thing, even though the only things on his chin were a few bright-red pimples. Toby had a long way to go before he would ever be like Daniel, as far as Jessica was concerned.

Jessica and Toby had many of the same personality traits and interests, but that's where their similarities ended. They looked nothing alike. She didn't look like Daniel or Jamie either. The one thing that set Jessica apart was her hair, beautiful and strawberry-blonde. She was the only child to have inherited their father's hair color. He always called her "Berry." It made her feel special because he didn't have nicknames for any of her siblings.

Jessica carried the bucket into the house and set it down next to

Jamie. Her sister stared at the mantel with a distant look in her eyes. *Hmm*, Jessica mused to herself. Never one to resist an opportunity, she took advantage of her sister's distraction.

"Boo!" she yelled, grabbing Jamie by the waist.

Jamie leapt into the air. "Don't do that. You know I hate it."

"I know," Jessica said, laughing. "I just had to. Got you real good this time."

"Yes, you did. You should feel my heart beating. One day you are going to scare me to death."

"Sheesh. Don't be so dramatic. Getting scared is good for you. Keeps you on your toes. You need more water?" Jessica asked, still chuckling.

"No, this should do it. You're really going to stay home?"

"Heck yeah. I hear the fish calling my name. Can you hear 'em?"

"Don't be silly. You do know you upset Mother, don't you?"

"What did I do?" Jessica asked, her green eyes flashing with a hint of indignation.

Jamie put her hand on Jessica's shoulder. "She doesn't want you to stay here by yourself. Why don't you just go with us?"

"I don't want to. But try and talk her into bringing me home a piece of candy."

"I'll try. And don't mess up today or you'll never get to stay home alone ever." Jamie gave her little sister her best wiser-than-you stare.

"I won't."

"And don't ruin that dress. There's not enough fabric for me to make another one."

"I know. I won't." Jessica walked over to the table. She stuffed her pockets with an apple and a chunk of bread her mother had wrapped in a rag for her.

While heading to the barn to get her fishing pole, Jessica thought of what Jamie had said. Overwhelmed by a sudden desire to thank her mother, she turned and headed back to where her mother was hanging clothes to dry. Jessica wanted to thank her father again, but he and Daniel had already left to go hunting. She would have to thank him later.

"Got my chores done. Thanks for letting me go fishing, and you don't have to worry. I'll be careful," Jessica said as she approached her mother from behind.

"Oh!" Sarah said with a slight tremble in her voice. "You startled me. Did you get the food off the table?"

"Yes, ma'am."

"Are you sure you don't want to go with me? I'd feel a lot better knowing you weren't going out there by yourself. You know how dangerous it can be."

Jessica stood and listened to the cautions she knew by heart. She and Toby had been lectured many times about the dangers of the Devil's Fork River: how swift the current was, how it swallowed anything that entered, and how they must only fish in the small inlet leading off of it.

Jessica knew it was impossible to catch fish in that river anyway because she had seen Toby try it once. The current was too strong, and it had snagged his line as soon as he had tossed it in. She had watched in horror as Toby jumped onto one of the boulders close to the bank to free it. She'd been furious. They both knew the rules. Toby had begged her not to tell a soul, and he had even made her pinky swear, the most sacred promise a ten-year-old could make.

Jessica continued listening to the speech she could have made herself. She shifted her weight from one foot to the other, annoyed at the delay and repetition.

Jessica crossed her arms in front of her chest. "I'm not a baby," she said. "I'm ten years old."

Wringing out another piece of clothing, Sarah continued. "I don't care if you're thirty. You will always be my baby."

"I'll stay away from the river. Promise. So don't worry."

"That's what mothers do. You'll understand that when you grow up, get married, and have children of your own."

"I'm never getting married. Boys are disgusting," Jessica said, wrinkling her nose.

Sarah smiled down at her daughter. "I think someday you will probably change your mind."

"No, I won't!" She pinched her lips together.

"Well," Sarah said, "let's not argue about boys. I'm sure we'll have plenty of discussions about them when you're older. You be careful today. I don't know what I'd do if something ever happened to you. Maybe you should come with—"

"Nothing is going to happen," Jessica interrupted, sensing her opportunity slipping away. It was time to go before her mother changed her mind. "I'll be all right."

"Oh, very well," Sarah said. She gently took hold of Jessica's chin, tilting her head back so that she could look directly into the young girl's eyes. "You don't put so much as a toe into that river. Is that understood?"

"I won't, Mama," she said, practically bouncing with excitement. "I promise."

"I mean it," Sarah said, reiterating her words as she leaned down and kissed Jessica's upturned cheek.

Jessica hugged her mother's aproned waist tightly in an unusual outpouring of affection before turning and running toward the barn.

She heard her mother yell. "Stay out of the water!"

"I will," she called over her shoulder as she waved a final goodbye.

CHAPTER THREE

Jessica saw Toby brushing the morning's dirt and manure from his arms. She couldn't resist the opportunity to tease him.

She sang, "One scoop, two scoops…"

Toby bent down as fast as he could and picked up a clod off of the ground.

"Makes Toby smell like poo—"

He hurled it at her, yelling, "You're so stupid!"

Jessica ducked, narrowly avoiding being hit by something firm and foul smelling. It soared past her head and hit the barn door with a thud.

"Ha! You missed me," she said, sticking out her tongue.

"You're such a pain in my—" Toby said but stopped himself. If his mother heard him, he'd get the switch. Today was going to be a great day. He wasn't going to let his little sister get him into trouble, not today.

Fishing pole in hand, Jessica hurried out of the barn, determined not to let anything delay her further. The fishing spot wasn't far, but would take her short legs half an hour to get there. It didn't matter to her how long it took, really. She loved the walk and had done it so many times with Toby she could do it in her sleep if she had to.

Jessica walked confidently, pole over her left shoulder, feeling as if she could conquer the world. In her other hand she carried a stout stick she found along the way. She swung it through the air, fighting off hidden enemies as she continued.

The woods were blanketed in colors. The vibrant scarlet, honey, and ginger hues enhanced the red in her hair, as it gleamed in the bright morning sun. Many of the trees were already losing their leaves, carpeting her path in beautiful autumn foliage. She might have been old enough to gain temporary independence, but wasn't too old to enjoy kicking the small piles of leaves into the air as she made her way along.

Rounding a small bend, she came upon what she considered to be the finest fishing hole in the world. She didn't actually have any experience with other fishing holes, as this was the only place she had ever fished. This spot probably wouldn't seem great to anyone else, but through the eyes of this ten-year-old girl, it was magical.

Jessica turned over several rocks, grabbing any worms she spotted before they could burrow back into the ground. She held half a dozen captive on a curved piece of elm bark. She settled onto her favorite rock situated between the Devil's Fork and the small cove she considered her own, and then baited her hook.

She studied the worm as it squirmed on the sharp tip of her hook. *I'd rather kiss this worm than kiss a boy.* Jessica was still bewildered that her mom would think she would ever fall in love with a boy let alone marry one.

With her line in the water, she sat listening to the crashing water of the nearby river. The sound calmed her. She'd once been so relaxed she had fallen asleep, only to be jerked awake by the sound of Toby yelling, "You got one!" It had been a trick, as it was her brother tugging on her line. She usually liked having him around. At times like that, though, she had to fight the urge to push him in.

Her mind drifted back to her conversation with her mother. She usually jumped at the chance to go to town, but not this time. Her father had made her a new cane fishing pole and she had been eager to try it out. Besides, she thought, *what girl would want to go to town when they can go fishing*. At her age, there wasn't much she could do to contribute to the family. When it came to fishing, though, she was the best.

Sitting there, she came to the conclusion that her mother was just going to have to accept the fact that she was growing up. She was only ten, but she could take care herself.

Toby got the horse and wagon headed toward Granite Falls with a smart snap of the reins. His sister, Jamie, sat in the back on an old, folded up quilt, and his mother sat on the wooden seat beside him. For Toby, too, this was one of the best days ever. Usually when they went to town, he was stuck riding in the back with the girls. On the rare occasion their father couldn't escort their mother to town, the job had always fallen to Daniel. Finally, Toby felt like the man in charge. He was proud his father had finally trusted him with the responsibility.

There was rarely any trouble in town. Even so, Toby had brought his rifle with him so he was prepared. He was very good with a gun and had already made several successful hunting trips with his father and brother.

Toby pulled up to the hitching post and helped his mother and sister down. The serene little town was a hotbed of activity on that fall day, and he watched the people walking the streets, their booted feet kicking up dust as they hurried along. Toby tried to stand taller than his thirteen years, chest puffed out with pride while he waited next to the horses.

Mr. Carlson greeted the women as soon as they entered the store. "Good morning Mrs. Pratt, Miss Jamie. Jacob is out back unloading some feed." He winked at Jamie.

Smiling, Jamie thanked Mr. Carlson before practically skipping her way toward the back of the store.

Sarah went about collecting the things she needed. She took her time, remembering being young and in love; how her heart used to feel like it was bursting out of her chest when she saw James. Her smile widened at the thought. Sarah truly couldn't think of a nicer young man for her daughter. Jacob was nice-looking, polite, and financially secure. His family owned Carlson's. If things worked out the way she hoped, she wouldn't have to worry about the young couple struggling to put food on the table.

Standing in the back doorway of the store, Jamie called out, "Hi Jacob."

"Jamie!" Jacob said. He beamed as he dropped the feedbag off his shoulder. "How are you today?" He brushed the dust off his shirt as he made his way over to her.

"I'm fine. And you?" Jamie's cheeks turned a bright shade of red as she wiped a few remnants of grain from his shoulder, enjoying the feel of him beneath her fingertips.

"Much better now that I get to see you. I was hoping you'd be in today. There's something I've been wanting to ask you. Been wanting to ask for a long time. Just not sure how to say it."

Jamie's heart beat like a drum. It thumped so loud in her ears she thought for certain Jacob could hear it too. The day she had dreamed about for so long was here. At least, she hoped it was. She swallowed the lump in her throat. "Mother always says if you have something to say, just go on and say it." Jamie held her breath.

"I don't know if you are aware of it," Jacob said and then cleared his throat as he searched for the right words, "I like you. I like you a lot. I'm not sure how you feel about me, but I would like to spend more time with you. Get to know you better."

"Oh, Jacob, I would like that very much," she said, trying her best not to sound like an anxious schoolgirl.

Jacob's smile widened. "I'd like to come by your house this

evening and have a talk with your father. Do you think he will give us his blessing?"

"I think he will. I heard him tell Mother once he thought you were a fine young man."

"Well, will he still feel the same when I tell him I want to start courting his daughter? I know how protective fathers can be."

"I think he will give us his blessing. Father is a kind man. I can't think of any reason why he wouldn't approve of us."

"I'll be out at your place this evening as soon as I get my work done," he said. Looking past Jamie, he saw Sarah standing at the counter. "It looks like your mother is ready to go. Let me walk you in."

Jamie whispered, "And don't be scared of Father. I think he will be happy for us."

Jacob walked up to the counter. "Hello, Mrs. Pratt. Let me load your things for you."

"That really isn't necessary, Jacob. I didn't buy much today and we can manage," Sarah said, motioning through the large plate glass window for Toby to come inside. "Besides, I'm sure you have more important things to do."

"It's always my pleasure to help," Jacob said. He grabbed the two largest bundles from the counter and headed toward the door. Jamie watched his broad back and shoulders as he met Toby in the doorway and handed off a sack of dried beans. She grabbed the bag of coffee and hurried outside to join them, leaving her mother standing at the counter.

"Mrs. Pratt, can I help you with anything else?" asked Mr. Carlson.

"No, I think I...oh, can I get four of those?" Sarah asked, pointing to a glass jar on the shelf behind him.

Mr. Carlson dropped four of the sweets into a small paper bag. "Will that be all?"

"Yes, and thank you." She smiled, sliding the bag into her dress pocket. "You have a blessed day."

"You too, ma'am," he said as he made his way toward the back of the store.

Jacob tipped his hat to Sarah as he passed her on his way back to finish unloading the feed.

A group of four very rough-looking men exited the Rowdy Rabbit Saloon down the street. So drunk they could barely stand, they whistled and jeered at several women passing by. The obvious leader of the group stumbled his way toward Carlson's store with his cronies following closely behind. His gaze immediately locked onto Sarah Pratt, who was helping Toby and Jamie arrange their purchases in the wagon. He walked up next to them, and tried to take a sack of flour from Sarah's hands.

"Here," he said, noisily spitting tobacco juice into the street, "let me help ya with that." A trail of brown spit rolled down his chin, which he carelessly wiped on the sleeve of his shirt.

"No," Sarah said, trying her best to hide her disgust. "We can manage, but thank you just the same."

"Aw come on now. Don't be like that. Name's Jake. What's yours?"

"Uh...Sarah," she said, reluctantly.

"Well, that's a pretty name. Matches the face," Jake said and then snorted.

"We're in a hurry. I told my husband we wouldn't be gone long."

He released a long, slow belch. "Husband. Well, that's one lucky som' bitch," he finished with a hiccup and a pained look on his face.

"Look, we don't want any trouble. We just need to be on our way."

"Don't have to run off. I know a place where we can go. Just you and me." He gave her a wink.

"Jamie, get in the back. Toby, untie the reins. Look mister, I don't mean to be rude, but we have to be on our way." Sarah tried her best to remain calm as she climbed up on the seat and placed Toby's rifle on her lap.

"Well, hurry on home! Wouldn't want that husband to worry," Jake said with a hiss. He used a fat finger to flick the brim of his hat.

One of the men, a skinny blond, approached the wagon. He brazenly lifted a strand of Jamie's hair, letting it play loosely through his dirt-encrusted fingers. The act was made even more offensive by his crooked, tobacco-stained teeth, flashing yellow and brown through a malicious grin.

Jamie was overwhelmed by the foul stench of his breath. Unable to hide her disgust, she pulled away, shoving his hand aside. Those beady eyes narrowed even further, and his cheeks flushed an angry shade of crimson at having been rebuffed so publicly.

"You rude bitch!" he shouted as the wagon pulled away.
Toby's heart raced. He snapped the reins, the wheels kicking up clouds of dust as they sped away. Looking over his shoulder, he was relieved to see how quickly he'd put distance between them and the men standing in front of Carlson's.

"Slow it down," Sarah said, her voice quiet yet commanding. She gently held Toby's shaking hands, preventing him from snapping the reins again.

Toby's lip trembled and his heart pounded as the wagon rolled out of Granite Falls.

CHAPTER FOUR

After the discovery in Sutter's Mill, news of gold spread across the country like wildfire. People flocked to the area via the Oregon and California Trails. The Pratt family was one of many who made the journey west in search of a better life.

The exponential population growth brought prosperity to the towns of the region. New roads branched off from the trails as new cities grew along these routes. One such road led to the town of Granite Falls.

James Pratt had found a promising parcel of land just outside the town. Standing in a natural clearing, he studied the slow-moving stream through the ponderosa pines, and an old, long-forgotten barn. Even though the structure was dilapidated, he sighed, contented. He looked beyond the roof of the barn to the towering presence of Mount Perish. Its summit rose majestically in the distance. James knew he was blessed to find such a beautiful place. He visualized bringing new life back to the barn, and more importantly, where he would build the new house for his family.

Mount Perish could be seen from hundreds of miles away. The largest peak in a long range of mountains, it inspired awe in all who gazed upon it. The mountain rose so high, crest disappearing into the clouds, it appeared to touch heaven. The statuesque mass was adorned by thousands of acres of untamed wilderness growing from its slopes. Areas of lush green vegetation provided shelter for a vast array of animals—grizzly bear, beaver, deer, and fox, to name a few. On the west face, glacier-polished granite crags formed enormous pinnacles. Projecting skyward, they gave a castle-like appearance.

The towering pines cast their shadows on a plethora of descending waterways cascading down the sides of the mountain. Some trickled, looking for the best route, polishing stones along the way. Others would jet and spit off of the face of the sheer granite walls, screaming to be let off the mountain.

Three massive waterways ran down the mountain's east face, converging into Devil's Fork River. This vast, fast-moving current was named because of the pitchfork shape it made just above the convergence. Thousands of gallons poured into the river there, creating a waterfall of epic proportions. Devil's Fork was hundreds of miles long, its downward flowing twists and turns creating numerous white water rapids.

A portion of the river surged at the wide-ranging base of Mount Perish, separating the mountain from the three towns nestled in its foothills. It provided a natural protective barrier for the mammoth mountain. The ferocity of the rushing water was enough to deter most from attempting to cross. Those foolish enough to try would find themselves overcome by the deluge or risk having their bones snapped, mere twigs against the massive boulders. As such, Mount Perish had been untouched by humankind.

Granite Falls, Ely, and Big Oak were the three towns settled in the foothills of the mountain. A narrow, well-traveled dirt road ran though the towns and beyond. The northernmost, oldest, and largest of the towns was Granite Falls, named after the massive waterfall nestled in the woodlands just six miles from the town's center. What had once been an old military fort had been transformed over the years. It was now home to Carlson's General

Store, Granite Falls Stables, Doc Tilson's office—in the back of which he resided—and the Rowdy Rabbit Saloon. Though small, the town was busy and thriving.

The shop owners did well for themselves, but none so well as the Rowdy Rabbit Saloon. The establishment was the first and only two-story building in Granite Falls. The ground floor housed the saloon, while the second story was reserved for business of a more risqué nature. Preferring to trade coins for drink rather than save their money, most of the men heading through town spent their time at this local watering hole. The colorful ladies who worked there were kept as busy as the bartender.

Most men wanted two things from the town: whiskey and women. The Rowdy Rabbit offered both.

The four men outside the saloon on the day Toby brought his mother and sister to town were not there looking for honest work. They were scouting the area trying to figure out how to make some fast, easy money. Their thirst had brought them into Granite Falls that day. Uneducated and unskilled, except at causing trouble, they survived mostly on canned beans washed down with cups of tar-like coffee. These small, petty thieves wasted no time in relinquishing whatever cash they acquired at the local saloons.

The two men who headed up this ragtag team of misfits were Jake and Clay Roberts. They had no interest in their father's dream of his sons following in his footsteps. Farming was hard work. The brothers wanted no part in breaking their backs over a plow.

They had assumed finding gold would be easy money. Much to their disappointment, they never had any luck. These days the drifters spent their time stealing, drinking, and harassing women. They loved to play cards and would sit down at any table that would have them. More than one establishment had thrown them out for cheating. Jake and Clay were nasty guys, the kind of guys that, if you saw them on the street, you would cross the road so you wouldn't have to get too close.

Jake was the older and meaner of the two brothers. He was homely, overweight, and downright vile. Greasy black hair topped a face scarred by acne. Dirt and grime filled the deep craters partly hidden beneath a scraggly beard. Not one to smile much, few noticed his teeth were rotten. His black eyes and constant sneer vied with his foul odor.

The younger man, Clay, was the physical opposite of his brother. So scrawny he appeared emaciated, he almost disappeared when standing behind Jake. Clay, like Jake, also had terrible hygiene. He was dirty blond, with only a few sporadic hairs on his baby face. His yellow teeth could be more easily seen due to the mindless grin he always wore.

Clay had no formal education and relied on his brother to help make any kind of decision. What Jake said was the law, and Clay would follow orders without question. Years of abuse from his older brother had taken its toll on Clay, robbing him of empathy. He enjoyed watching Jake beat someone to the brink of death. He liked the sight of fresh blood and was always willing to join in a good fight, or a bad one. If he could get in a few good licks on some poor, defenseless guy, or animal, he was even happier.

Willard Fulton and Chester "Pinky" Riffle were the other two men with the Roberts brothers that day. They were nobodies, really. They weren't even friends. Circumstances had placed them across the poker table from Jake and Clay. Lacking direction, their main fault was being easily roped into anything guys like the Roberts boys dreamed up.

Willard wasn't the smartest duck on the pond. What he lacked in brains, though, he made up for in brute strength. Mean from the day he was born, most people did what he said. Those who didn't had a tendency to find themselves in a pine box.

Chester was a different sort of fella. He hadn't been born mean, but rather raised that way. He had been going by the name "Pinky" for as long as anyone could remember. The way he told the story, his infamous missing digit had been bitten off during a fight. What his narcissist mother would say, if you knew where to find her, was tough ole Pinky lost that finger when he was a small boy.

When Chester was five, his father thought it was high time the boy learned to ride a horse. He sat Chester on the back of a horse and gave it a hard smack on the rump. It bolted. Needless to say, Chester didn't stay on long. He was lucky it was only his hand that got trampled. It as easily could have been his head. Young Chester saw all that blood, his blood, and cried. His father had enjoyed picking on him, and this provided yet another cruel opportunity.

"Stupid boy, can't even stay on a horse. Talk about worthless," he had said, walking away. He was just a child but that didn't matter to his parents. They truly enjoyed belittling their son. The more they mistreated him, the meaner Pinky got.

Clay tried not to show his embarrassment at being snubbed by Jamie Pratt. He hoped the gang of misfits wouldn't bring attention to the rejection. However, they began to antagonize him almost immediately, fueling his temper.

"Girls like that don't want the likes of you touchin' her," Pinky said with a chuckle.

"Shit," Clay said, "she couldn't handle a man like me. If I got 'er alone, I'd make sweet love to her and she'd be beggin' for more."

The three men laughed in his face, only adding to his rage.

"You are right about that, jackass. She'd be beggin' all right. More like beggin' for ya to get off her," Jake said. He spat another long stream of tobacco juice.

"I'd go after her and show y'all, but her father is waitin' at home."

This earned another round of laughter from the goons.

"Big talk for a little man," said Jake, flashing rotten teeth through a mean smile. "You ain't showin' shit."

Clay's face burned. Knowing the other men might notice him blushing only made him angrier. His lip curled, another involuntary response. He felt his hands ball into fists; his shoulders rose.

"Lookit!" Pinky said in a mocking tone. "He's puffin' up like a chicken!"

Willard and Pinky laughed. Jake took a step closer to his brother, looking down at the smaller man.

"What are you gonna do?" he asked, his hot, stinking breath in his brother's face.

Clay's chest rose and fell. He did his best to stare his brother down. Fingernails drew blood in his clenched fists. And then he turned and started walking. The other men laughed, forcing it out louder to humiliate Clay. He kicked a stray dog on his way back toward the saloon, earning more guffaws from the others as they followed along behind.

CHAPTER FIVE

The nervous staccato of Toby's boot on the toe board was the only sound breaking the awkward silence hanging over the wagon.

"Are you all right?" Sarah said, placing a hand on his leg.

"What is Father going to say when he finds out I just stood there?" Toby asked, his eyes betraying him, filling with tears.

"There was nothing you could've done. You didn't just stand there. You got us away from trouble. Your father will be proud of you. I know I am."

Toby's bottom lip trembled. "I didn't say anything to them—didn't do anything to make them stop."

"Son, you learned a valuable lesson today. Some men are just no good. You have to know there is no way to win against men like that. Sometimes it's better to walk away and say nothing. They just wanted to cause trouble. Don't ever stoop to their level."

Jamie leaned up from the back. "Toby, you did exactly what Daniel would've done. He knows when it comes to people like that, it's best to walk away. It doesn't make you weak. It makes you much stronger than them."

"Your sister is right. Do you think Daniel would have gotten into a fight with those men?"

"Uh...probably not," Toby said as he tried to inconspicuously wipe away the tear rolling down his cheek.

"What do you say we all forget about those men? Let's not let them spoil this fine day," Sarah said. She reached into her pocket for two pieces of candy. "I was going to wait until after supper to give these to you, but I think you should have them now." She handed a piece to each of them.

~

Toby pulled the wagon up to the house, and helped his mother and sister unload their purchases. The confrontation in town had frightened him. He had tried his best to hide his fear, but he was relieved to be home.

As the women started preparing a pot of venison stew for supper, Toby headed to the barn to tend to the horses. He brushed them down, taking his time, trying to calm his nerves that were still on edge from the encounter with the drunken men in town. He'd felt like a man earlier. Now, angry and riled up by his failure to act, he felt like a boy again.

Toby threw in some hay and latched the stall door behind him. He grabbed the bucket to fetch some water from the stream. As he did, Jessica came tearing around the corner.

"Toby! Just look at the fish I caught! Aren't they monsters?" She squealed with delight.

Nerves still tied into tight bundles, Toby jumped, fists up. He regained his composure by placing his hands on Jessica's shoulders and taking a slow, deep breath. He was about to speak when he was interrupted by a scream from inside the house.

"You get in the stall with Dakota and stay there. Don't come out until I come for you," Toby said, commanding her in a terrified whisper. He paused long enough to grab his rifle from the wagon seat. The old bucket with the rusted handle lay forgotten as Toby sprinted to the house.

Jessica hated it when Toby told her what to do. Just because he was three years older didn't give him the right to boss her around. This time was different. Hearing the terror in his voice, she did exactly as she was told. She ran into the stall, latched the door shut, and completely buried herself in the hay.

Toby burst through the door. He stopped dead in his tracks, recognizing the intruders instantly. They had been followed home.

His mother, the quiet, soft-spoken woman who would never hurt a soul, was bent over the table, dress hiked up to her neck. Her torn undergarments lay on the floor next to her.

Willard and Pinky stood around the table looking on as Jake raped Sarah, eyeing the spectacle like a prizefight. Toby could not see his mother this way. He looked away, locking his gaze on his sister. Clay Roberts had Jamie in a bear hug from behind, pinning her arms to her sides. Pinky lunged at Toby, wrestled the rifle out of fear-crippled hands before the boy could react.

Jake paused long enough to yell, "Take that damn kid outside!" He then resumed forcing himself onto Sarah before her son was out the door.

Sarah tried to remain calm for Jamie's sake. This was something no daughter should ever have to witness. Sarah was restrained, on her stomach, against the redwood table James had made her after he had finished building the house. He had told her, "Sarah, this room, all of us seated around the table, this is the heart of our home." If there was any truth in that, then that heart was being broken.

Sarah knew she was going to have to stay strong if they were going to make it through this. She didn't dare look at Jamie, fearing if she did, her daughter would see how terrified she really was. Instead, she focused on the little clock sitting atop the mantel; oblivious to the fact her fingernails were clawing scratches into the surface of the beloved table. Shocked and staring, Sarah willed the clock's frozen hands to move, to count her family out of this nightmare.

Jamie didn't want to look. She turned her head away in horror and shame. Each time she did, Clay would twist her head back in her mother's direction, forcing her to face the sordid scene head on. Red handprints blossomed against her cheeks, the hard slaps penalty for closing her eyes. Jamie stared, deadpan, eyes cold and flat. She focused on the fact that her father and brother would be home any minute.

Could be home any minute.

Should be home any minute.

Clay whispered in Jamie's ear. "Ever been with a man? Mmm…bet not," he said, moaning. His voice alone was enough to make her skin crawl, even if it wasn't hot and scented with whiskey and decay.

Taking his time, Clay lifted the hair from the nape of Jamie's neck, clumsily kissing her tender skin. She retched as his fetid breath assaulted her, leaving her with a bitter taste in her mouth. He rubbed himself against Jamie's backside, the bulge in his pants prodding her through the thin fabric of her dress.

Jamie said a silent prayer as Clay continued to push himself against her. *Please,* the terrified young girl pleaded with God, *please let Father and Daniel get here soon.*

Clay had never been a man of patience. He was impulsive, if anything. With a quick temper and a short fuse, he wasn't the kind of guy to stand around and watch anything. He was always one of the first ones in, and he was tired of watching. Without warning, he jerked Jamie by her arm. She screamed as he pulled her toward the door.

Her daughter's scream was all it took to pull Sarah's eyes from the clock. She lifted her head off the table and cried out. "No! She's just a girl. Take me instead."

Her pleas fell on deaf, uncaring ears. Jake pushed her face flat against the table and continued his assault.

Toby, still restrained out on the porch, watched as Clay shoved Jamie through the door. He tried to muscle free from the tight grip Pinky had on him. His strength was no match for his captor. Toby watched in helpless terror as Clay shoved Jamie off the porch. She hit the ground hard.

"Get up," Clay shouted, "or I'm going back in the house and put a bullet in your mama's skull."

Knowing he would do just that, Jamie stood unaided and continued on to the barn without resistance.

Under the hay in Dakota's stall, Jessica could hear the commotion outside. She wondered if Toby might be returning. Peeking out of the hay enough to see through a knothole in the wood, she watched as a man she had never seen threw Jamie to the ground so hard she swore she felt the vibration beneath her. Jamie cried harder and gasped for the air that had been knocked out of her.

Jessica saw a stream of blood roll down her sister's chin. She wanted to storm out of the stall and beat him with her fists. Her body wouldn't move, though. She was too afraid to make a sound. Her teeth began to rattle, and she thought for sure the echoing chatter was going to reveal her hiding spot.

What was about to happen in the barn was a violation in more ways than one. The heinous act would rob Jessica of her innocence.

The man bent down and hiked Jamie's dress up so far the hem rested on her neck. She resisted, pulling her dress down, desperately trying to remain covered.

"This is going to happen—so you can fight me if you'd like," Clay said, his voice sinister, "but I promise you are not going to win." He raised his booted foot and kicked Jamie in the ribs. She yelped as she curled onto her side in a protective ball.

Clay bent down and squeezed her face. "So what's it going to be?" he asked, looking her dead in the eyes.

Jamie, hurt, traumatized, and defenseless, didn't speak.

Clay took her silence as acknowledgement of his control. "Good," he said with a sneer. "Now, roll over on your back and raise your damn dress. And don't make me ask again."

Fearing more violence if she resisted, Jamie did as she was

told. She rolled over. With trembling hands, she slowly lifted her dress above her waist.

"Higher," he ordered. "I want to see you—all of you."

Jamie obeyed.

"Mmm...perfect," Clay said as he bent down. He pulled off her undergarments and tossed them to the side.

Jamie turned her head away, lips and chin trembling, as the gravity of the situation set in. She was totally powerless, but knew it would be over much sooner if she didn't resist.

Clay reached down and removed his belt, letting his pants fall to the ground.

Jamie dug in her heels and did her best to scoot away from him. She was too scared to worry about the consequences.

Clay snickered. "And where do you think you're goin'?" he asked, grabbing her by the ankles and pulling her toward him, scraping her back against the hard barn floor.

Jessica could tell by the looks of him the man was mean. She also knew whatever he was about to do to Jamie was bad, monstrously bad. Out of the corner of her eye, Jessica saw the pitchfork leaned up against the wall. She envisioned herself sneaking out of the stall, grabbing it, and thrusting the tines into the man's back. She was still paralyzed, though, frozen with fear. She couldn't move a muscle.

Jessica watched powerlessly as the man fell on top of Jamie, pushing his way between her thrashing legs. With one hand he pinned Jamie's hands above her head. With the other, he reached down between his own legs and, in one quick move, did something that made Jamie cry out.

Jessica watched the man's body move over Jamie's motionless form. Jessica grew even more concerned when she saw that all the color had gone from her sister's face. The man's movements reminded Jessica of a fish flopping when it's out of the water. She wondered, bizarrely, if she would ever be able to look at a fish again.

Then, it appeared to Jessica as if the man was being shocked by an invisible force. He released a long, protracted moan, and then his flopping slowed to a stop. It seemed an eternity to Jessica. In truth, the whole sickening scene was over in minutes.

∿

Inside the house, the assault on Sarah continued. Her eyes still focused on the ornate clock, an attempt to block out the reality of the hell her family was going through. She forced her mind to go back to the day she had gotten the clock. Sarah had been fond of it since she was a small child. Knowing this, her mother presented it to her on her wedding day. Sarah couldn't have asked for a more perfect gift. To her, it was more than hands and gears; the clock was a piece of her mother, still with her. Someday, she would pass it down to Jamie. She panicked when Jamie came to mind. She couldn't even let herself think about what was happening to her right now.

Finally finished with Sarah, Jake fell heavily onto a chair. He was exhausted, panting, and dripping sweat. He was not used to any type of physical activity.

Willard was eager for his turn. He flipped Sarah over onto her back and undid his pants. Grabbing a handful of her hair, he kissed her roughly. His weather-beaten skin left small abrasions on her soft lips. Sarah felt as if she would never come clean again.

Outside the house, Toby was still trying to escape and help his family. Realizing his struggling only caused Pinky to tighten his grip, he somehow managed to calm himself.

When Willard finished with Sarah, he went outside to speak with Pinky. "We need to get out of here. Now."

Distracted by the conversation, Toby felt Pinky's grip start to loosen. This was his chance.

Toby tore away, and the chase was on. He ran toward the barn, his brain racing faster than his feet, and he lost his footing. He rolled, head over heels. When he came to a stop, he looked up, and saw Pinky standing over him. The last thing Toby saw was the butt end of a rifle.

∼

"Get up," Clay said as he fastened his trousers. "And stop crying or I'll give you something to cry about!"

Clutching Jamie by the arm so hard it was bound to turn black and blue, he escorted her out of the barn.

Jamie saw her lifeless brother as soon as she emerged. The sight gave her a burst of panicked strength. She broke free from Clay's grasp and ran to Toby. She dropped down and cradled his bloody head in her lap, careful to avoid the large laceration running down the right side of his forehead. Jamie pleaded with him to open his eyes, her tears falling on his ashen cheeks. Her brother was gone. She looked to the sky and released a bloodcurdling scream.

Jessica heard her sister's wail. Though terrified, she felt an urgent need to see what was happening. She crawled on hands and knees out of the stall and across the exact spot on the barn floor where her sister had been violated. She reached the barn wall and found an old knothole she could peek through.

Jessica watched Jamie cradling their brother in her lap. She stared at Toby's lifeless body, praying for him to get up. She wanted more than anything to run to him. Instead, she stayed rooted in place, unable to move again. Jessica pressed her ear firmly against the hole and listened as the rifle wielding man standing over her siblings spoke.

"Didn't mean to kill the little bastard. Just wanted to keep him from gettin' away."

"One less witness, right?"

Jessica recognized the voice as that of the blond man from the barn.

"We need to get out of here," the man with the gun said.

"Go ahead. Don't give a shit what ya guys do, but you're gonna miss out on this sweet thing!" the blond man said, pointing down at Jamie.

Jessica put her eye back to the hole and watched the blond man yank her sister off the ground. He manhandled her as he drug her back to the house. The other two men hurried to their horses and rode away.

Clay flung the door open. His calloused brother sat eating the stew the women had prepared for supper, at the very table where he had violently assaulted Sarah. Clay loosened his grip on Jamie and she ran into her mother's arms.

"Where are you hurt?" Sarah asked as soon as she saw all the blood on Jamie's dress.

"It-it's not m-m-mine. It's Toby's," she stuttered between sobs. "They killed him!"

"Jamie, breathe." Sarah's tone was eerily calm. She gently wiped the dried blood from her daughter's chin with the saliva-dampened hem of her dress.

It was as if Sarah hadn't heard the words or her mind refused to believe them. Either way, she did not acknowledge what Jamie had said.

Clay pulled out a chair and plopped down at the table beside his brother.

"Get him some food!" Jake snarled.

Sarah wanted nothing more than to smash the bowl on his head. Knowing their lives depended on it, she sat a steaming hot bowl in front of Clay. She returned to tending to Jamie's busted lip.

Sarah reached down for the hem of her dress and felt the bag of candy in her pocket. Her mind shifted to Jessica. She glanced the ceiling, put her palms together, and said a silent thank you. It was a true blessing Jessica was at her fishing hole. The men had no idea she existed. Sarah prayed her younger daughter would stay far away from the house, and if she did come home, she would somehow know to hide.

∼

James and Daniel headed back to the house. In years past, James would have been upset about coming back empty handed. This year, however, they had already hunted enough to get them through the winter. The burden he had felt in previous years did not exist. His mind was on his family as he walked back to the house with his son, heart filled with pride. As they approached the house, his thoughts shifted and he thought about Jessica, his little Berry. He wondered how many fish he would have to help clean, as she usually caught more than she could carry.

"Bet Berry caught her weight in fish today," James said.

Nodding, Daniel replied, "I reckon you're right about that—bet we'll be cleaning fish 'til dawn."

They both chuckled out loud at the thought as they stepped onto the porch.

Jessica's heart beat faster when she saw her father and brother. Salvation had finally arrived. Jessica wanted to yell to them, but she was still in shock and unable to make a sound. *Look this way*, she silently pleaded, hoping their eyes would land on Toby's body sprawled out in the dirt.

Hearing voices out front, Jake and Clay drew their pistols and pointed them toward the door. The intruders opened fire the moment the Pratt men swung it open.

Sarah and Jamie let out heart wrenching screams as James and Daniel fell backward onto the porch.

Jessica's mouth was opened wide, but her silent scream hung on her trembling lips, unable to escape.

Choking on lingering gun smoke, Jake turned to Clay and yelled, "Shut those bitches up!"

"Shut the hell up!" Clay shouted. "Wanna just shoot them too?" he asked, pointing his pistol at Sarah and Jamie.

"Dammit! Just go get some rope and tie them up. I need time to think," Jake shouted.

Clay did as he was told and tied the sobbing mother and daughter in chairs next to the table. When the knots were good and tight, he sat next to them and returned to his meal.

Jake rubbed his sweaty palm down his pant leg. "We need to get the hell out of here."

"Why? I haven't finished—"

"You dumbass! We need to get the hell away from this town. You know damn well they'll be sending a posse out after us. If they catch us, we'll be swinging by our necks," Jake said, snapping at his brother.

Clay took one last, heaping bite of food as he stood up. "What are we going to do with them? We can't leave them here. They know what we look like. Maybe we should burn this place to the ground?"

Jake used his pistol to push up the brim of his hat and scratch his forehead. "Hmmm." He nodded happily. For the first time ever, he thought his nitwit brother had come up with a good idea. Jake walked over to the mantle and knocked off the oil lamp, watching as its contents spilled across the floor.

Sarah knew what was about to happen. "Don't do this, Jake!" she pleaded. "Please! I'm begging you. I swear we'll never tell anyone. I'll do anything you want. We'll go with you."

Jake looked down at her, a look of loathing twisting his already unsightly features. "Why the hell would I take you anywhere? Woman, you wouldn't give me the time a day when we were back in town. Not good enough for ya then, was I? Now, all of a sudden you want to come with us? I see right through you, lady."

Knowing she couldn't get through to Jake, Sarah began pleading with Clay. "I know you like my daughter. I think she would make a great wife for you. Take care of you the way a man should be taken care of. Please, please just spare my daughter!"

Clay scratched his chin, as if considering Sarah's words. Before he could form an answer, Jake shouted at him.

"You are about the dumbest man I have ever met! You honestly think that girl would ever marry the likes of you? First chance she got she would run to the sheriff and tell him everything we done."

Clay said, "You're right. You're always right. I was just thinking…"

"That's what you have me for. I do the thinkin'," Jake said. Without another word, he struck a match on the heel of his boot and tossed it. It caught as soon as it hit the flammable liquid. They stepped over the two bodies near the doorway and left without any thought at all for the women left inside.

Sarah had been trying desperately to loosen the rope binding her hands as she pleaded with Jake, but all she had managed to do was tighten the knot. With no way to free their bindings, the one thing she could do was calm her hysterical daughter. She forced herself to smile as she turned to face Jamie, who was crying uncontrollably beside her.

"Sweetheart, look at me. It's going to be fine. We are going to get out of this. Jessica is out there. She'll save us," Sarah said, coughing from the black smoke already filling the house.

Terrified and panicked beyond the point of reasoning, Jamie could not be calmed. She managed nothing more than a scream or two in between her bouts of coughing and her gasps for air.

It was only a matter of seconds before flames were shooting out of the door. Jessica could hear her mother and sister screaming. She placed her tiny hands over her ears in hopes of stopping the sounds that seemed to shatter her eardrums. No matter how hard she pressed, the sounds of their suffering could not be silenced. Only after the house was engulfed in flames did the screams stop. The only sounds Jessica heard now were the crackling and popping noises emitting from the inferno.

The two men seemed to be amused as they watched it burn. Jessica looked on as the blond man who hurt her sister relieved himself onto the flames. Fearful they would torch the barn too, she crawled backwards until she bumped up against the loose board in the back; the one her father had never gotten around to mending. The gap was barely wide enough for her to squeeze her tiny body through.

Once she was out of the barn, she ran for her life into the fading light. She never looked back.

CHAPTER SIX

Fueled by fear and adrenaline, Jessica raced to her fishing spot in half the time it had taken her hours earlier. Had the route been less familiar, the darkness would have swallowed her. This was the only place she thought to go. Granite Falls had never even crossed her mind. The usually safe and familiar area now seemed totally foreign as the eerie darkness cast ominous shadows everywhere. She had never been here at this hour. It was no longer the place she knew.

She collapsed onto the ground and gazed at the moonlight reflecting on the Devil's Fork. Any other time she would have found the shimmering lights beautiful. Now, they resembled dancing flames. Even over the roar of the river, all she could hear were the screams of her mother and sister. They were all gone. She would never see them again. The faces of those horrible men who had shot and burned her family flashed in her mind.

Are they are coming after me? Panic and fear replaced her shock and sadness. Jessica couldn't go home. The river would swallow her if she tried to cross. In her frenzied state of mind, only one option remained. She followed the flowing rapids downstream in hopes of finding help.

Foliage and water were the only things she could make out in the scant light of the waning moon. Thorn trees and briar bushes along the riverbank grabbed at her with spindly claws, tearing into her arms and legs. She was too scared to worry about cuts, scrapes, or pain. Her progress was slow, and her body tired with every step.

She stumbled across a large tree, its base hollowed out from years of rot.

They won't find me in there.

Jessica crawled inside this teepee of dead wood and curled into a fetal position. She shivered uncontrollably, her torn dress inadequate to keep the cold from her bones. The screams and gunshots ringing in her ears were not silenced until her tears carried her off to sleep.

∼

A small beam of early morning sunlight found its way through a crack in the tree and onto Jessica's eyelids. It slowly drove her from slumber. Dirt and dried tears caked her eyes. She could barely see as she shimmied her way out of the damp, musty tree.

She stood and rubbed the crust from her swollen eyes. Across the river, a massive waterfall poured down a granite wall and spilled violently into the river. The exploding droplets of water created an epic lightshow, a rainbow of colors dancing across the surface. Jessica paid it no mind. She sat on the ground next to her crude shelter and looked at her ragged dress. It was the one Jamie had made her for her tenth birthday. She only had two dresses to her name, and now she had ruined the one that had meant so much to her.

Jamie is going to be so mad at me for ruining my dress. Mother will give me the switch. Then the realization hit her, like a slap across the face. *They won't do anything. They are all dead.* She placed her face in her hands and bawled.

A twig snapped, and Jessica's heart leapt out of her chest. *They're here.* Glancing over her shoulder, she sighed with relief when she spotted a small red fox. The animal was more scared of her than she was of it.

Her relief did not last long. The horrific events from the night replayed over and over in her mind. Scared, she crawled back into the tree and lay there until she fell asleep again. Jessica's dreams propelled her back to the barn. She was hiding in the stall when someone started removing the hay she hid under. He found her. It was the skinny blond man who had been on top of her sister—the Devil himself.

Jessica shot straight up as she screamed herself awake, slamming her head into the tree. A stream of blood trickled out of a small, crescent-shaped wound on her forehead. Her tiny hand smeared dirt and blood across her brow.

She crawled back out into the daylight, bloodshot eyes blinking, feverishly, trying to adjust to the sun. The hollow ache of her hunger, and fear of the men who had murdered her family, motivated her to keep moving.

Without another thought, she ran. She ran away from everything she had ever known. With her mind racing as fast as her legs, she leapt over logs and ducked under branches, a speck in a vast ocean of trees and green. She prayed she would find someone —anyone who could help.

She ran until she couldn't take another step. She stopped, panting and parched. Her only thought was to quench her thirst. The water of the river she followed enticed her. She moved slowly, making her way nearer to the bank, looking for any place that might give her easy access to drink.

Jessica spotted a small embankment and pushed her way through the dense brush. Despite stepping carefully, she lost her footing on the muddy ground, and slid straight toward the rapids.

She reached out, grabbing for anything she could grasp to keep from plunging into the river. Seconds before she fell in, she latched onto an old log. Jessica and the log tumbled into the river. Cold shocked her body as she fought to keep her head above water.

The Devil had her now. Her mother's warnings about the river came to mind. She knew her only hope was the log, which she held onto with all her might, riding out the violent rapids.

With each submersion, water shot up her nose and down her throat. She coughed and gasped, barely able to take in a breath before the next attack. Over and over the wild beast tried to devour her. It swallowed her whole and spat her out. It threw her at boulders trying to crush her, determined to crack her skull like an egg. Repeatedly it attacked. Repeatedly it was thwarted. No one had ever survived the river's grasp, but this child, somehow, was conquering it.

She managed to ride out the most savage part of the rapids and made it to a stretch that was a little less violent. Retching up water, she saw an enormous, fallen redwood spanning partway across the river. It was still anchored by some roots, almost as if put there on purpose to reach out and help her. It was her only hope.

She kicked wildly, steering herself toward the tree. Panic mounted as she drew closer. Jessica fought against her tensing muscles, trying to maintain control. If she failed, she would die.

She released the log and stretched her arms out as far as she could as the tree came within reach. Somehow her tiny fingers managed to clamp on. She began pulling herself across, despite the onslaught of rushing water crushing her small frame against the tree.

Inch by inch she went, until she was safely on the bank. She collapsed to her knees, purging up mouthfuls of river water as she struggled to catch her breath.

Her gratitude for solid ground faded when she realized she was on the wrong side of the river, the uninhabited side. Her heart sank. Jessica watched as the water ripped the tree from the ground with a thunderous crack. Even it was no match for the river's awesome power. The mammoth piece of lumber hurtled downstream and was soon lost from Jessica's sight.

Broken in body and spirit, Jessica slowly got to her feet and scanned the river. She found no sign of human life in either direction, just wilderness. She backed away from the raging river with no real thought as to where she was going, dazed by grief and loneliness.

Jessica came upon an impassible granite wall. Exhausted, she slumped against the rock face and slid down until her bottom touched the ground. *I'm so hungry. I'd eat a worm if I had one.*

She put her hands on her stomach to calm the rumblings and felt a lump in the pocket of her torn dress. She reached in and pulled out a filthy rag. It took her a few seconds to realize it was the piece of bread her mother had wrapped for her to take fishing. The contents now looked like a soggy ball of dough that had been rolled in the dirt. Beyond hungry, Jessica didn't care how it looked or tasted. She popped the tiny morsel into her mouth and swallowed. She stuck out her tongue to catch droplets of water trickling from a rock above.

With her thirst and hunger somewhat appeased, she stood up and stretched. Jessica tried to ignore the pain in her tired, aching feet, and the throbs emitting from her many lacerations. She needed to keep moving. Unsure of how much daylight she had left, her best chance was to get to higher ground for a better view of the area.

She decided she would approach the rock wall the same way she did the big oak out by the barn. That had been intimidating at first, too. Step-by-step, she found it wasn't as hard or scary as she thought it would be. Jessica found a foothold and began her ascent. Though climbing as quickly as she could, she wasn't making much progress. Her legs already felt like they were on fire. She continued upward, occasionally glancing over her shoulder. She saw nothing but treetops.

The sun was sinking low in the sky. She studied her surroundings, hoping to find a safe place to rest for the night. Spotting a small opening in the rocks above her, she continued on until her shaky legs could go no further. With what little energy she had left, she pulled herself onto a breath of a ledge, and crawled into a small cave. Once again she curled into a ball. She fell asleep instantly, too exhausted to be scared of the unfamiliar sounds as darkness swallowed her

∼

A tiny droplet of water condensed on the ceiling of the cave. Its silent splash against Jessica's dirty cheek eased her awake. She stretched her legs. They were stiff and cold from sleeping with them tucked up to her chest. It had been a long night filled with dreams of fire and flopping fish, and what she wanted more than anything that morning was to wake up to the smell of her mother's cooking. Tears welled in the corners of her eyes as she realized they were gone from her forever.

If only I had been brave enough to warn Father. She couldn't help feeling the death of her family was somehow her fault. She'd been paralyzed with fear, unable to do anything at all to help. Frozen. Useless.

She shivered, the crisp air raising goosebumps under her raggedy dress as she made her way out of the damp cave. The heat of the sun's glaring rays felt good on her skin. She stood on the small ledge, basking in the warmth, hugging herself as if to hold onto the heat.

Anxiety settled in as she took in her surroundings. She was completely lost with no idea where to go or even which direction would lead to help. The baby of the family never had to make decisions before. Now, every choice was hers alone. Jessica's stomach growled, loud and painful. Her body, at least, knew what she needed to do.

She climbed until she reached an area where she could get off the rock wall. Surveying her surroundings from this new vantage point, Jessica was extremely disappointed. All she could see was more trees. She stepped into the unfamiliar forest. After wandering for what felt like an eternity, Jessica searched for something edible, anything to lessen the pain in her gut. She found a cluster of mushrooms growing at the base of a tree. Her mouth watered as she stared at the fungi. She could almost taste them.

They weren't worth the risk. She didn't know if they were poisonous. *Father would know.* She wiped more tears away as she abandoned the potential meal. An uneasy feeling came over her. She stopped and scanned the dense forest. A growl shattered the silence, and she spun around.

Jessica found herself facing a large grizzly bear. Only thirty yards away and muzzle up, the bear sniffed the air. The girl would make a good, full meal for the hungry animal. Winter was coming and it would soon be time to hibernate. The beast needed its fill.

Inexperience and terror took over. Jessica ran as the bear gave chase. Her short legs were no match for the ravenous carnivore. The distance between predator and prey narrowed. Jessica tripped and fell. Her head smacked against a large rock sticking out of the ground. She rolled over, stunned, confused, and disoriented. The last thing she saw before her world went dark was the bear lifting its enormous paw, claws spread.

CHAPTER SEVEN

Smell was the first sensation to tickle Jessica from unconsciousness. Aroused by the persistent gnawing in her stomach, she smelled something and it smelled delicious. The mouthwatering aroma reminded her of her mother's cooking and for a fleeting moment she thought it had all been a horrible nightmare.

Was it just a bad dream? Are they all sitting around the table waiting for me?

The moment she opened her eyes, Jessica knew the nightmare was real. This was not her home. She was warm and dry, and immediately thankful to be in a comfortable bed, not curled up in some rotten tree or damp cave, but she didn't know where she was. Her eyes adjusted to the light of a fireplace as she looked around.

The bed was against a wall in a small cabin. She could tell right away it was only one room. From her vantage point, she could see the whole place except what was in the loft above her. Even in the poor lighting, it was clear the place hadn't seen a good cleaning in quite some time.

Tiny, hand-hewn log tables flanked the bed. Floor-to-loft shelving lined the walls, each shelf crowded with old rusted tins and jars of various shapes and sizes. Some were clear and full of bizarre substances. Others were so covered in layers of dust she could only imagine what might be hidden within.

Next to the shelves was the large stone fireplace, the only source of light in the cabin. A few inches above the mantle hung a familiar looking rifle. Her father had owned the same model. For a second she thought maybe he'd rescued her, and brought her to this place. Then she remembered watching his body fall.

Her eyes welled up. Her father taught her to shoot using that very gun. Although she had never killed anything with it, she had managed to hit a few old bottles he had placed on the fence as targets.

A large cast iron pot glistened in the flickering light. It must hold the food, its aroma still tickling her nose. Her stomach growled again in protest. In front of the fireplace sat two weathered rocking chairs made from twisted branches. Again, she remembered her father, sitting on his lap in a similar chair, sharing stories or being read to. She pushed the thought from her mind.

In the center of the room sat an old, scuffed-up table with four wooden chairs pushed in around it. Opposite the fireplace was a large, plank door. Next to it was a long, waist-high cabinet with a window above it. Shutters covered the lone window, but it was obvious from the strands of cobwebs they hadn't been opened in quite some time. The wall directly across from the bed had traps and tools hanging on it. Another reminder of home—they'd had similar instruments in the barn.

The floor was so filthy it was hard for her to tell if it was made of wood or simply hard-packed soil. Unfamiliar plants hung drying in bundles from the ceiling. Small, wooden statues rested throughout the cabin. They varied in size, and their likeness to toys intrigued her. They were carved with great detail: horses, cows, pigs, and even figurines of people. She found it odd toys would be in such a strange and peculiar place.

Who lives here? Jessica wondered with a mix of fear and curiosity. As if in answer, the latch clicked and the door flung open.

"Are you finally up, youngin'?" the woman asked as she puffed on a soapstone pipe. Plumes of smoke followed behind her as she walked toward the fireplace.

Although the voice seemed kind, Jessica was wary. She watched as the woman made her way to the pot hanging above the fire and gave it a quick stir. It reminded Jessica of a witch stirring a brewing cauldron, but for some reason she wasn't frightened. The woman was older than her mother and dressed much differently. She wore a dirty shirt and an old pair of pants. The ensemble was topped off with a black hat with a large eagle feather sticking up from the band.

Before Jessica could respond to the question, the woman said, "You've got to be starving child! The name is Frieda McGinnis. What might yours be?" She tapped her pipe on a stone, knocking the burnt tobacco into the fire before placing the pipe on the mantle. She turned to face the young girl.

"Jess…Jessica Pratt," she said. Her voice was barely above a whisper.

Frieda grabbed a wooden bowl from a shelf and opened one of the old tin containers. She sprinkled some of its contents into the bowl, added a small ladle of water, and gave it a stir. She set the bowl on the rickety log table next to Jessica, and took a seat on the edge of the bed.

Jessica peeked into the bowl. She could tell by the sight and smell there was no way she was going to eat it, no matter how hungry she was. Frieda pulled a handkerchief from her raggedy pants pocket. She snapped it in the air a couple times and dipped it in the bowl. Gently and carefully, she cleaned Jessica's cuts with the damp cloth.

"Child, you look like you got into a fight with a briar patch and lost." She used her finger to wipe away a lone tear that slid down the girl's cheek.

Jessica stayed silent. As Frieda tended to Jessica's wounds, she hummed softly, hoping to calm the young girl's nerves. She went back to the fireplace and returned with a bowl full of delicious soup. Jessica took the steaming bowl and dished spoonful after spoonful into her mouth. She was too grateful to speak; too hungry to care it burnt her tongue.

"Slow down, girl. There's plenty more if you're wanting it," Frieda said. "You'll make yourself sick, keeping up like that."

Jessica's belly filled up quickly, having shrunk from going so long without food. When she finished, she slid back down on the old straw mattress, burrowed under the blanket, and fell asleep almost instantly.

Dreams of screams and fire filled her restless sleep. Jessica woke herself by calling out for her mother. In her left hand was one of the carvings she had noticed earlier, a small wooden horse. Frieda sat holding her other hand.

She squeezed Jessica's small hand and told her, "I'm here and I promise you're safe."

Frieda had no idea what this little girl had gone through, but she knew whatever it was, it had been bad. She was shocked the little girl had managed to make it across the Devil's Fork. No one crossed it, let alone a child.

Frieda knew Jessica was in a fragile state, but she was desperate for information. In the gentlest voice possible, she asked, "Want to tell me how a little girl like you managed to get on the mountain?"

"I fell in the river," she said, whimpering.

"I have to say, you're lucky to be alive. Never heard of anyone making it across."

"Well, how did you get here? Did you fall in, too?" asked Jessica.

"No child, I crossed years ago. There was a bridge on the other side of the mountain. Washed away in a flood before you were even born. Your parents must be worried sick. For all they know you drowned."

"My parents are gone. I don't have anyone. Not anymore."

"Oh, I'm sorry. I didn't know. Who's been lookin' after you? They have to be worried about you."

"You don't understand. Men came to our house and killed them. Father, Mother, Daniel, Jamie and Toby are all dead." Jessica broke down and sobbed.

"Oh, Jessica. I am so sorry."

"My brother told me to hide in the barn underneath the hay. I saw the men kill all of them. I didn't know what to do." The words spilled out of her. "I just ran. It's all my fault. If I had only called out and warned Father they were in the house…"

"Child, I'm sure as I'm sitting here, there was nothing you could have done. If they saw you they would have hurt you, too. You did the right thing, running away."

"I didn't even run to town for help. I got lost in the woods and fell in the river." Jessica pushed her face into the pillow, ashamed, as her tears soaked the cover.

"Someone has to be worried about you. You got other kin?"

"No. I don't have anyone."

"Well, child, that's not true. You got me." Frieda placed a reassuring hand on the young girl's back. "Why don't you get some more rest? You've been through hell. I'll be right here when you wake up."

Jessica curled up under the blanket and closed her eyes. Beneath her lids, she could still see the fear on Jamie's face, the filthy man on top of her. Eventually the screams echoing in her head were replaced by the sound of Frieda's voice. She sat holding Jessica's hand, singing a soothing melody, until the girl fell asleep.

There really was no way to comfort someone after an ordeal such as that. Loss was something Frieda knew about all too well.

∾

Frieda hadn't always lived in the isolated cabin on Mount Perish. Before being blessed with a head full of white hairs, her life had been much different. Nathaniel, her husband, had gotten it into his head they should head west. He told her repeatedly the lands there would be more bountiful. Pennsylvania had been over trapped and it was damn near impossible to make a living there anymore. Nathaniel felt that Illinois, a newer state, had much more to offer and could be the beginning of a new, prosperous life for them. Frieda was finally persuaded to leave her home.

In 1835, they loaded a few possessions and their only child, Patrick, into their wagon. Frieda felt a little melancholy at having to leave so many things behind, but there wasn't room for anything nonessential. The load had to be light and manageable for their team of mules to pull.

It was a difficult trip and everyday there seemed to be a new hardship. The weather wreaked havoc on the old dirt paths they followed. When the rains poured they became a treacherous, muddy mess. They were thrilled if they made it fifteen miles in a day.

After traveling west for three and a half weeks, life changed suddenly and forever for Frieda and Nathaniel. They were somewhere in northern Indiana when Nathaniel came down with influenza. Frieda spent that night and the following day tending to him in the back of their covered wagon, trying to cool his burning fever. He became delirious, speaking gibberish. He was in dire need of help.

With no other choice, Frieda made the fateful decision to have Patrick take over the reins and drive the team. They would have a better chance of getting to help if they were moving. Staying put meant waiting for death in the middle of nowhere. Even though Patrick was only twelve and had never driven the team before, Frieda decided to push on through the darkness, hoping to find help before it was too late.

The wagon moved along while Frieda tended to Nathaniel. Later that night, either from fatigue or distraction, Patrick dropped one of the reins. He bent down to reach for the swinging leather strap, lost his balance, and fell headfirst from the wagon.

Frieda would never forget the sickening sound and feel of the wagon's wheel crushing her child.

She managed to stop the mules. Frieda jumped from the wagon and ran to Patrick as fast as she could. She sat there on the ground, holding him tight against her chest, and let out a blood-curdling wail that could be heard echoing across the land. She held him close, rocking him back and forth as if he were still her baby.

God knows how long she stayed that way. In such a state of shock, she lost the ability to cry. She rocked back and forth, devoid of spirit, completely devastated by her loss. The world around her lost all meaning.

Rapt with grief, she was oblivious to the approaching horses. So focused on her only child, she didn't blink when a pair of buckskin moccasins stepped into view. Frieda sat, unafraid, of the men surrounding her, or anything else. One man bent down and tried to take Patrick from her arms, breaking her trance. She tightened her grip, clinging desperately to her son. The man mumbled a few words. She didn't know what he said, but understood by his tone he meant her no harm. He wanted to help. He continued speaking, his tone soft, until at last it had its desired effect.

With a faint moan of protest, Frieda let go of her lifeless son. The stranger took the boy. The hand of another man reached down to help her to her feet. His face was painted. The men were careful and respectful of her son as they placed him in the wagon next to her husband. One man jumped onto the driver's seat and motioned for Frieda. She took the seat beside him.

Lost under a haze of sorrow, time lost all meaning. Frieda had no idea, then or now, how long it took them to reach their home.

She had never seen a native village before. A fire blazed in the middle of a field. Wigwams dotted the landscape. The small group of people that had been dancing around the fire stopped and watched as the wagon approached. The driver shouted orders. Three men approached and, still careful, still respectful, took Nathaniel from the wagon and into one of the wigwams.

The women gathered round, reaching out to Frieda. They wanted her to follow them, and she did. In a warm wigwam next to the one Nathaniel had been taken into, the women huddled around Frieda, chanting softly. It was if they, too, were feeling her pain. All the women seemed to understand the devastating loss of a child.

Once Frieda was out of sight, two men took Patrick's body from the wagon and disappeared into the woods. They returned just before sunrise. The men waited outside of Frieda's wigwam for the grieving woman to join them.

Frieda couldn't sleep. She stared blankly at the women surrounding her. For a brief moment, she felt like a goat lying in the center of a lion cage. It was an irrational thought, an illusion brought by loss, and she knew it; this group of women had spent hours comforting her. Frieda knew in her gut they were kind people.

Morning came. The village sprang to life around Frieda. She understood their intentions only through kind faces and gestures. She gratefully accepted water and a piece of dried corn cake, even though she wasn't the least bit hungry.

Grabbing her by the hand, the oldest woman in the group led Frieda outside where the two men were waiting for her. They motioned for Frieda to follow them into the woods. They brought her to an ancient oak tree. Beneath it was a pile of freshly placed rocks. She didn't need to be told what was buried under the pile. What little strength she had left went out of her and she dropped to her knees. Seeing that pile of stones opened some kind of floodgate, and Frieda let her tears flow.

One of the men placed a comforting hand on Frieda's shoulder. He motioned at the sleeve of her dress, his intention obvious to Frieda. No longer caring about such petty things, she did as instructed and handed the man the torn sleeve. He tied the fabric to the end of a long stick. Jammed into the ground at the head of the small pile of rocks, it marked the small grave so the Great Spirit would know where to find him. The small group walked away silently, leaving Frieda the privacy to continue mourning the loss of her child.

With some comfort in knowing the natives were caring for Nathaniel, Frieda spent the next few days sequestered inside of a wigwam in an inconsolable state. Periodically, a woman would bring her food and drink, but it would remain untouched. Frieda didn't want to live anymore, and the toll of her deep heartache was starting to show.

On the fifth day, an old, white-haired woman of the tribe entered the wigwam and tugged on Frieda's arm, in an effort to pull her to her feet. She spoke loudly and with purpose, and although Frieda had no idea what the words meant, it was evident the woman wanted her outside. Frieda staggered on her way out, squinting in the bright sunlight. The old woman took Frieda by the arm and led her down to the creek, motioning for her to get in and bathe.

Frieda stepped into the rolling water. Her clothes, stiff from days of filth, loosened and flowed around her. She dunked her head under and screamed as loud as she could, her cry muffled by the calming water. As she rose, she understood why the old woman had brought her there. The water not only cleansed her body, but it was therapeutic as well. Screaming like that seemed to release all the pent up emotions she had been keeping bottled up inside. She felt a glimmer of her old self, a new spark of strength to help her get on with her life.

It took Nathaniel several weeks to recover from his illness, and many more months for him to fully regain his strength. If it hadn't been for the old medicine man of the tribe, there's no doubt he would have been reunited with Patrick.

Nathaniel took the news of his son's death extremely hard. He knew if he hadn't pursued the move to Illinois, Patrick would still be alive. The weight of the guilt crushed him and it would plague him until the day he died.

The Dothka tribe was good to Frieda and Nathaniel, adopting them into the village as their own. They helped the newcomers deal with their grief by keeping their minds and bodies occupied. Busy from sunup to sundown, Frieda and Nathaniel were never given the opportunity to sit around and feel sorry for themselves. Finding the native customs fascinating, they persevered, pushing on through their pain, eventually even learning the strange language.

As soon as Nathaniel had regained his strength, the men of the tribe taught him how to construct the frame of his own wigwam. The women took Frieda to collect elm bark, and then methodically attached it on the wigwam frame. They used tanned deer hides, another skill they taught her, to cover any openings on the outside of the rounded shelter. It was unlike any home they had ever lived in and, although small, it was right for what they needed.

The women of the tribe worked hard in the fields, and they taught Frieda how to plant crops in the way of their ancestors. Bare-chested, their tanned skin glistening with beads of sweat, the women spent their days in the fields, unprotected from the scorching sun. Uncomfortable with the nudity at first, Frieda eventually gave up her inhibitions. The woman from Pennsylvania found her true self, becoming more of a free spirit. Little by little, Frieda shed a bit more of the restricting white man's ways, as she had her old clothes.

After long hours in the sun, the women couldn't wait to get back to the village and jump into the cool waters of the creek. Young and old, they stripped off their animal hides and ran, laughing like children as they splashed, tan bodies gleaming in the sun.

The months flew by during the winter, and the well-built wigwam kept them nice and warm. Discussing their future night after night, Frieda and Nathanial decided in the spring they would continue their trip to Illinois. They told the tribe they would leave as soon as the weather was favorable.

Big Antler, chief of the Dothka tribe, told them when the rains slowed in the spring, a chieftain from far away would come to his village. He would ask him to help guide Frieda and Nathaniel in the direction of the setting sun. They never imagined the journey to come would take them far beyond the boundaries of Illinois.

∼

As Frieda continued watching the young girl sleep, she reflected on her own loss. Her pain was still as raw as the day Patrick had died. Frieda knew how Jessica felt and wanted nothing more than to help the orphan cope with the tragedy, just as the Dothka people had done for her all those years ago. The best way she could help the young girl overcome her grief was to keep her mind busy and not allow her to dwell on the despair that was sure to threaten her sanity.

In the morning, Frieda would begin by teaching Jessica some of the things she had learned over the years.

CHAPTER EIGHT

The modest little structure Frieda called home had become dilapidated from years of neglect. Nestled in a sea of trees beside a stream, the place was once lovely. It still would have been, had it been cared for. It was nothing more than hand-hewn logs mortared together with mud and straw, and a roof covered in a thick layer of bright green moss. The weathered cabin, despite its condition, was home.

The most charming aspect was the covered porch of wood planks spanning the front. On it sat two crudely carved chairs fashioned from old stumps, seats worn smooth from years of use. Attached to one side of the dwelling was a rickety lean-to with a small grazing area, enclosed by a failing split-rail fence. Having housed no livestock in years, the structure was home now to rodents and other vermin. The paddock was so overgrown that portions of the fence surrounding it had all but disappeared.

Inside was not much better than the outside. It was dark and dingy, and perpetually musty, despite Frieda's best efforts.

Jessica took an interest in the old home as she healed and regained her strength. Wanting to contribute, she set about cleaning up the place. It was the least she could do after everything Frieda had done for her.

The efforts renewed Frieda's interest in the old cabin as well. She helped Jessica fix up the loft above her bed. It wasn't the home Jessica knew and loved, but she was happy to have a personal space to call her own. Frieda, though sad about Jessica's situation, couldn't have been happier for the company.

Each day, life on the mountain exposed Jessica to many new experiences. Frieda spent endless hours teaching Jessica how to hunt, clean and prepare meat, and tan hides. No matter what kind of animal it was, Frieda knew how to dress it. Jessica was a quick learner, soaking up all the knowledge her new mentor had to offer.

On hot summer days, when the chores were finished, they would strip off their clothes and race each other to the creek, laughing and splashing as the cold water soothed their hot skin. Evenings were spent sitting out on the stump chairs underneath the covered porch. Frieda whittled and smoked her pipe, telling Jessica about her life on the mountain.

~

When first arriving on the mountain, constructing a shelter was Nathaniel and Frieda's first priority. Initially, they built and lived in a wigwam. Even though Nathaniel was impressed with the versatility of the native-designed shelter, he knew a cabin would be more suitable for him and his wife. He appreciated and was grateful for all he had learned from the Dothka tribe. Nonetheless, he was a proud white man who chose to stick to what he knew best.

The couple lived in the wigwam while they worked on their cabin, toiling sunup to sundown to complete their new home. Trees were chopped down, their logs hand-hewn and notched. Each rock was inspected with great care before making its way into the stone fireplace. Even selecting the right piece of timber for the mantel was done with great care.

Frieda was never one to ask for luxuries, but there was one

thing she yearned for in a home. Back in Pennsylvania they had always had dirt floors. Nathaniel wanted nothing more than for Frieda to have wood floors for the first time in her life. She deserved it. Frieda had, after all, uprooted her previous life, and lost a son to get where they were.

It took weeks to split all of the logs. Cuts and blisters covered their sore hands. In the end it was worth it because Frieda finally had her puncheon log floor. With the cabin completed, the couple began work on a shelter for their horses.

They enjoyed nine years together on the mountain before Nathaniel's health began to decline. He spent the last two years of his life bedridden. Nathaniel knew he had become a burden, and welcomed the approaching reunion with his son. He was at peace knowing Frieda was strong and capable. She would do all right without him.

Frieda took good care of him, but eventually his body couldn't take any more. He slipped away in his sleep, passing away in her arms in 1847, eleven years after arriving atop Mount Perish.

Frieda buried him underneath a beautiful sycamore, cocooned in a bear pelt. Their wigwam, their first home on the mountain, had sat in the same spot. After covering the hole with dirt and placing rocks on top, she tore off the sleeve of an old shirt and tied it to a stick. She jammed it into the ground, marking the spot as it had been done at Patrick's grave so long ago in Indiana.

Frieda spent her time hunting, foraging, and fishing. Experience had taught her staying busy was the best remedy for loss. Still, she neglected her home's appearance. She sometimes felt bad about the layers of dirt lining the grooves of her wood floor, but survival was her priority. She was one woman, with only so much energy. It took everything she had to simply get through her days. On lonely evenings, she sat on the porch whittling and humming songs she had learned from her time spent with her native friends.

Frieda's one true pleasure was smoking Nathaniel's pipe. One day she noticed it sitting next to his old brass spill on the mantel.

The sight of it alone was enough to bring on such a vivid memory of the smell of the smoke she had become dizzy with emotion. The aroma had been gone for so long and she hadn't realized until then how much she missed it. She smoked it from that day forward. Tobacco was not readily available on the mountaintop, but Frieda found several herbs and plants she liked to smoke. Her favorite was a blend of mugwort, huckleberry, and nettle leaf, which she always kept hanging in bundles inside the cabin to dry.

∼

Jessica listened to Frieda's stories, watching in fascination as one animal or another came to life from a piece of wood. The woman carved them without effort, her knife never pausing while she spoke. Jessica was thrilled when Frieda handed her a knife.

"It was Nathaniel's. Thought you might want to give it a try. Just be careful not to cut off a finger," Frieda said, only half teasing. She kept the blade razor-sharp.

"Thank you," Jessica said, eager to create her own figures. "I'm going to make you a deer."

"That would be lovely." Frieda smiled at the girl's confidence. She felt a surge of pride.

It took three weeks to complete her first carving. It was so hideous and lopsided it wouldn't stand upright. Even so, Frieda bragged about it as if it was a blue ribbon winner. She propped the wooden deer up against a tin, smack dab in the middle of the table where it would remain thereafter.

Life on top of Mount Perish hadn't been an easy transition for Jessica. Frieda tried her best to keep her young mind engaged. Still, the gruesome memories managed to creep in. Most of the time Jessica quickly pushed them away, tucking them safely into the deepest recesses of her brain where they could do her no harm. Other times, especially at night, in her loft bed, those thoughts would come crawling out to bite. Her breath caught in her throat as her eyes burned. The memories were heavy, holding Jessica back as she tried to escape into sleep.

Some nights she dreamed about fishing with Toby or sitting on her father's lap, while others were filled with the faces of evil. On the bad nights, sweat soaked, tears streaking her cheeks, she woke to find Frieda sleeping next to her in the loft. The sight of Frieda always comforted her, particularly after a bad nightmare.

Jessica was now part of a new, if smaller, family.

~

The next two years flew by for Jessica. Busy, work-filled days meant she spent much less time at play than other kids her age. She learned how to sew using animal pelts for fabric. Jessica couldn't help but think about her sister every time she pulled her bone needle through the tanned animal hide. Jamie had loved to sew. These memories were tamed by time and didn't hurt as much. Now, the act of sewing helped Jessica feel closer to her sister.

Plants played a pivotal role in mountain life; learning which were edible and which were poisonous was as important as understanding the medicinal properties of each. Frieda taught her about wild roots, leaves, flowers, and fruits. Jessica learned how to make an antidote for snakebites, how to use tree sap to stop infections, and endless other remedies.

Life on the mountain was often extremely hostile. Brutal winters seemed as if they would never end. The snowy months were long and hard for the pair. They huddled inside, sometimes for days on end, while nothing moved outside. Frieda, determined the young girl would get an education, thought this the perfect time to channel the always-active youngster's energy into learning.

Lethargic and bored, Jessica had little interest in reading, writing, and arithmetic. Why would she need to know such things? Like other girls her age, she would get lost in daydreams, her mind racing with thoughts of so many other things she wished she could be doing. *Trapping, fishing, hunting, anything would be better than this.* A quick, calculated clearing of Frieda's throat always brought Jessica back to reality. In the end, Frieda would succeed in enlightening another mind, much to Jessica's dismay.

Frieda wanted to make sure Jessica could survive on her own in any situation. She taught her the importance of the stars and moon cycles, and how to use them. Vital not only as instruments of time, these heavenly bodies were used for guidance and as a guidepost on the movements of the nature that surrounded them. They called the months of the year by moon names, which took Jessica some getting used to at first. Her favorite month was the Harvest Moon, or September, when the huckleberries ripened. Huckleberries were her favorite.

Sometimes Frieda would point to an object and call it by name in a different language. The words sounded funny to Jessica, but she thought it was fun and did her best to learn each new word she was challenged with.

One of the most important lessons Frieda taught Jessica came in the spring. Nathaniel had been an expert at trapping beavers, and he had passed his knowledge on to Frieda. She, in turn, passed the trade along to the young girl. Once caught, beavers had to be skinned carefully and with skill.

First, Frieda would scoop out the brain and mash it in a bowl. Next, she would add her urine to the bowl, mix the contents, and smear the salty mixture on the pelt. The hide would be nailed to the side of the old cabin, the shape kept as round as possible. The dried pelts made excellent parkas, mittens, and hats. They were essential in keeping the women warm when the air became bitter cold and the ground turned white with heavy snow.

Summers were spent picking fresh berries along the mountainside, the excess carefully dried. When Frieda and Jessica weren't harvesting fruit, they hunted for red meat, fish, and fowl.

Drying meat was a summer priority. Once it had dried, it was pounded into a powder, mixed with hot fat and dried berries, and then mixed into small cakes called pemmican. The cakes were unremarkable on the surface. In the dead of winter, when it was too cold to leave the cabin and food became scarce, they tasted wonderful and calmed hunger pangs.

Chopping, splitting, and stacking wood also took up a lot of time. Somehow the two of them always managed to put away enough to get through the harsh winters. Summers were busy and filled with hard work, but all of it was necessary. Winter on the mountain proved fatal if one was not properly prepared.

Jessica needed less and less supervision as time went on. She reveled in the independence her abilities gave her. This was exactly what Frieda had hoped for. Jessica may have only been twelve, but she had been catapulted into adulthood. No longer the helpless little girl, too scared to come out from under the hay, she now bore a growing portion of the burden as her beloved mentor aged.

One afternoon, not far from the cabin, as Frieda insisted she was never to venture too far, Jessica was out checking on one of her snares. She bent down to check the trap when a rattling noise stopped her cold. She had never heard the sound before. Like rocks shaking in a tin can, the rattler gave little warning before sinking its fangs deep into the flesh of her right forearm. When the snake finally released, Jessica ran back to the cabin.

"It bit me!" she screamed, face chalky white, arm cradled in excruciating pain.

Frieda was out front plucking feathers from a dead grouse. She dropped their dinner, and ran to Jessica, already pulling an old handkerchief out of her pocket. She wrapped the makeshift tourniquet around Jessica's upper arm. Pulling out the knife hanging from her hip, she sliced Jessica's arm right across the two puncture wounds. She put her mouth over the cut, and began to suck and spit.

Frieda's lips and tongue were numb before she was confident she had gotten most of the poison. She carried Jessica into the cabin and put her in bed as the room began to spin around the girl. Frieda retrieved an old jar off of the shelf; mixed the contents with a ladle of water, and feverishly shook the mixture. She lifted Jessica's head and held the jar up to her lips.

Jessica knew she would die without it, but still her body involuntarily retched as she tried to swallow the bitter drink. After getting it down, Frieda tossed the jar aside, and carefully lowered Jessica's head onto the pillow. She removed the tourniquet from the rapidly swelling arm.

"I don't want to die."

"I won't let you. You're going to be just fine," Frieda said in the most reassuring tone she could muster. In all honesty, she had no idea if Jessica would survive. She was scared to death. What had been a long day turned into an even longer night. Worsening, burning with fever and hallucinating, Jessica screamed. Once again the faces of evil men haunted her fevered mind.

"Frieda! They're coming. They're going to find me. Frieda… where are you? Help me!" Jessica said, crying out.

"Child I'm right here. No one is going to hurt you. I promise you. I won't let anyone hurt you, ever again." Frieda tried to soothe the tormented girl. Not being able to pull Jessica from her nightmare was heartbreaking. Her lip and chin trembled even more at the realization it was the first time Jessica had called out for her instead of her parents during one of her terrifying dreams.

Frieda never left her side. For the first time in many years, she prayed. She prayed all night. By morning, the fever had broken. Her girl was out of danger. Once again, Jessica owed her life to the old mountain woman.

CHAPTER NINE

It was impossible to tell who needed the other more. Jessica and Frieda had only each other. The bond between the two became like that of mother and daughter. Jessica adored the older woman, and had anyone witnessed their interactions, it would have been obvious Frieda felt the same way.

As the years passed, Frieda imparted more skills Jessica needed to continue living on the mountain. One of the most essential was how to make arrows. Frieda had learned the method years ago from Nathaniel, and passed the vital technique and craft to Jessica. Since their gunpowder was almost depleted, they relied primarily on the bow to hunt.

Even though she was only fifteen, Jessica had become a pretty good craftsman, able to fix just about anything. She put her skills to use on the cabin. Their home was in better shape than it had been in years. It had problems, as most aging things do, the main one being the roof. It did a decent job of keeping the rain out, but during serious downpours, they had to catch invading water in jars and pans.

Years of labor took their toll on Frieda. Arthritis set in, gnarling and distorting her hands. She continued whittling figures until she could no longer grasp the wood. Even packing her pipe became too painful for her inflamed fingers.

Walking slightly bent at the waist now, Frieda ended most days in a great deal of pain. Jessica massaged a salve of chopped huckleberry leaves and stems onto Frieda's back each night, but this remedy was becoming less effective. Jessica was frustrated at her mentor's helplessness. Frieda had done so much for her. She was able to repay the older woman less and less.

Frieda's legs also betrayed her. Most days they swelled with a slight inward bow. She couldn't get anywhere without her sturdy, oak walking stick, its knots like those on her knuckles.

One evening after dinner, Frieda asked Jessica to join her outside. "Sunset is going to be something to see this evening."

"Let me fix you a pipe and I'll be right out," Jessica said.

"That would be lovely, dear. Thank you." Frieda swayed side-to-side as she made her way out onto the porch.

Jessica brought her the pipe, already lit, and took a seat on the old stump chair. She picked up a small piece of wood and began whittling, the hobby having become her own. The sky burned a pale orange, mixed with swirls of red and yellow. A soft breeze blew bits of wood shaving into a dance around their feet.

Watching Jessica's blade digging into the soft wood, Frieda's mind drifted back to a harrowing event that had taken place many years before. Focusing her gaze on Jessica's young features, Frieda asked, "Are you frightened by Indians?"

Jessica's hands stopped carving. She looked up at Frieda. "I heard my parents talk about them when I was little. The stories I heard scared me. But I've heard you tell stories about your time with them. How kind they were to you. I guess maybe some are good and some are bad. Why?"

"I used to think, when I was young, that Indians were horrible people…mean and ruthless. But I was wrong about them. I don't want you to fear them."

"Why—do you think they will come here someday?" Jessica asked.

"Don't you fret about that. I'm saying don't just assume they're going to hurt you and don't you try and hurt them either. I used to consider them all to be savages. They killed my father. The tribe that took me in years later softened the anger and hatred that had settled in my heart. Loving and kind, they accepted me as one of their own, and if not for their teachings I would never have known how to survive on my own all these years."

"But they killed your father. How can you ever forgive them for that?" Jessica asked.

"They did kill my father, but they were provoked. They were only protecting their way of life. How would you feel if a man came here and told us that we had to leave this place? That this was his property now. Would you just leave peacefully or would you stand up and fight for our home?"

"What would give him the right to do that?" Jessica's expression hardened.

"Exactly. The Indians have been living here long before the settlers came to this country. What gave us the right to claim that we owned the lands and tell them they had to leave—to go somewhere else that wasn't their home?"

Jessica bit her lip, a sure sign she was concentrating. "That's terrible. I can understand why they fight. I would too."

"So promise me, if you ever meet them, you will be kind."

"I promise," Jessica said. She could sense there was more Frieda wanted to say, but she kept it to herself for whatever reason. Jessica didn't ask. She was more focused on getting Frieda to talk about her past. "I'm sorry you lost your father. You've never told me what happened."

"I wasn't much older than you were when you came to live with me. I remember that horrible day as if it happened yesterday. It was a beautiful autumn day and the trees had just begun to change. My father was a damn good trapper, and it wasn't unusual for him to be out checking his traps on a day like that. Trapping was considered to be man's work, but since my father was never blessed with a son, he sometimes took me with him—

but not that day. Oh, how I had wanted to go with him when he left that morning."

"I liked to go with my father too," Jessica said, chiming in, "but I had brothers and they were the ones who usually got to go."

"I guess I was lucky then," Frieda said, smiling. "Looking back, I cherish the time I got to spend with him out in the woods." She paused and then frowned. "That day, however, my mother insisted I help tend to the garden to begin the fall harvest. My sister and I did as we were told. It seemed unusually quiet, except for the birds. It was like they were sitting on my shoulder, singing just for me. Right before it happened, they got quiet. It was like they knew."

Frieda grew quiet for a passing moment. She stared into the distance, lost in thought, before she continued. "Howling screams filled the air. The hair on the back of my neck stood up. Our neighbor ran out from the woods so fast he couldn't speak. He had to catch his breath first. His face was white and his eyes were wide."

"What happened?" Jessica's eyebrows shot up.

"He just screamed 'They shot him!' My mother ran to him asking: Who? Who was shot? The corn fell out of her hands. I think she already knew." Frieda stared intently at Jessica.

"He said, 'Jasper!' Then collapsed, face down in the dirt. That's when we saw the arrow sticking out of his back. I can still see the dust flying when his head slammed into the ground. Jasper Saylor, my father was out there, shot. I knew right then our lives were changed forever."

"I can still see bad things too. I think I always will." Jessica wanted to know more, but didn't want to ask. She could tell by Frieda's expression how painful the memory was. Her own eyes welled up, thoughts of her own family filling her mind.

"I think you're right about that. Some things just get etched in our minds, unfortunately." Frieda shook her head, and returned to her story. "I saw a group of dark-skinned men with painted faces riding over the ridge. They yelled high-pitched war cries. I thought we were next, but then they turned their horses and rode out of sight. Before my mother ran to Father, she ordered us to stay where we were. I suppose she didn't want her little girls to see him like that. My heart breaks that you had to see such things."

"I wish there was a way to unsee the bad things."

"Me too, dear."

"Why did they kill him?" Jessica asked.

"I learned the Indians were very angry with us white folk. They felt we were depleting their food supply and forcing them off their lands. They were right about that. Men, women, and children…so many lives lost on both sides. It's a shame."

Jessica sat in silence as Frieda continued telling her story.

"The years after Father's passing were tough on Mother. Lavina and I always worked hard to take some of the burdens off of her. I think she was actually relieved when I met Nathaniel. He came to our village one summer to visit with his cousins. He was a fine man, and like Father, he could trap anything. I think Mother felt I would be taken care of and she wouldn't have to worry about me as much if I got married—like my sister did. Lavina married a man named Elgie Wilson, and they moved to Philadelphia the year before I met Nathaniel."

"Was Elgie a trapper too?" Jessica asked.

"No, dear, he was a book-learning kind of fellow," Frieda said with a chuckle. "Elgie was studying to be a lawyer. Anyway, I felt as if I was her last burden. I knew she loved me, but I knew she worried about my future too. I wasn't attracted to Nathaniel in the beginning, but over time our friendship grew deeper and he finally won me over. I agreed to accept his marriage proposal under one condition—we had to stay and take care of Mother."

"I wouldn't have left my mother either. I miss her so much."

"I know you do. It's not fair what happened to you. You lost so much and it breaks my heart," Frieda said with a pained expression.

"So, did you?" asked Jessica.

"Did I what?"

"Stay there and take care of your mother?"

"Yes. Nathaniel was a kind man. He had no problem with that. We settled into a nice life together, had our beautiful boy, and looked after my mother. Our little town grew over the years, and I became the local teacher. I enjoyed my time with the children. I will never forget those years."

"I wish I got to know Nathaniel and Patrick."

"Me too, Jessica," Frieda said, eyes filling with tears.

"I know how that feels to miss someone so much. It's a pain like no other."

"It's something that you and I will carry for the rest of our lives. But we both have fond memories we keep in our hearts," Frieda said with a sigh.

"That's true," Jessica said, nodding.

With an unfocused gaze, Frieda continued on with her story. "We stayed in Pennsylvania until Mother passed away. Nathaniel had heard talk that the lands to the west were plentiful with all sorts of animals, and with the animals all but gone in our area, he was more than ready to take us away and make a new start. Having just lost Mother, I still wasn't quite back to myself yet. I guess you could say I had just been going through the motions. I was thirty-three years old, and like Nathaniel, I wanted to see what another state had to offer."

"So that's how you ended up here?" Jessica asked.

"Not exactly. We were planning to go to Illinois, but that all changed when we met a chieftain from another tribe who came to the Dothka village. After speaking with him, we made other arrangements, and eventually made it here."

Frieda sighed. The embers in her pipe, forgotten in her hand, had grown cold. "If I had stayed in Pennsylvania, my boy would still be alive. The guilt of that decision has been so hard to live with. I don't know that it was fate or a grand plan or anything like that at work. Sometimes things just work out the way they do. I spent years of my life questioning the Great Spirit. Why this, and why that? But, I do know this: if I hadn't gone through all of that, I would have never been here for you. You are the ray of sunlight radiating out of my darkness. Because of you, I know the loss of my son was not in vain."

Chin trembling, Jessica reached for Frieda's withered hand. The sun had long since set, and the once-perfect breeze now blew cool across the porch. She could tell by the faraway look in her old friend's eyes the story had taken a lot out of her. Jessica stood and took the pipe from Frieda's lap. Frieda allowed herself to be led by the hand into the cabin. The old woman fell asleep as soon as Jessica tucked her into bed.

Jessica lay awake for quite some time, mulling over everything Frieda said. She didn't think she'd ever be half as strong as the woman softly snoring below her.

CHAPTER TEN

1861

Jessica nocked an arrow onto the bowstring. A large elk stood grazing in the meadow, completely unaware of the sharp projectile trained on it. A light gust blew. Jessica held her shot, waiting for the right moment. The soft twang of the string was the only sound as the arrow flew toward its mark. Her aim was true. Tip through its heart, the animal dropped.

At seventeen, Jessica had become a tall and beautiful woman. With high cheekbones, chiseled jawline, and emerald eyes, her face was stunning; the only blemish being a crescent-shaped scar on her forehead. Though dressed from head to toe in loose-fitting, buckskin clothes, it was obvious her body was well built, lean, and muscular from years of mountain living. No longer the frail little girl who hid in the barn, Jessica was now a strong, young woman.

Jessica knelt beside the fallen elk, giving thanks as she always did when taking an animal's life. Frieda had taught her to acknowledge the Great Spirit for providing the sacrifice. In her mind, she didn't do exactly that. She whispered silently to herself, giving instead a small thank you to her father and brothers who she felt were always with her on her hunts.

Her long, ginger hair tumbled in the wind as she field-dressed her kill. She wasted no time, working fast with the large blade. She wanted to get back to the cabin as quickly as possible to check on Frieda. Her mentor was not recovering from the illness that had befallen her during the winter. Frieda's health was deteriorating by the day. No longer able to make it out of bed, Frieda depended solely on Jessica for everything.

The bedridden woman spent most of her days worrying, plagued with anxiety, agonizing about what would become of Jessica after the Great Spirit came for her. She knew it would be soon and didn't want Jessica to stay isolated and alone in the old cabin. The young woman had no experience living in a town as an adult. This frightened the ailing woman to the point where she spent most nights staring at the loft above, fretting over what to do.

After many sleepless nights the solution came to her, and on one of her better days, she motioned for Jessica to come sit next to her. The girl's radiant smile illuminated her entire face, bringing a similar expression to Frieda's. Jessica sat beside Frieda and held her hand, grateful the old woman seemed to be feeling better.

Frieda said, "You're going to have to leave here and go make a new start in the world."

Jessica's smile cracked a little. "I'm not going any—"

"Now hold on just a second and hear me out, girl," Frieda said. Her rigid tone erased what remained of Jessica's smile. It wasn't unusual for Frieda to be stern with her. But this was different than the tone she took when Jessica had misbehaved or needed a push on her schoolwork—more urgent somehow.

Frieda's hand squeezed a little tighter. Jessica let out a long sigh, grateful for the small show of affection. "I know you don't want to face it, but I'm not going to be around here forever. I've thought long and hard about this. You are going to have to leave here."

"Leave and go where?" Jessica cocked her head to the side.

"There's a place called Ely—"

"There isn't even any way to cross the river. You said the

bridge washed away years ago," Jessica said, interrupting. She was confused and more than a little scared.

"There never was a bridge that got washed away. I just told you that. The river can be crossed. I've done it before. That's how Nathaniel and I got up here. There's a secret crossing. The Indians that led us here showed us the way," Frieda finally confessed.

"Why didn't you ever tell me?" Jessica asked, dumbfounded by the revelation.

"You were young and besides, what difference would it have made? I would've taken you across years ago if you had kin searching for you, but you told me you had no one. I guess maybe I was wrong not to tell you. I'm sorry." Frieda shrugged her shoulders.

"No reason to be sorry. I wouldn't have left you. What do you mean by a secret crossing?" Jessica asked with raised eyebrows.

"Long ago, way before our time, when this mountain was being formed, somehow a natural granite crossing was made in the river. It's like a bridge hiding beneath the surface. Nathaniel said it was a large slab of granite that broke off the mountain long before men were even walking the earth. It can't be seen even if you're looking right at it, but it's there. On the north side of the slab is a jagged ledge. Sticks up about three feet high and runs the entire length. The force of the river hits that instead of your legs. Keeps you from being swept off your feet."

Jessica had no desire to leave and opened her mouth to say so, only to be quieted by Frieda's raised hand.

"Let me finish. It's a tough world out there. It's hard enough for a man to survive, but damn near impossible for a single woman to make it on her own. You, of all people, know how cruel some men can be. Do you think a beautiful woman could just walk into a town alone without drawing unwanted attention? Think about that. If a man walks into town alone no one gives two hoots. I'm telling you, when you go, you're going to have to do something so that you don't stand out. You have to change the way you look."

"What do you mean? I don't understand," Jessica said, rubbing the crescent-shaped scar on her forehead.

"To be safe, I want you to dress like a man. Do this one thing for me, please. I need to know that nothing will happen to you."

"Dress like a man?" Jessica stood up, her green eyes flashing with confusion. "I'm not sure you're thinking clearly today. Why don't you get some rest?" She reached down to feel if Frieda had a fever.

"Now dammit, I don't need rest and my mind has never been more clear. You can do this. I haven't been off the mountain in years, though, so I have no idea what Ely is like after all this time. You don't have to do this forever, just go check things out. See what it's like."

"You're serious?"

"Never been more serious about anything," Frieda said with stern expression.

"How am I supposed to look like a man?" She bit her bottom lip.

"We can work out those details later. Will you go?"

"What if it's a bad place?"

"It might be and it might not…I don't know. Why don't you go down and see? Just go look and then come back here and decide what you want to do. You can always go back down. Why don't you sleep on it, and we can talk about it some more in the morning."

A coughing fit took Frieda's voice away. When she pulled her handkerchief from her mouth, both women tried to disguise their alarm at what they saw. Blood splattered the rag, a small shotgun spray of red.

∽

The talk of leaving troubled Jessica. She tossed and turned in bed, restless. The distress followed her when she finally found sleep. Her eyelids fluttered and a loud moan escaped her lips. Wicked figures from her past found her hiding in the hay. They gave chase. Jessica ran in the darkness, filled with a terror she never knew possible. She woke with a start, sweat-soaked, bile rising in her throat. She stared at the dark ceiling, trying to get the disturbing nightmare out of her mind. Her wandering thoughts turned to Frieda and their conversation from the night before. She replayed Frieda's words over and over, dissecting them while weighing the pros and cons.

The more Jessica thought about it, the more the idea made sense. She knew better than anyone bad men did indeed exist. The thought of living in a strange town where she wouldn't fit in frightened her, but the idea of living alone on the mountain with no human contact was equally as daunting.

By dawn, she had reached a decision.

While feeding Frieda breakfast, Jessica announced her intentions. "I'll do it when the time comes, but then and only then. I'm only going down to look and then I'm coming back here."

Frieda sighed. The lined features on her face relaxed, her relief obvious. "I need you to get into my trunk. Take out Nathaniel's shirts and my old dresses and bring me the tanned outfit underneath," Frieda said, pointing past Jessica.

In all the years Jessica had been there, she had never looked in the weathered trunk sitting at the foot of the bed. She knew whatever was in the trunk was important to Frieda, and that it had something to do with her past. Jessica had respected her privacy. Now, she did as she was told and opened it. Two neatly folded outfits were placed on top of the clothing. Her breath caught from the sight. She knew whose they were, but she didn't bring attention to them. Not wanting to upset Frieda, Jessica sat Patrick's clothing aside with the utmost care. Beneath the remaining shirts and dresses lay a beautiful outfit made of buckskin adorned with fringe running down the sides of the sleeves and pants. The clothing appeared as if it had never been worn.

"My friends made them for Nathaniel and presented them to him on the day we left the village," Frieda said in between coughs. "He just never was comfortable wearing such an outfit. I want you to have it and wear it when you go. I know you're not that big up top, but still you're gonna have to do something to hide your chest."

"Hide my chest?" Jessica crossed her arms over her bosom.

"Yes. Cut up one of my dresses and wrap it around your chest. A man can't have chesty bulges. There's something else you'll need, too. Fetch me that tin off the shelf," Frieda said as she pointed to it.

Jessica handed the tin to Frieda and watched as the woman struggled to open it. It was sad to see someone who had always been so strong become frustrated with her own hands. They wouldn't cooperate for such a small undertaking. Jessica took it gently and opened it with one deft twist.

"Thank you, dear. Over the years, I did have some luck." Frieda shook several gold nuggets from the tin onto her palm. "I never needed to exchange them for money. No need for it around here. Underneath my bed, dead center, remove the loose floorboards and you will find more." She placed the small nuggets in Jessica's hand, saying, "Take one of these when you go. Hide it. Use the money I have first. You don't want to do anything with the gold unless you have to."

As the old woman handed her the gold, Jessica noticed how emaciated Frieda had become. She must have seen these changes before, as she had been bathing her for some time. The talk of her leaving and going to Ely finally forced her mind to accept the reality of the situation. Jessica fought back tears and forced a smile, appreciative of the gifts. She had no idea of their true value.

It was the beginning of March when Frieda revealed her plan to Jessica. From the moment it was hatched, Jessica spent every day perfecting the scheme. She attempted to adopt the mannerisms of a man, recalling how her brother Daniel had carried himself. Her muscular physique, gained by extremely rugged mountain living, helped provide the illusion of masculinity.

During the day, she practiced speaking in a lower tone. When she was alone, she said random things aloud to get in the habit of doing so. "The sky is blue, the grass is green, and snow is white." Over and over she chanted, deep-voiced, the forest her backdrop, and the trees her audience.

Jessica couldn't help but think about Toby. She remembered the time she was hiding up in a tree and Toby was trying to get his own voice to change. He had sounded so silly at the time and Jessica had laughed at him. She had so many regrets about picking on him. She would give anything to see him one more time, to tell him how sorry she was and how much she loved him.

In the following weeks, Frieda made suggestions, hoping to fine-tune their plan. As Jessica let the thoughts turn in her mind, she stewed, still unsure if she could even pull off such a masquerade.

"Tell me about Ely," Jessica asked one evening, trying to get a handle on what she was getting herself into.

"Well, it's not really a town like you might be thinking of. It's just a trading post or at least it was the last time I was there. They were just starting construction on a couple more buildings back then, so by now I reckon there's more than the trading post."

Frieda went on to explain it would take her six days to make the journey. She'd made the trip with Nathaniel a couple times when they needed supplies. Once he died, she never again left the mountain.

"It is only possible to cross the river when the spring rains stop. During the summer months. It's the only time of year the water level lowers in the river. Any other time the water would be over your head. When the moon grows half-full, it will be time to leave. By the time you get to the crossing, the light of a full moon will light your way, but you need to cross in the dead of night."

"Why at night?" Jessica asked.

"No one can ever see you making the crossing. If anybody saw the river could be crossed, they would invade our mountain. They would come and decimate the lands as they always do. Only cross in the privacy of night. That's why you gotta wait for the full moon."

Jessica nodded.

"Start out by following the stream. Follow it to the lake, and then you'll see six tall sycamores side by side to the east. The space in the middle of the tree line marks the path. Once you get on the path, you'll notice trees along the way that have special markings pointing out the route. Look carefully for them every fifty yards or so. Nathaniel and I notched them years ago so they may be hard to find, but they are there."

"What do they look like?"

"They look like antler rubs. No rhyme or reason to 'em. The key is to look at the bottom of the marks. They point in the direction you need to go."

"Do you think after all these years that the path is still there?"

"I'm sure it's overgrown by now, so pay close attention and find those marked trees. That will keep you heading in the right direction. As soon as the sun begins to set, it will be time to look for a place to rest for the night. Every morning when the sun comes up, make sure you start out in that direction. Follow the river south when you get there. The most important thing is to keep that river on your left and to never lose sight of it for any reason. Stay well hidden under the trees. For all I know folks could be living along the other side of the river by now."

"I'll make sure no one sees me."

"By late afternoon on the fifth day, you need to watch for the crossing. A crooked tree will mark it. You'll be able tell it wasn't naturally made that way. It's oddly bent at the trunk. Directly across the river from it is another tree, same kind of bent trunk. This will be the only spot to cross. Stay between the two trees or you'll be swept away."

"I have to be honest. That scares me," Jessica said, eyes wide.

"Just go slow and feel with your feet. You'll be fine. Keep your leg up against the ledge on the north side of the river. Once you cross, rest until the sun comes up. Then, continue walking ahead and eventually you'll come to Ely. Take as many beaver pelts with you as you can carry and sell them at the trading post. That will give you some extra funds to start with. Remember, only one piece of gold goes with you, but don't do anything with it until you need to. Like I said, I haven't been there in years and I have no idea what you can expect. Beaver pelts are one thing, but gold is something else altogether. You don't want to do anything to bring unwanted attention to yourself if you don't have to. So be careful if you do anything with the gold."

By the end of May, Frieda's health had deteriorated to the point in which all rational thought frequently left her, sometimes for days on end. Jessica stayed by her side. Some days the woman who raised her from a young age no longer recognized her. On good, lucid days, they talked about the 'plan' and enjoyed each other's company. They knew they didn't have long together, and they wanted to be as prepared as possible for when the time came.

Jessica did a trial run to see what she would look like dressed as a man. She took one of Frieda's old dresses out of the trunk, the buckskin outfit, and Frieda's hat. She went outside and placed everything on the stump chair out on the porch. She cut the dress into long strips, which she wrapped tightly around her chest. The fabric concealed her breasts as Frieda had said it would. It wasn't as uncomfortable as Jessica had expected. She put on her shirt, buttoned to the top, and then donned the pants and the coat. Her long locks she tucked away, hidden under Frieda's hat.

She walked to the bed where Frieda was sleeping and waited for the fragile woman to wake.

Frieda blinked hard when she woke, trying to focus on the outline of the figure by her bedside.

"It's me, Jessica," she said in her practiced low tone. "I've fixed you some squirrel stew."

Frieda ventured a small bite from the offered spoon. "Mmm," she said, enjoying the savory taste. Frieda's watery eyes traveled up and down Jessica's buckskin clad figure. She nodded in approval. "I know you don't want to look like that, but it makes me feel like nothing will happen to you down there."

"Do you think I will fool people?"

"I do. If I didn't know any better I would think I was looking at a young man. Thank you for doing this for me."

"I still can't believe I'm going to do it." Jessica eased onto the bed beside Frieda. She felt the older woman's forehead. "How are you feeling?"

"Not good, but here until the Great Spirit comes. Don't think I'm going to be around for your birthday this year. Hard to believe you're turning eighteen. Where has the time gone?"

"Don't say that. You're gonna be just fine."

"All right, if you say so, child." Frieda smiled.

Frieda ate more of the warm stew, trying her best in between bites to assure Jessica she'd have a successful journey. She tired quickly. Stew broth ran down her chin as she rested back on the pillow.

Jessica wiped it away with her handkerchief. "You get some rest."

Frieda spent the next few days in and out of awareness. Lost in a fog of confusion, she called out to people who weren't there. Sometimes she would yell for Patrick, other times for her late husband. Jessica continued her round-the-clock care, always trying to comfort and calm Frieda. Whenever she asked about Patrick, Jessica told her he was fine, merely sleeping in the loft above. *Surely this one small lie could be overlooked given the circumstances*, she thought.

Jessica was sleeping on a chair, head on Frieda's bed, when Frieda cried out, "Where's my daughter? I can't find her. She is lost in the woods! Help! Help me!"

Jessica stroked the frightened woman's forehead. "It's all right. Shhh," she said, trying to soothe her companion. Frieda had never mentioned a daughter. Jessica wondered if it was the delirium talking, or if there was something in Frieda's life too painful to talk about. She didn't have time to give it much thought, because Frieda grabbed her arm.

"There you are! I have been looking everywhere for you. I thought you were lost in the woods. Don't run off again." Tears rolled down her cheeks as she spoke.

The sentiment behind Frieda's words was not lost on Jessica. She couldn't hold back her own tears. She had never known for certain until that moment Frieda had considered her a daughter all these years.

Jessica kissed the frail woman's brow. "I love you," she said, voice trembling. "You mean the world to me. Always have."

"I love you too, dear, always and forever. I'm so tired." Frieda's voice was fading.

"You can go with the Great Spirit. Don't you worry about me. I'll be fine. You get some rest now." Jessica hugged her. It was a moment Jessica would carry in her heart until the day she died.

Jessica continued to sit vigil over Frieda and listened as her breathing changed into a ragged gurgle from somewhere deep within her chest. Over the course of hours, it slowed and quieted to a tiny wheeze. Jessica remained close by, watching over the woman who had cared for her so lovingly over the years.

Jessica thought back to the times as a young girl when Frieda had sat watch over her bedside in the same way. Only now did she really appreciate how difficult those times must have been for her, especially after all of the loss Frieda had endured herself.

Frieda had been able to open not only her home to Jessica, but her heart as well. She taught her not only how to survive, but to become a strong, independent woman. That Frieda didn't take her back down the mountain and hand her off to someone else was a true testament to her character.

The rise and fall of Frieda's chest finally stopped. Jessica sobbed and continued to sit, holding the hand long after the delicate fingers had turned cold. It was a devastating loss for Jessica—a feeling she had not experienced since before coming to live at the cabin. Her heart was being ripped from her chest. Without

Frieda, she didn't know how she would ever cope. Time lost all meaning as Jessica sat next to Frieda. Holding the lifeless, contorted hand, she swallowed hard. A lump caught in her throat as she tried to speak.

"Frieda…there are no words I can say to tell you how much you've meant to me. You took me in and cared for me as your own. You taught me so much and I owe my life to you. I am the person I am today because of you. I was so lucky to have been found by you and I just wish we had more time together. I'm going to miss you—more than you can imagine. I know someday I'll see you again, and I'll get to meet Nathaniel and Patrick. I feel that somehow you're with my family too. I can see you with them. I'm sure they're thanking you for taking such good care of me. It gives me some comfort knowing you are all together. We are all a family and someday we'll all be together again. I love you."

Jessica kissed Frieda's hand before tenderly placing it on the bed. After one final kiss to the forehead, now free of the lines creasing its brow hours earlier, Jessica rose and removed the bearskin hanging from the wall at the head of the bed. As gently as she could, she picked Frieda up in her arms. The woman, who had been so strong, was now so light, wasted away from weeks of illness. She placed the body carefully on the pelt.

She took one last look, and then gingerly wrapped the body of the woman who had meant so much to her in the hide. Frieda had been fifty-nine years old. Jessica went outside and dug a hole underneath the large sycamore next to Nathaniel's grave. With the utmost care, she carried Frieda's body outside and lovingly placed the beloved bundle in the hole.

After replacing the soil, she stood staring at the newly mounded pile, tears streaming down her cheeks. She had no idea how in the world she was supposed to go on now. Jessica hauled small rocks from the stream to the grave. She made trip after trip, working nonstop, not finishing until the sun began to set. Satisfied she had enough, she knelt down once again, carefully arranging the rocks. Once the last stone was in place, there was only one thing left to do.

She returned to cabin and got into Frieda's trunk once more. She took out one of Nathaniel's shirts, and tore off one of the sleeves. She made her way back to the grave where she tied the piece of fabric to a branch and stuck it in the ground, marking the spot so that the Great Spirit would know where to find Frieda. After hearing Frieda talk all of these years, it was important for her to carry on the ritual Frieda had continued after her devastating loss in Indiana all those years ago. Jessica stared at the ground even after the sun had fled and the shadows swallowed it. *At least she's no longer suffering.*

At peace knowing Frieda was once again beside her beloved Nathaniel, Jessica washed up in the stream. As she splashed cold water on her face, she chanced a glance at the moon growing larger with each passing night. She knew there was nothing holding her back now from embarking on the plan she and Frieda had cooked up together.

Her stomach turned, and her breathing quickened in a surge of fear of the unknown, of the great big world out there. But then Jessica felt another new emotion surge within her: anticipation of what the future may bring.

CHAPTER ELEVEN

Frieda's passing devastated Jessica. In an effort to keep her mind off the deep sorrow threatening to drown her, she focused instead on the things that needed to be finished around the cabin. Mending the leaking roof was not only helpful for keeping tears at bay, but it was also an ideal time to practice her lower pitched voice. Repeatedly she chanted random, nonsensical sentences, rehearsing verbiage in her new tone. Before long, Jessica no longer had to remind herself to speak in a lower tone.

Her anxiety grew as she finalized preparations. The last task was the one she dreaded most of all. Jessica studied the rippling image reflecting back at her in the stream. She separated a long, silky lock of her hair, winding it softly around a trembling finger. Closing her eyes for a moment, she fondly remembered Frieda brushing her hair when she was young. She didn't give herself time to lose her nerve. Pulling the razor-sharp knife from its sheath, another gift from Frieda, she sliced off the beloved strand of hair. With steely resolve, she continued to cut as clumps of hair drifted lazily downstream, her heart aching as if it too was floating away, adrift, powerless in the current.

Staring at her reflection once again, she barely held back tears, as hair that once reached her hips now scarcely grazed her shoulders. She stood and brushed stray remnants from her arms. *Good Lord, it's only hair,* she told herself.

When the morning finally arrived, she gave herself a pep talk. "I can do this," she repeated as she readied, wrapping her chest with the strips of cloth and then getting into costume.

Concealing her femininity was a fairly easy task. She put on a long sleeve shirt, buttoned it up to the top, and then slipped into the buckskin pants. With the coat and Frieda's old feathered hat, the illusion was complete. She secured supplies to her waist: knife, powder horn, shot pouch, a large bag of jerky, and canteen. Last, she poured the contents of an old tin into her hand, and placed the coins into a small leather pouch. It was Frieda's life savings and she would be careful to spend it wisely. Jessica secured one gold nugget, Frieda's allowance, in her breast binding for safekeeping. If she ran into trouble along the way it wouldn't be easily found. Over one shoulder was a roll of thick beaver pelts and a deerskin, supported by a long, rawhide strap. Her leather pouch and rifle were flung over the other. Taking one final look around the place, she was as ready as she could be. She walked outside and closed the door behind her.

The sun was just rising on that mid-June day. The instructions Frieda had given her were fresh in her mind, each word still clear. They gave her a sense of peace: she would not be alone. Frieda would be with her.

She turned back for one last look at her home, letting the loving memories wash over her. She pushed them out of her head and stepped into the forest, saying goodbye to her old home, and to Jessica. Now, and for the foreseeable future, she was Jesse.

Jesse followed the stream until it spilled into the large mountain lake. She had been here many times over the years, but had never given much thought to the six sycamore trees lined up in a row to the east. She followed the directions and discovered the faint trail Frieda described between the third and fourth trees. The path was overgrown with weeds and shrubs; even small trees grew sporadically.

She moved slowly, examining trees as she went. It wasn't long before she found one with the special notches carved into the bark. She ran her fingers over them and thought about Frieda and Nathaniel standing at this exact place all those years ago. A lump welled up in her throat and in that moment it was hard for her to swallow. The marks were old, barely visible. She used her knife, their knife, to redo the markings. There was some relief in finding them. Now, she knew exactly what she was looking for.

The beginning of the descent was fairly easy, not too rocky or difficult. Jesse found each marked tree along the way, taking a few extra minutes to deepen the cuts with her knife. Her bulky pack of supplies and pelts weighed her down. By midday, sun directly overhead, she felt as if she was baking, even though shaded by the ample canopy of the trees. She had to pause for a break.

Jesse was in top physical shape, but the added weight was taking its toll. By the time the sun started to set, she was exhausted. She dropped her provisions and collapsed to the ground. She snacked on some deer jerky and washed it down with water from the canteen. Darkness and sleep both came quickly. There, under the massive star-filled sky, the old deerskin embraced her like a warm hug.

The second morning started out rough. Her body was sore and her muscles ached even before she set out. The landscape was magnificent and pure; the clean air and the sounds of nature filled her senses. The scenery was a welcome distraction from the grueling task at hand.

The routine for the next few days was monotonous. She continued east, always descending, studying her surroundings along the way.

On the fifth morning, she heard the sounds of rushing water. She found herself standing on the west bank of the Devil's Fork, water roaring fiercely before her. Boulders were scattered throughout the raging torrent, the crashing water exploding high into the air as it collided with the jagged rocks. The river was still flanked on each side by thick, dense woods, as she remembered. There were no signs of people anywhere.

Jesse dropped her belongings and removed her coat, enjoying the cool breeze. She sat on the ground to admire the beautiful yet daunting sight. Shaking her head in disbelief, she was shocked she had made it across the river alive when she was a young girl. It had been a miracle. Someone must have been looking down on her to help guide her across such wild, deadly waters.

"Keep going." Jesse shuddered, certain she had heard Frieda's voice on the wind.

She hefted her belongings and began to head south, keeping a watchful eye on the river flowing on her left. This part of the trip was more difficult than descending the mountain had been, as the roots of the ever-present trees became thick tangles underfoot. Perhaps the change in altitude or nearby water had provided better growing conditions. Whatever the reason, the woods were much thicker near the base of the mountain, the footing more treacherous.

Jesse stumbled upon a well-worn deer path, making navigation easier. It was obvious more than deer had been using the path. She had to be careful to avoid occasional piles of bear scat as well; the excrement the only sign of life she saw. The day proved to be as lonely and isolated as all the ones before.

Stopping abruptly, she was caught off guard by the spectacle before her. A tree loomed like a misshapen and out-of-place arm flexing its muscle. The trunk was oddly bent only a few feet up from the base, as if something had made it grow horizontally for a time and then released it to grow vertically. It looked like no other tree she had ever seen and her heart soared in excitement.

This has to be it.

Jesse searched across the water and found an identical, disfigured tree standing on the far riverbank. Walking closer to the edge of the embankment, she stared into the fast moving current, trying her best to see the granite crossing hidden beneath its surface. She knew it had to be there, the hidden underwater bridge between the two route marker trees. Frieda told her the granite slab path was invisible beneath the water, even if someone were looking right at it. Jesse would feel a whole lot better if she could at least catch a glimpse. No matter how long she stared, she saw nothing but rolling water. The longer she looked, the more anxious she became. She had to cross, or at least attempt it, even if she died trying.

But first, she would rest. She camped beside the mighty river, oblivious even to the howling of wolves off in the distance.

An owl's screech woke her from her slumber. She stretched her arms and legs, shaking them to get the blood flowing again. Jesse double-checked everything was securely fastened to her. By the light of the full moon, she had no trouble making her way down the grassy embankment.

She held her rifle with both hands, chest level, for balance. The cold made her suck in a breath as she put a foot in the water. Her next step dropped her waist-deep into the torrent. Her muscles tensed.

Sliding her feet around, she bumped up against the knee-high granite ledge, and gauged the passage to be about six feet wide. She made sure her left leg was always as close to the ledge as possible. She had to lean a little to counteract the force of the water against her. Gripping her rifle firmly, she continued moving forward. Jesse focused on the bent tree ahead. Slowly and cautiously she shuffled, unaware the bottoms of her moccasins were becoming slick.

The passage was going well until her right foot slid out from under her. She fell, dropping her rifle when her elbow hit the underwater ledge. She grabbed the submerged rock with one hand, her other flailing for a lifeline that didn't exist. Jesse struggled against the current, trying to keep her grip and her head above water. It took all her strength to pull her body up against the ledge. Clinging with both hands, she gasped for breath and tried to stand.

Back on her feet, she steadied herself and grabbed the

swinging rifle. Her neck stung where the leather thong had rubbed her skin raw, but without it her weapon would have been lost. Coughing, lungs and throat still on fire, she crept onward. She was more careful this time with every short step.

She collapsed, shaking and wet, when she made it. Pain throbbed in her arm. A tear rolled down her cheek as stared down the river. She thought of Frieda and how proud her old friend would be.

She sat, unnerved by the senseless oversight that had almost cost her her life. She knew the bottoms of her moccasins became slippery when they were wet, but she had been so focused on all the other details of the plan she had overlooked that critical fact. Future crossings would be made without them. Her bare feet would give her better traction.

Frieda must have known it could be deadly to cross in moccasins, but in her delirium she had forgotten to warn her. Jesse hoped there was nothing else Frieda had failed to mention. Drained of all energy now and shivering, Jesse wanted nothing more than to light a fire and get warm. She chose to forego one that night, fearing it would draw unwanted attention.

Jesse noticed the missing feather when she removed her hat. She pushed aside the twang of guilt, telling herself, *No, Frieda would be proud that I made it this far. I could have lost much more.* She wanted to get out of her wet clothes, but knew they wouldn't be dry by morning without a fire. It was a nightmare getting into wet leather.

Jesse cut pine boughs for bedding. A layer of branches would protect her wet body from the heat-stealing forest floor. She curled up in a ball and arranged the rest on top of her. Knowing her rifle had been rendered useless and her pouch of gunpowder was ruined, she slept fitfully, knife in hand.

∽

She cringed as she woke to the feeling of wet leather against her skin. Chilled and sore, she started walking, hopeful the activity and the sun would soon put a stop to her shivers. Jesse's nervousness intensified with each step. Could she really pull off this charade? *What happens if I get caught? What will they do to me? Do I really need to look like this?*

A sick feeling returned to her already queasy stomach. There was curiosity mixed in with her fear. After having lived so long on the mountain, she was afraid to do what most people do every day. Although scared, she also wanted to experience life in the town. She smiled, recalling visits to Granite Falls as a youngster. Visiting Carlson's store had always been exciting. She got to see other people besides her family, and it was where her mother would buy her a piece of candy.

After several more hours of walking, she saw buildings off in the distance. She was relieved at having made it without getting lost. There was no turning back now.

Jesse made it to Ely late in the afternoon. It was obvious the town was much more than a mere trading post now. She saw movement in every direction and all types of people going about their business. Beautifully dressed women walked along the road, their hems dragging the dirt behind them. Men of all dress milled about, their noises mixed in with children who ran in all directions. Their laughter combined with the other street noises overloaded Jesse's senses. It had been years since she had heard any human sounds besides Frieda's voice.

Word there was gold in California had brought people into the area years ago. Even though most were simply passing through, Ely thrived. The town was still growing; men pounded nails on the new buildings being constructed alongside the road.

Jesse stood frozen, taking in the sights, and trying to get a feel for the area. Galloping hooves shot past her and interrupted her observations. Her first lesson—don't stand in the street or you were likely to get run over. She drew a few looks on her way through town, but no one gave more than a quick glance. She seemed to blend in.

Frieda was right.

Coming across a building with a sign offering rooms for a dollar, she thought a warm place to sleep for the night was well worth spending some money on. She entered into a room with a fireplace and a couple of empty chairs. A woman greeted her warmly the moment she stepped inside. She was pretty, with a slender figure and long, braided hair pinned up in a bun.

"Well young man, you look like you could use some rest. I take it you'll be needin' a room?" the woman asked.

Jesse nodded and followed to a room down the hall. There were three other doors, which she assumed were also bedrooms. Not trusting herself to say too much, Jesse said, "Thank you, ma'am."

"Welcome, and the name's Edith," she said, her voice kind.

"Jesse McGinnis." She nodded.

"Well, Jesse, if you'll be needing anything just give a holler."

"Just need to get some sleep."

Jesse thanked her once more before closing the door. She fell back on the soft feather bed, instantly relishing in the comfort. It was a far cry from the old straw mattress up at the cabin. She stared at the knotty pine ceiling, grateful to have made it this far without having been found out.

I can't believe she called me young man. Maybe I can pull this off, she thought. It calmed her fears. She soon drifted into a deep, refreshing, and comfortable sleep.

A firm knock on the door woke her a few hours later. "It's Edith. You hungry?"

It was uncharacteristic of Edith to offer food to a customer. She had always made it clear to her guests, without being rude, the Tin Plate would be happy to accommodate them if they got hungry. There was something different about her newest lodger. Jesse's despair and sadness were almost palpable. Edith had a pretty good intuition, and an even bigger heart. Maybe that's why she broke her own rule and took pity on the worn traveler.

Jesse opened the door.

"I made a pot of stew and thought you might be hungry," Edith said, standing in the doorway.

Hungrier than she realized, for a hot meal no less, Jesse was more than happy to accept the invitation. "Thank you ma'am. That's kind of you to offer." Her voice was still raspy from sleep.

"Well, follow me," Edith called out over her shoulder, already heading to the kitchen. She was already dipping the ladle into the steaming pot when Jesse caught up. "Pull up a chair. I'll take care of ya," Edith said.

"Thank you," Jesse said. She took in a deep breath. *It smells so good.*

Edith pulled up a chair and sat across from the newcomer. "That is quite the outfit you got on. Did you make it yourself?"

"No ma'am," Jesse said, "it was a gift."

The whole ensemble impressed Edith, being a seamstress herself. Edith spoke as Jesse ate. "My husband and I actually started the trading post here in town. After Isaac died, it got to be too much. I sold it to a fella who made me an offer too good to pass up. Turned our home into the only hotel in Ely. I know it's not much. Four bedrooms and a couple fireplaces, but it will keep the rain off your head and it's a nice place to get some rest."

Noticing Jesse's empty bowl, Edith stood to get more. "Where are my manners? I haven't let you get a word in."

Jesse didn't mind at all. She had been alone for a while. It was nice to hear a kind voice again. "Thank you, ma'am, but no. I've had plenty."

"You sure?"

"Yes, ma'am."

"You're welcome. So, where ya from?" Edith asked as she sat back down.

Jesse was caught off guard by the question. Not once in all the months of preparation had she given any thought as to what she would say should someone ask that. Why would she? This was supposed to be a scouting trip only.

She had to think of something on the spot. A small wooden

barrel of potatoes against the wall gave her an idea. Jesse blurted out, "I'm from Barrel." The lie rolled off her tongue too easily for her liking.

"Huh. Never heard of it."

"Yeah...it's really small."

Edith didn't think it odd. People from all over passed through the area. "I noticed you have some pelts with you. Are you taking them to the trading post?"

"Yes."

"Well, when you go in there and drop your pelts on the counter, you tell Felix I said to treat you right. He's an honest man, but he runs a business and sometimes he starts out with a low-ball offer." Edith leaned over the table and whispered, "He's kind of sweet on me. Been flirtin' with me for years."

Jesse thought it was funny Edith felt she had to whisper. It was only the two of them, and yet she acted like someone might over hear her.

"All right, I will and thank you for everything." Not wanting to get caught up in any more lies, Jesse finished by saying, "I think I'm going to turn in for the night." She stood, excused herself from the table and started back to her room.

Edith stuck her head out in the hallway and called out, "I'll bring a fresh pitcher of water to your room in a few minutes so you can wash up."

"Thank you, ma'am."

Edith always had a sixth sense when it came to people. If a person was good or bad, she could feel it in her gut. Even though Jesse didn't have much to say, Edith felt Jesse had a kind and gentle soul. She watched thoughtfully as Jesse closed the bedroom door. There was something unusual about the new guest that intrigued her.

CHAPTER TWELVE

Jesse did not sleep well. She woke in the predawn hours still tired, wanting nothing more than to crawl back under the soft quilt for a few more hours of sleep. It was pointless. She sat on the edge of the bed, weary, mind awhirl with her strange surroundings. After a few minutes of contemplation, she decided it was as good a time as any to check out the sleeping town.

She splashed her face with water Edith had left in a china pitcher atop the worn bureau. The tepid water shocked her into full wakefulness, the desired effect. Her rifle was still unusable, but she took it with her. The sight of it would hopefully deter any trouble she might run into.

The street was empty as most of the businesses were still closed for the night. Light emitting from a nearby window piqued her curiosity. The closer she got, the more the aromas inside excited her grumbling stomach. She'd been too overwhelmed upon her arrival to notice the wood-planked Tin Plate sign above the door, now illuminated from light within.

Inside, she was greeted by a brunette woman seated at a table. "Oh, mornin.' You're up and at it early. Have a seat and I'll be right with you," she said, getting up and taking her plate to the back.

Except for wooden chairs and tables, the place was empty at this early hour. Jesse chose a spot next to the window, placing her rifle and hat on the chair next to her.

The woman approached Jesse's table. "You wantin' the special?"

Jesse had no idea what the 'special' was, but nodded, eager to put a taste to the smell.

"Just put on the coffee. I'll bring ya a cup as soon as it's ready. Usually don't get many people in this early," the woman said over her shoulder, returning to the back of the establishment. "Got us an early riser, Joe. Need one special," she called out.

Jesse's vantage point offered a view of a long stretch of the street. Without the overwhelming bustle, the size of the town wasn't nearly as intimidating. She caught her own reflection in the window. She wondered what Frieda would think of the changes to the town, and to herself.

The woman placed a large plate of food in front of her, startling her back to reality. Her mouth watered at the sight: two fried eggs, four pieces of bacon, and two slabs of toasted, buttered bread.

Setting down a steaming cup of coffee, the woman asked, "Ya needin' anything else?"

"No, ma'am. Thank you."

"All right, then. Enjoy." She returned to the back.

It smelled amazing. She dug in, soaking up egg yolk with the toast. It was better than she had eaten in years. Jesse felt bad for thinking so, but knew Frieda would be happy for her. The coffee was perfect, too.

The woman returned as Jesse was finishing the first cup. "How was it?" she asked, pouring a second cup.

"Very good." Jesse smiled.

"Glad to hear it. I'll leave ya to it. No rush. Not like we are needin' the table."

As Jesse sipped her coffee, her thoughts shifted to her family. Years had passed since she had smelled bacon. Images of sitting around the table with her family, eating her mother's cooking, came rushing back. She could almost feel them sitting next to her. She was so lost in the recollection the waitress had to repeat the price of the meal before Jesse acknowledged her. She had no idea how long the woman had been standing there.

Jesse apologized for her inattention as she reached into her pouch and handed over a few coins.

"You look like a man with a lot on his mind."

"Sorry. I just got lost in a thought," Jesse said.

"Well, let me fetch your change and I'll be right back," the woman said, glancing at the coins in her hand.

When she returned with the change, Jesse was already gone. *What a nice fella to leave such a generous tip,* she thought.

Walking around the still-quiet town, Jesse felt relief. She had passed as a man again. She took her time exploring the strip of closed businesses along one side of the road before ending up at a corral on the southernmost end. A variety of horses circled inside the fence. Watching them frolic, it wasn't long before a curious buckskin walked right up to her, nudging her hand with his nose. He resembled her father's horse, Dakota. She felt drawn to him by the uncanny similarities. Jesse spoke quietly to the light tan horse with the black mane, rubbing his face, and scratching him behind the ears.

The instant connection with the horse evoked such strong feelings of nostalgia that Jesse was sad when the sun made its appearance along the horizon. She could have stayed there all day.

"You wantin' to buy?"

Startled, Jesse turned from the fence.

The man dropped his cigarette and ground it in the dirt with his boot. "You won't find a better horse than that buckskin right there. He's well broke and ready to ride. Won't find a better price, neither. Hell, I'll even throw in all the tack you'll need—for the right price, that is."

The few coins in her pouch weren't enough to buy a horse. Jesse turned away, fumbled in her shirt, and pulled out a small, shiny nugget. She turned back to face him, extending her hand with the nugget in the center of her palm.

"Want to trade?" she asked.

The man grabbed the gold chunk. He placed it in his mouth and bit down, looking jubilant as he pulled it away. "Hell yeah, and I'll even throw in saddlebags and a scabbard for your rifle," he exclaimed, tone higher than before.

Jesse could tell by his eagerness she might be overpaying. She pointed to the pistol hanging on his hip.

"I'll need your gun too," she said, calm and confident.

"You got yourself a deal, fella!" he said.

After shaking hands, he pocketed the nugget. Jesse followed as he led the horse into the barn. She studied his movements carefully as he saddled the horse. It had been years since she had seen her brothers and father do it, and she'd never had the opportunity to try herself. Jesse made mental notes of each step of the process.

After attaching the saddlebags and leather scabbard to the saddle he said, "Let me see your rifle."

She handed it over and watched as he slid it into the scabbard. It was a perfect fit.

He removed the pistol and holster from around his waist and handed it to her.

"Ever shot one before?"

"No, sir," she said. "Never have."

"Well let me show ya," the man said.

Outside, he explained how to load the gun. He aimed at a bale of hay up against the barn and fired. "See? Nothin' to it!" he said, handing it over. "Take a shot."

She took the gun, aimed, and fired. Bits of flying hay marked her shot. Impressed with the small pistol, Jesse strapped it around her waist, cinching it a few notches tighter.

"Appreciate the business," the man said. He shook her hand one last time before handing over the reins.

"Thank you. Come on, Buck." Glowing, she led her new

purchase out of the barn, completely satisfied with the trade. She hadn't a clue what the nugget was worth, but either way it was fine. Right now, she needed a horse more than she needed a piece of gold.

Her gaze fell upon a building down the street called Felix's Trading Post. She stopped at the hotel for the roll of pelts, and then led Buck back to the Post. She slowly tied him to the hitching post, giving herself some extra time to calm her nerves.

A bell jingled above her head as she entered. Two old men sat by a barrel moving game pieces around a board. They briefly glanced at her before turning their heads back to the playing surface. She was inconspicuous, as Frieda had intended.

Jesse walked to the counter and dropped her pelts. "You Felix?"

"Yes, sir."

"Edith said to tell you to treat me right."

The short man behind the counter, his hair slicked back and shiny, picked them up. "She did. Well, I wouldn't want to upset Miss Edith. She can be a little spitfire," he said, grinning as he started to sort through the pelts.

Whatever he used on his hair, he also used on his mustache. It had the same glossy appearance. Jesse tried not to stare. She had never seen one like it before, so thick and long that it curled in circles on the ends.

"I don't really buy beaver pelts anymore. They can be hard to sell these days. But these are some nice ones. Fantastic quality." He scratched his head like he was deep in a thought. "I know a furrier—lives down in San Francisco. I'm thinking he'd be interested in these. He comes through here a couple times a year. I don't want to overpay or get stuck with 'em." He paused again, considering potential offers. "I tell you what, I'll give you two dollars each and I'll see how it goes. You interested in doing some trading?" He pointed to the merchandise behind her.

Glancing around the store, Jesse saw items she was definitely interested in. She grabbed a book, candles, two traps, rope, gunpowder, ammo, nails, twine, a coffee pot and coffee, and a sack of horse feed.

"Give me just a minute to do some figuring." Felix took the pencil from behind his ear and scratched some numbers down on a piece of paper. "All right, I still owe you," he said as he reached in his cash drawer.

"Thank you, sir," Jesse said, taking the money.

"Welcome. And when you see Miss Edith, give her my best." He finished with an ornery wink.

Jesse walked out, put her purchases into her saddlebags and returned to get the bag of feed. Before she could leave again, Felix called out, "Hey, I'm not sure he'll buy these," he nodded down at the pile of pelts, "but if he does, he may want more. Do you have more if he asks?"

"Not with me, but I can bring some next year," she said as she hoisted the bag of feed over her shoulder.

"I don't know how this will pan out for me. Tell you what, you bring them by next year. If he purchases these, and wants more, then I'll buy those off you too."

"All right. I can do that."

She was just about out the door when Felix called out again, "What's the name?"

"Jesse, and thanks again."

Jesse led the encumbered horse back to the hotel. She collected her belongings from her room and loaded them into her saddlebags. She found Edith outback, mucking out one of the stalls in the barn.

"Mornin', Jesse. I was wonderin' what happened to you. I was going to make you some porridge this morning, but there was no answer when I knocked on your door."

"Couldn't sleep, so thought I'd go for a walk."

"You hungry? I can still fix you a bowl," Edith asked, squinting, as she massaged her shoulder with her fingers.

"No, ma'am. I got some food at the Tin Plate."

"Oh. All right. You heading out already?"

"Yes, ma'am. But first, let me do that for you," Jesse said, reaching for the pitchfork.

"That's kind of you to offer, but you don't have to do that."

"It won't take me long, and I'm happy to do it for you."

"You're an angel. My shoulder is giving me fits today. Usually it ain't this bad."

"I'm happy to help," Jesse said. "Can I help you with anything else before I leave?"

"No. You just come inside when you're done," Edith said.

"All right. I'll be in shortly."

Jesse started scooping up the manure and putting it in the wheelbarrow. After filling and dumping a load and a half, she cleaned her hands in the trough. She found Edith in the kitchen.

"All finished. How much do I owe you for the stay?" Jesse asked.

"One dollar, the food was on me. And I made you a little something for your trip," Edith said, handing Jesse a small burlap bag.

Peeking inside, Jesse noticed a loaf of bread, and a piece of smoked pork. "This looks delicious, but you didn't have to do that."

"I am happy to do it," Edith said, smiling.

"Thank you for everything." Jesse returned the smile.

Edith followed Jesse outside after they settled the bill. "That's a beautiful horse," she said, rubbing Buck's neck.

"Just bought him. Should make traveling a lot less lonely."

"Congrats on a fine purchase. Just so you know, when you come back, the price of the room includes a stall for your horse. Will you be returning soon? You are always welcome here."

"Not this year, but I'll be back next year to do some trading. Thank you again for everything, ma'am."

"You're welcome. And please, call me Edith."

Jesse smiled and tipped her hat as both said their goodbyes. Heading out of town, Jesse got the feeling she looked a little ridiculous. She didn't care. It had been years since she had ridden, and until she had some privacy she wasn't going to make a fool of herself. Horse in tow, she walked until they were back in the solitude of the woods.

Once away from watchful eyes, Jesse stopped. She slid a foot into the stirrup and mounted the horse. She sat completely still for a moment, afraid to breathe, wanting to give him a chance to get the feel of having her on his back. He had no qualms with his new passenger. After a few minutes, she gave him a gentle nudge to the flanks.

Every time he stepped over a fallen log, she rubbed his neck, praising the achievement. She could tell Buck was a tame horse. It wasn't long before all she had to do was relax and enjoy the ride.

They reached the river crossing with plenty of daylight left to burn. Jesse decided to use the time to get a better feel for the horse. She removed the supplies in a nearby clearing and steered her mount toward the small glade. After a few laps around the meadow, she felt the urge to increase his speed. With another tap of her heels, Buck transitioned into a smooth trot. She knew he could run much faster if she chose to let him, but this was plenty fast for now.

Jesse pulled back hard on the reins after a few laps. Buck, obedient, came to an immediate stop. Jesse kept her momentum, realizing her mistake as she went catapulting over the front of the horse. She struggled to regain the breath forced from her lungs when she hit the ground.

A more pressing matter arose once she came to her senses. With her hand held up in front of her face, she stared at her contorted middle finger. It instantly reminded her of Frieda's fingers, only worse. The twisted finger throbbed, but she had to straighten it. Waiting would make the process unbearable. She picked up a stick and placed it between her teeth. Jesse grabbed the finger, simultaneously pulling and twisting, until the crooked knuckle popped back into place.

Next time don't pull on the reins so hard, she thought. She was thankful that she hadn't broken her neck. She practiced walking with the horse directly behind her until she was satisfied she could lead him across the river. Jesse walked him back to her belongings, praising him the entire way. When she removed the saddle, she paid special attention to the knot. She would need to know how to retie it later.

Jesse let Buck graze. As the horse ate, she had her own small meal of smoked pork and bread. She couldn't help but wonder if it was crazy to consider doing what she was about to attempt. Frieda and Nathaniel had crossed with horses, but she still had doubts. As night closed in, her uncertainty grew.

Under the cover of darkness, she removed her moccasins as panic washed over her. Buck was gentle, but she had no idea how he would react once he stepped into the wild river. If he panicked, they would be swept away to their deaths.

She grabbed him by the reins, and slowly led him down the embankment. Buck's ears flickered back and forth at the water's edge. Jesse wondered what he was thinking. She gave him enough slack to bend down and smell the water. After a few snorts and tosses of his head, the flickering of his ears slowed.

Jesse moved forward until his front two legs were in the water. As soon as the force of the water hit Buck's legs he yanked his head back, threatening to pull her off of her feet. She gave him more slack. Buck tossed his head wildly, wide-eyed with flaring nostrils. He was suddenly a different horse. Jesse did her best to calm him before he pulled them both in.

"Easy, boy. Easy." She spoke in the most reassuring tone she could muster, rubbing his neck, and scratching him behind the ears. She wasn't sure who she was trying to encourage more— herself or the horse.

Jesse stood with him until she saw his temperament soften. She took him by the reins under his bit, and cautiously walked forward. She prayed he wouldn't panic. If he did, she would have to release the reins and let him go. Buck followed right behind her, once again trusting in his new companion.

Jesse didn't give him even an inch of slack. Slowly, step-by-step, she led Buck across the moonlit river. Once safely on the opposite bank, she praised him repeatedly. They kept walking until she felt they were well hidden on Mount Perish.

Jesse fell asleep watching the soft yellow glow of fireflies blinking all around her in the darkness.

The next morning she woke to the throbbing pain of her swollen and bruised finger. She managed to saddle the horse despite the discomfort.

She followed the river, keeping it on their right for the return trip. With each step, her confidence on horseback grew. She and Buck spent three days traveling ever upward. Each evening they stopped and bedded down for the night.

When they were close enough, she decided to give Buck a rest and walk for the remainder of the journey. With his help, she would now be able to make the trip in four days instead of six. Buying a horse had been one of the best decisions she had ever made.

The sight of the cabin gave her mixed emotions. It was good to see home again, but it felt empty without Frieda. She wasn't sure how she was going to handle life on the mountain now. Keeping busy would be the best thing to keep her mind off of her loneliness.

Jesse spent the remainder of the summer practicing her riding and shooting skills, and working on the preparations for the coming winter. Her first priority was getting the lean-to repaired. She cut and hewed several trees, and used the wood to patch up the old lean-to and mend the split rail fence.

It didn't take long for Buck to become accustomed to the place. During the day he roamed around freely. He spent his nights in the safety of the lean-to.

Most of Jesse's days were spent using a machete to cut down areas of green grass, which she dried, bundled, and tied with twine. The bundles were stored inside the cabin with the large bag of feed to keep them dry. By the time she was done, there was an entire wall of the bundles piled from floor to ceiling; supplemental food for Buck during the long winter months that lay ahead. Jesse had also managed to kill and smoke a couple of deer, as well as making several loaves of pemmican. She felt a sense of accomplishment; she was more than ready to make it through another winter season.

Jesse was already looking forward to her upcoming trip to Ely next year.

CHAPTER THIRTEEN

1862

Winter was one of the warmest in recent memory. Jesse ventured away from the cabin on a few pleasant days. The fresh air did wonders for her body and soul.

Having Buck around was also a welcome reprieve from the solitude. If not for him, she'd be feeling more isolated and alone than ever before. A part of each day was spent tending to her equine companion, and she found herself truly appreciating his steadfast company.

She stayed huddled inside by the fire on brutal days, sipping hot coffee and reading the book she had purchased on her trip to Ely. She wasn't the best reader, but she was able to sound out the unfamiliar words thanks to the education Frieda had provided over the years.

The book, *The Scarlet Letter*, was exactly what she needed to keep her mind occupied while the snow flew outside. All alone in a world of white, the only sounds she heard were the howling winds and her crackling fire. At times, she thought she would go mad from the restraints placed on her by the unforgiving climate. Reading became an escape, if temporary, from the solitary confinement of her cabin cell.

Unfortunately, the book also triggered a great deal of anxiety.

The townspeople in the story persecuted Hester for her sin. What would happen if the good people of Ely were to find out she deceived them? That she was really a woman? Would they make her stand on a scaffold in the middle of town with a capital letter on her shirt too?

The scene played out vividly in her mind, with her in the middle of the road in Ely, her shirt bearing a larger than life L, as Edith, Felix, and the waitress all shouted at her, "Liar!"

Maybe the letter F, for fake, would be more appropriate, she thought.

By the time spring came, she had read the book seven times.

Jesse's anxiety intensified with each passing day. A plan that made perfect sense when hatched now raised all kinds of concerns. She liked the peaceful little town, and she didn't get the sense the people were vengeful. But how could she ever go back to town as Jessica Pratt? How could she go there looking like a woman when some of the folks there knew her as a man named Jesse? She hated the deception. Frieda told her she wouldn't have to do it forever, but what other option did she have? The masquerade had already begun. Frieda wasn't here to ask, and she hadn't a clue on how to right what now seemed a terrible wrong. No longer did the evil men of her childhood haunt her dreams—the good people of Ely did. Some nights she wore the letter L; others, the letter F.

Finally, after what seemed like an eternity, the birds began to sing their songs, heralding the return of spring. Elk sprouted new antlers. The fresh smell in the air excited her anticipation for the thaw. The drip-drop of snow melting from the trees told her it wouldn't be long before it was time to set her new traps.

Jesse had spent a lot of time over the winter compiling a list of things she wanted to buy with her profits. The first item was more coffee. She had grown quite fond of the taste and couldn't imagine a morning without a cup. She also decided if she were going to have a horse, then a scythe would be a must. Cutting grass with a machete was hard work. A longer-handled instrument would make the chore much more bearable. Another priority was more books. Reading helped pass the hands of time during the long, lonely winters.

Jesse released her pent-up energy by making repairs to the old cabin. She repaired and cleaned everything she could, and stacked firewood along the interior walls of the lean-to. Buck still had plenty of room. The stacked wood served as a better windbreak for the building, while the roof of the small shelter protected the wood from the elements.

Her new traps did not disappoint. Soon she had amassed a nice stockpile of pelts. There would be no need to worry about money for supplies on her next trip. Not that she had to worry, anyway. There was more gold if she needed it. For her, this was a matter of pride. She wanted to prove she could make it on her own merits.

After another day of hard work, Jesse sat staring at the old wooden deer carving with the uneven legs, still the centerpiece on the table. Rubbing her thumb along the rough grain, she couldn't help but tear up. She thought of Frieda, and the day she first divulged her scheme.

Just because Jesse pulled it off once was no guarantee she could do it again. She hated to change her appearance, but knew she had to continue the charade. She couldn't come up with an alternative.

Keeping her eye on the moon, she knew it wouldn't be much longer. In the morning she would have to do what she had been dreading for months. She would go to the stream and cut off the hair which had grown over the last year.

On the evening of the half moon, she spent the night tossing and turning, dreaming of scenarios that would expose her for who she really was.

She woke feeling as though she hadn't slept a wink. Short-tempered and edgy, and with very little enthusiasm, she donned the dreaded masculine attire and loaded the supplies onto Buck. She poured one last cup of coffee, but ended up dumping most of it out on the ground. It was the last thing her already jumpy nerves needed.

Jesse had spent the lonely winter looking forward to going back to town. She kept reminding herself of the feeling as she secured the door behind her.

～

With Buck's help, Jesse made it to Ely in four days. She decided to stay in town two days this trip. She had to get back across the river before she lost the brightness of the full moon. If she missed her window of opportunity to cross, then she would be stuck in Ely for weeks until the moon was bright enough to light the way again. She had no desire to stay that long, especially when she had to pretend to be someone else.

The landscape of the town had changed noticeably since her last visit. Even more new businesses had popped up in the growing town. Riding directly to the hotel, she was delighted when she saw Edith again. The woman approached her with a smile.

"I'm so glad you came back. I got something special just for you!" Edith exclaimed.

Once Buck was happily munching on a rare snack of oats in the barn, Jesse followed Edith inside the hotel.

"You can just head on to your room if you want. Same one you had last time. I'll be right behind you."

Edith went to her own bedroom across the hall, and then entered Jesse's room. She handed Jesse a neatly folded outfit. "I made these just for you," she said. "I hope I got the size right."

Edith earned extra money by making and selling clothes at the trading post. She'd thought to provide more practical garments than her guest's usual attire.

Jesse was at a loss for words and deeply appreciative. She hadn't had any new clothes in several years.

"Try 'em on and then come out and let me see how they look

on ya," Edith said as she walked out of the room, closing the door behind her.

Jesse undressed and put on the pressed shirt and trousers. She opened the door to find Edith standing sentry outside.

"You look like a new man. I have to say the fit is damn near perfect! I have something else that might fit you," Edith said before disappearing again. She returned with a nice-looking pair of black leather boots.

"These used to belong to Isaac. I have no use for them and all they do is collect dust. You might as well get some use out of them. Might be a little larger than what you're used to, but take these, too." She handed Jesse a thick pair of wool socks.

Jesse had never tried on boots like these before, but she could remember her father and brothers wearing something similar. She had only worn tall moccasins for years. Standing in the hallway, Jesse slid into one sock and then the other, and then into the polished boots. The extra bulk from the socks made the boots fit perfectly.

"Thank you, ma'am—Edith. Thank you for everything!" Jesse's voice rose higher than intended. "I have something for you, too." Jesse pulled a tin container from the saddlebag in her room. "I made this for you. Whenever that shoulder gets to bothering you, just rub some on. It should help."

"I can't believe you remembered about my shoulder. I can definitely use this." Edith hugged a somewhat-reluctant Jesse. "Thank you, Jesse. And you are more than welcome, young man. You're going to have the young ladies of this town smitten in no time."

The comment amused Jesse. *As if that would ever happen.*

They headed into the kitchen where there was a loaf of bread cooling on the table. As they ate, Jesse filled Edith in on some of the things she had done since the last time they saw each other. She kept secret it all had taken place on Mount Perish. Once her stomach was full, Jesse thanked Edith again for the outfit and food, and then politely excused herself to get some sleep.

Jesse woke in the dark, the faint glow of the moonlight spilling in around the edges of the curtain. She got up and went to the window. Her body was stiff from the journey, and also from sleeping on her back. She'd been trying not to wrinkle her clothes. Staying dressed seemed safe. The night sky was full of clouds. Jesse hoped when it came time to return up the mountain, the weather would be more congenial. Even though a light rain was falling, Ely bustled with activity.

Jesse freshened up a little and strapped on her pistol. She reached for the door handle and stopped. A man was whispering out in the hall. She slowly cracked the door about half an inch to take a peek. She'd recognize that mustache anywhere—Felix. Jesse had no idea what he had whispered, but Edith must have found it amusing. Edith giggled softly and placed her hand over Felix's mouth to keep him quiet. Jesse watched as he grabbed Edith by the waist and teasingly guided her backward into her bedroom across the hall. He closed the door behind him with his foot. Neither had noticed Jesse's door was ajar.

Jesse quietly closed her door and waited. Understanding played across Jesse's face. She wasn't the only one with a secret. Even with her inexperienced eyes, it was obvious to her they were quite fond of each other, acting like two silly kids in love.

When she felt the coast was clear, she walked softly out to the barn to check on Buck. She spoke to him as if he could understand the words. After a few parting rubs, she was off to check out the source of the boisterous sounds.

Closer to the saloon, Jesse could hear women singing. She couldn't resist having a look. She walked in The Foxtail, took a seat at the bar, and ordered a shot of whiskey.

She had never tasted alcohol, but understood how it worked—in theory. She took the drink in one swift gulp, trying to calm her nerves. Fire burned from her throat to her gut and she wasn't sure how she managed not to cough up a lung. Somehow she regained her composure. Once her eyes quit watering, she willed herself to breathe normally. The warm sensation radiated outward, tingling in her cheeks. Feeling a little calmer already, Jesse ordered another. She left the second drink untouched and swiveled in her seat to look around.

Several saloon girls flitted about in brightly colored skirts, with petticoats peeking out beneath the short ruffles. Not at all shy about their bodies, the ladies had no problem shamelessly revealing their arms, shoulders, and legs. Their breasts protruded from their low-cut bodices. Lace, silk, and even net stockings were held up with garter belts. Makeup caked their faces and it was obvious, even to Jesse, their hair was not the color they were born with.

Jesse was appalled the women could so easily drape themselves all over the men. Many of the patrons were dirty and unkempt and reminded her of the man who had lain on her sister in the barn all those years ago. The recollection was so startling nausea and dizziness flooded her body briefly, though part of the feeling could have been from the whiskey. Jesse thought perhaps she should stick to coffee.

She felt bad for the women and wondered what could have happened to make them desperate enough to resort to such a lifestyle. She didn't care how poor she was, she would rather starve to death. One of the painted ladies made her way to Jesse and took a seat next to her.

"How's about buying a thirsty girl a drink?" she asked.

Not wanting to be rude, Jesse motioned for the bartender to bring the woman a shot. The woman tried to start up a conversation, but the words fell on deaf ears. Jesse, completely caught up in the activity around her, could barely pay attention to the attempted conversation. Realizing a better customer awaited elsewhere, the woman moved on to find her next target.

It was standing room only in the smoke-filled saloon. A gentleman, already intoxicated, quickly snatched the newly vacated seat. He wasted no time and ordered a shot. He tilted his head and aimed at the spittoon near his feet. He missed.

What an ass. "Hey mister, next time watch what you're doing,"

Jesse said, pointing at the thick glob of tobacco juice dripping from her boot.

"Actually...looks like," he said and then hiccupped, "my aim wasn't too bad. Consider it a free s-s-shine," he said, his words slurred. The drunk picked up his shot of whiskey, gulped it in one swallow, and slammed the glass upturned on the bar. He motioned for a refill before turning to face Jesse. "And if I wanted to be nagged at, I'd be at home with the wife. Now, don't bother me, boy."

Jesse could feel her blood starting to heat, but she remained silent. *Calm down. Ignore him. He's drunk.* She turned her attention back to the wall behind the bar. Behind the bottles was a long mirror. Jesse sat staring, transfixed by her own reflection. Her appearance stunned her, and she did not recognize herself.

The dancing girls on stage finished their routine, and the stage went dark. A single bright light shone on a central platform as the piano started playing again. The most beautiful woman Jesse had ever seen took the stage. She wore a flowing, crimson dress, arms and shoulders bare, which exposed a hint of cleavage. Her presence on the stage was resplendent and of a different caliber altogether than the tawdry girls who had preceded her. Her dress had a slit that traveled all the way up to the top of her thigh, revealing a well-formed leg covered in a silk stocking and garter of the finest lace. Her flaxen hair was piled loosely on top of her head and fixed in place with a jeweled pin. Her full lips and alabaster complexion required little makeup. She used just enough to enhance her natural beauty.

It was obvious from the cheers this woman was a crowd favorite. Men lost interest in their cards, their gazes drawn to the source of the voice that had quietly started to sing. The resonating timbre of her voice flooded the room as she sang. Her voice gained power with each note as she stepped down and moved slowly past the tables, lightly brushing her hand across the backs of the card-playing men seated next to the stage. She had a powerful effect on them, earning fidgets from even the stern-faced among them.

The woman had an effect on Jesse as well. Jesse turned back to the mirror, suddenly insecure about her appearance. It had been years since she had looked like the girl from her past: pretty dress, long hair, and soft hands. She missed it and she couldn't help but fantasize about how she would look if she were all dolled up. *Would I look that pretty?*

The entertainer finished her song and took a final bow to a deafening explosion of cheers. The singer made her way toward the bar, thanking men along the way. Jesse stiffened as the soloist leaned in between her and the drunk to her left.

"Has Boone been in yet?" the woman asked the bartender.

"Not yet."

"Can you tell him I want to see him when he comes in?"

"Sure thing, Abby."

"You gotta light?" Abby asked Jesse as she glanced at her fancy filtered cigarette.

The drunken man rubbed against Abby. "I's-s-s got a light for ya," he said, slurring his words once more as he reached for Abby's breast.

Jesse grabbed his wrist, and twisted it in an odd angle, causing him to wince. She raised her voice. "Get your—"

The man lunged, shoving Abby backwards in the scuffle as he and Jesse crashed to the floor. He straddled Jesse and swung his fist. She saw the blow coming, barely turning her head in time. His knuckles glanced the side of her jaw. She balled her hand into a tight fist, and punched him right below the ribs, once, swiftly. The hard jab caused the man to lean to the side and Jesse rolled out from under him. She put him in a chokehold.

"All right, fellas. Knock it off," a man shouted.

Jesse looked up and saw the pistol pointing at them. She released the drunkard.

The man wielding the gun was employed by the saloon to

keep the peace. "That's enough you two. Let's go," he said using the barrel of his gun to point toward the door.

"Not him," Abby said pointing to Jesse. "He didn't start it." She picked Jesse's hat up off the floor.

"All right, come on you." The hired gun took the lout by the collar and tossed him out the door.

"The name is Abigail, Abigail Flanagan, but folks call me Abby," she said as she handed Jesse her hat.

Jesse put it on. She tipped her long-brimmed hat and said, "Thank you. Jesse McGinnis, and I'm sorry about all that. But he was a jackass. His poor wife. Can you imagine that coming home to you?"

Actually I can. The thought crossed her mind before she continued. "No reason to be sorry. I appreciate what you did," Abby said, extending her hand to Jesse.

Feeling the softness of Abby's hand, Jesse retracted her own. Her rough, calloused skin embarrassed her. She had no idea Abby was attracted to the strength and toughness she felt, a man who knew how to use his hands. By the look and feel of Jesse's, she could tell they were used to hard work.

Abby couldn't help but become a little aroused by Jesse's chivalrous gesture. She motioned to the barkeep, signaling for a round. "This one's on me, Jesse McGinnis," Abby said as she straightened Jesse's collar.

Jesse watched as Abby took her drink from the bartender. Moving with an unusual ease, she managed to make a task as simple as lifting a glass seem graceful. Abby, glass held high said, "Nice to meet you."

After tapping their glasses together, they downed their beverages. This shot went down a little easier than Jesse's first one.

Abby looked at Jesse and said, "So, Jesse McGinnis. What's your story?"

"Just came to town to pick up some supplies."

"Will you be staying for a while?"

"Heading home the day after tomorrow."

"Do you live far away?" Abby asked, hoping the attractive man lived close to the area, or near one of the towns where she performed.

"I'm from a town called Barrel. It's quite a distance from here."

The painted lady who had approached Jesse earlier returned. Jesse could hear the woman's loud whisper into Abby's ear. "I need to talk to you," she said, struggling too hard against the din. "In private!"

Abby stood up and leaned closer to Jesse. "That's my friend, Mabel. I have to go. I have never asked a man this before, but would you like to have dinner with me tomorrow night before you leave?"

"Um...I don't know if I can."

"Well, I'll be at the Tin Plate tomorrow evening at 6 o'clock if you'd like to join me," Abby said before she turned to walk away.

Jesse watched as the stunning woman made her way toward the back of the saloon.

Abby couldn't help but take another look at Jesse. She glanced over her shoulder and caught Jesse staring at her. They both smiled at each other before Jesse quickly turned her head. Abby's smile widened. *He looked like a kid with his hand caught in the candy jar.*

After settling the tab, Jesse headed back to Edith's place. *Should I go?* She had some thinking to do.

∼

Mabel took Abby to her room. Abby listened silently, heart sinking, as her friend told her story. "I'm going to have a baby. It has to be Earl's. He'll be back in town tomorrow night and I'm going to tell him."

Abby had met Earl several times and was not impressed with the man. It was obvious he was using Mabel for one thing. Somehow, he had convinced her he loved her, and because of that he was the one man Mabel never charged. Earl claimed he was close to making his fortune. When he did, he said he would take care of her the way she deserved to be taken care of. Mabel believed every word Earl said, but Abby didn't. She had tried voicing her opinion about him in the past, but it had only created a rift between her and Mabel. Now, hearing the hope in her friend's voice, she hugged and congratulated her, worrying in silence that Earl probably wouldn't take the news quite as well.

∼

Jesse lay on her bed and replayed the evening in her mind. The saloon had been too noisy and crowded for her liking, but she had enjoyed herself. She still couldn't believe how easy it was to pass as a man. She knew the clothing and hairstyle were a huge part of it, but there was more to it than that. She carried herself differently than the women in the saloon. Jesse was a woman, yet she felt nothing like the women in Ely. Having spent her teens isolated on the mountain, she thought perhaps she simply didn't know how to be feminine. Then there was Abby, who radiated femininity with her every movement. The thought of Abby's eyes, or her smile, or the touch of her hand made Jesse smile. She felt a flush of heat rush to her cheeks.

Jesse wasn't sure what she was feeling, but it felt both good and scary at the same time.

CHAPTER FOURTEEN

Jesse took her pelts and made her way to the trading post as soon as it opened. She couldn't help but think about Edith and Felix, and hoped when she saw him her face wouldn't give any hint she knew about their liaison. She smiled inwardly, knowing she wasn't the only person in town who had a secret.

She walked in and placed the rolled-up pelts on the counter.

"Jesse, right? Looks like you had another good season."

"Hi, Felix. Did he buy my pelts?"

"Everyone of them. And will definitely want these too."

Jesse was thrilled. She was making her own money, and knew Frieda would be proud of her. "Those new traps worked out great."

"Well, let me figure what I owe ya."

"I'm just gonna look around for what I need while you do that."

Jesse looked over the shelves, making note of the supplies she needed. She looked at a stack of men's shirts, wanting more than anything to hold one of the nearby dresses to her frame instead. The temptation of the soft fabric was too much. Jesse reached out to feel one of the nicer dresses.

"All right, I have the total. Do you know what all you want?" he asked.

Jesse spun around, hands flat against her sides. She cleared her throat and named off the things she would be back for first thing in the morning. Picking up a shirt she said, "But I'll take this now."

"That's fine, I'll see you tomorrow."

Jesse went back to the hotel to rest for the trip back up the mountain in the morning. She couldn't sleep. Instead she relived her encounter with Abby. *What is wrong with me?*

Something wasn't right about the whole situation. Jesse considered packing up and heading home. Then she thought about how nice it could be to make a new friend. *Nothing wrong with that.*

~

That evening Jesse washed her hair in the washbasin while having second thoughts about meeting Abby for dinner. She'd been wavering back and forth all day. She wasn't sure whether she was more excited or nervous. After a lengthy internal battle, she finally decided to go. She pondered the reason for her emotions as she dressed. Putting on the new shirt, she wished she was getting into the pretty dress she'd seen at Felix's instead.

Already late, Jesse brushed the dust off her wide-brimmed hat, took a deep breath, and hurried to the Tin Plate.

Abby was waiting when she got there. Jesse took a seat across the table.

"I was beginning to wonder if you were coming," Abby said.

"Sorry for being late. Time got away from me."

"It's fine. I'm just happy you made it. I hope you don't mind. I went ahead and ordered us coffee."

Jesse smiled, grateful Abby didn't press for details about her tardiness. "Coffee sounds great. Thank you. So, were you raised here in Ely?"

"I came here in '59, so...going on three years now. My best friend Mabel traveled here with me from Missouri."

Jesse asked, "Why did you leave Missouri?"

"Neither one of us had family or any kind of future there, so we figured, why not."

"What happened to your families?"

"Mabel's parents and older sister died from influenza when she was eleven. They stuck her in an orphanage. And my mother died giving birth to my sister when I was nine."

Jesse's own lost family flickered through her mind. She felt a sudden kinship. She met Abby's gaze and asked, "What about your father?"

Abby's blue eyes flashed. "I don't have a father. The day my mother died was the day I lost my father too."

"Oh Abby, I'm so sorry. What happened to him?"

Abby's lips tightened into a thin line. "When she died, he took comfort from the bottle. That became his only care." Her voice hardened. "I left home when I was sixteen, and never saw him again. I don't even know if he's still alive. I'm sure if he is, he's drinking as I speak. He's a mean drunk, and I don't like to talk about him."

Jesse's eyes widened, upset with herself for bringing up painful memories. "I, uh...sorry," Jesse said, stammering as she tried to think of how to lighten the conversation. "How did you end up in California?"

"Mabel and I decided to set out for a new start in life. She always lived kind of a wild lifestyle, if you know what I mean, so the easiest way for her to make money was in pleasuring men. And trust me, there are always plenty of men that need pleasing. She got me my first job performing at a saloon back in Missouri. The money was good. One thing you can count on—no matter how hard times get, men are always willing to spend their money on whiskey and women. I made ten dollars a week plus commission for any liquor I got the men to drink. I'd ask the men to buy me a drink and the bartender would serve me a shot glass of tea but charge for a whiskey. It's a big swindle, but I couldn't refuse. I needed the money."

Jesse listened; not raising an eyebrow, knowing the same trick was pulled on her the night before.

"Anyway, we took the stagecoach from Missouri to California. Cost us two hundred bucks each, and we made the journey. It was long, and god-awful, really. Weeks packed in a stagecoach is something I would never recommend, but at least it got us a new start."

"I bet you got to see amazing things, though."

"Yes, at first it was beautiful, but day after day. A person can only take so much."

"Never met anyone who rode one. What's it like?"

"It's hot, dirty, uncomfortable, and never ending. Nine of us packed inside that thing. It was so cramped that we sat knee against knee. You know how much dust a horse can kick up…well imagine being behind six of 'em. It's like sitting in a constant cloud of dust. You learned pretty quick to ride with your mouth shut or you'll be crunching dirt in your teeth. Most of the time it was hot, so that made it easy for the dirt to cling to your skin. Can you imagine how we looked when we stopped?"

"How often did you get to stop?" Jesse was enthralled.

"Not very often. Actually, we stopped mostly for the horses. Every now and then the horses had to be switched out for fresh ones. Those were very quick stops…maybe ten minutes."

"When did you eat or sleep?"

Abby said, "Speaking of eating, we should probably order."

"What would you recommend?"

"They have a wonderful sirloin." Abby motioned for the waitress.

Jesse had never had a sirloin. She was going to have to trust Abby knew what was best. "Is that what you're having?"

"I think so."

"I'll give it a try," Jesse said as the waitress approached the table.

The waitress looked at Jesse. "Have you decided?"

Jesse nodded toward Abby. "Ladies first."

Abby ordered a medium-well steak, along with a baked potato before the waitress turned her attention back to Jesse.

Jesse looked up at her. "I'll have the same."

The waitress gave an understanding nod and walked away.

Jesse picked up her cup of coffee. Before taking a drink, she asked, "Please, finish telling me about your trip."

"We stopped a couple times a day for food. Got about forty minutes to stretch our legs, get a bite to eat, and use the bathroom. Sleeping...I'm not sure I would even call it that. During the day, if you wanted to rest, you did it sitting up. At night we would stop at a farm along the way. The families would feed us and then we would stay the night."

"Like Edith's hotel?"

"Heavens no, Jesse." Abby grimaced. "We slept on dirt floors. Or at least tried to sleep. I'm not a princess by any means...but no one should have to sleep on dirt this day and age. At first light we were on the road again, and it was always in the back of my mind that we would be attacked by Indians or held up by a robber."

"I take it you didn't have any encounters?"

"Thankfully, we made it unscathed. Thanks to our driver."

"So how did you end up in here, in Ely?"

"Looking back now, Mabel and I were pretty foolish. We had no idea what we were going to do when we got to California or where we would even stay. We were just blessed to have one of the finest stagecoach drivers, Corky."

"Corky?" Jesse smiled at the strange name.

"It's his nickname. He told me when he was a kid he liked to talk a lot, and his older brothers were always telling him to put a cork in it. Well, one day they just started calling him Corky, and the name stuck with him since."

The waitress brought them their meals, and they continued talking as they ate.

"Anyway, Corky is one of the finest men I have ever met. It

was by happenstance we even got him as our driver. He was returning home from St Louis. He told me he had delivered a large sum of money there for the stagecoach company. We just got lucky to catch his coach on the way back to California. He kind of took us under his wing along the way. His hired gun didn't have to protect the strongbox, so to keep us safe, Corky had him ride inside the coach. He told me robbers knew if a man with a rifle was sitting next to a stagecoach driver, then there must be lots of valuables in the strongbox. Corky asked me to sit up there with him when we traveled through certain areas. We talked, mile after mile, and day after day. It wasn't hard for him to figure out that Mabel and I hadn't really thought out what we were going to do when we got here. By the time we reached California, he offered to let us stay at his place until we got things worked out."

"That was nice of him."

"Yes it was. We stayed with him for several weeks. It worked out for him and us because he was always gone, running the coach, so we never got in his way." Abby smiled.

"What?" Jesse asked in reaction to Abby's grin.

"I hadn't thought of it in a long time, but Mabel was so sweet on him."

"She was? Well, since she is here it mustn't have panned out for them."

Abby shook her head. "Corky just isn't that kind of man. I think he was just too busy to take on a wife. He is like a father to me. He got us here safe, took care of us, provided food for us, and he even got us our jobs. He knows a lot of folks all over California, and he introduced me to a guy down in Big Oak who owns The Drake. We both got hired on right away. Well, Mabel got hired no questions asked, but I had to audition for him. I had to go back that evening and sing for the crowd. If he liked their reaction then he would discuss wages. After the show, I got hired."

"You have a beautiful voice. He'd have been a fool not to hire you."

"Thank you," Abby said, bashful eyes drifting to the tabletop.

Jesse was amazed to see a slight blush coloring Abby's cheeks. Surely, with her amazing talents, she must be accustomed to such compliments.

Abby looked back up, smiled, and continued her story. "The owner made me an offer I couldn't refuse. He offered me a traveling job performing at the different saloons he owns. I decided, why not, and took his offer. I choose to stay in Ely most of the time because it's centrally located. Makes it easier to travel to the saloons north and south of here."

Jesse placed her fork on the empty plate. "That steak was delicious. So, does Corky drive you?"

"Glad you liked it. I wish he did. We have other men that take us. Corky does come through the area from time to time. I'll have to introduce you if you two happen to be here at the same time."

Jesse felt somewhat out of touch having lived isolated on the mountain for so long. She told Abby about life as a trapper and how her parents, Nathaniel and Frieda, had come to the Barrel area years ago. Of course, Abby had never heard of the place. Jesse assured her she probably never would, explaining it was so small it wasn't on any map. Jesse shared stories about hunting and the cabin, always being careful not to reveal anything that would indicate any of it occurred on nearby Mount Perish.

Abby stared wide-eyed, amazed as she listened to Jesse's tales of the harsh lifestyle.

Feeling like Abby's eyes were boring into her as she spoke, Jesse thought for sure her ruse was up. *Can she tell something isn't quite right with the man seated across from her? Maybe it's because I'm not big and burly like most of the other men around here. Maybe it's something about my voice.* Jesse's mind raced.

Jesse didn't realize it was because of the attraction Abby felt toward her. Abby had never met a man quite like Jesse. She was captivated.

Later in the evening one of the more risqué women from The Foxtail came rushing through the door.

"Lena!" Abby exclaimed, standing as the frantic woman made her way to their table.

Lena clutched Abby's forearms. "I have been looking everywhere for you! It's Mabel. She's real bad. You need to come, now."

Jesse was laying money on the table before Lena finished speaking. She followed the two women out into the evening air.

Out of earshot of the other patrons, Lena said, "A guy came in the saloon tonight. Told Mabel he could take care of her problem. Said he had done that kind of thing lots of times. She believed him and after he took her money they went up to her room. He did his thing and then took off. Now, she's bleeding real bad. I didn't know what to do."

Abby looked at Jesse. "I'm so sorry, I have to go."

"It's fine. Go, Mabel needs you."

Abby nodded and began to follow Lena. She stopped and turned back around, her words falling out in a rush. "I wish you weren't leaving in the morning. You aren't like the other men around here, and I really like getting to know you. My last stop this year is in Granite Falls—be there for the whole month of August. If you can, come and see me."

The blood drained from Jesse's face at the mention of Granite Falls. A sick feeling washed over her. For a moment she thought she might vomit on the street. She swallowed hard before replying. "I'll try," she said, eyes unable to meet Abby's for the first time.

Abby and Lena rushed to the saloon and up to Mabel's room. Two women were at the head of her bed, wiping her down with wet rags. Abby hurried to Mabel's bedside where she traded places with one of the women. She took the rag off of her forehead. "Oh, Mabes," Abby said in a consoling tone, "you're going to be just fine." She turned the rag over, placing the cool side down on her head.

With tears streaming down her face and the pain unbearable, Mabel squeezed Abby's hand. "It hurts. He did something wrong. The bleeding won't stop."

"Lena, go get the doctor!" Abby shouted. "Run!"

"I had to do it. When I told Earl, he said he wasn't havin' no baby with a whore. Asked me how in the hell I would know he was the father when I been with every other man in town. Said he wanted nothin' to do with me and left. You were right about him all along. I should have listened to you."

Abby wiped away the tears running down Mabel's cheeks. "I was hoping I was wrong about him. I'm so sorry."

"I really thought he was different. I went to find him but he was gone. I was sitting out back when Jules came out and saw me crying. I told her. She said there is this guy that could make my problem go away—said he was inside. He told me all he needed was a hairpin and just like that my problem would be gone."

"Why didn't you wait and talk to me?"

"Because I knew you would try to stop me. If I kept the baby, you'd want to help me raise it. I couldn't put that burden on you. It wouldn't be right—"

The door opened and Lena entered with the doctor. He set his bag down and told everyone to leave the room.

The women waited outside the door, pacing nervously, cringing every time they heard a scream from within. Abby felt guilty each time a thought of Jesse crept into her mind. She was starting to like Jesse already, and that concerned her greatly.

Jesse's night was filled with screams as well, but hers were also filled with fire. Just hearing the name Granite Falls brought back horrible memories.

∾

Jesse was thankful when sunlight came and chased away the nightmares. She dressed quickly and checked out, saying goodbye to Edith. Concerned about Abby and her friend, she decided to stop by the saloon before leaving town.

The Foxtail was silent; nothing like it had been just a few

hours earlier. Jesse was greeted by a man stacking clean glasses behind the bar. "Can I help you?" he asked.

"Is Abby around?"

"Sleeping, I suppose. Come back later."

"Can I leave her a note?"

"Be my guest."

Jesse was about to scrawl something when she saw Lena walking wearily down the stairs. "How's Mabel?" Jesse asked.

Lena walked over to Jesse and whispered, "She's better. Doctor got her bleedin' under control and gave her laudanum. Said as long as infection don't set in, she should pull through." She glanced toward the bar making sure the man didn't hear.

Jesse whispered back. "Is Abby with her?"

"Yes, won't leave her. Been by her side every minute."

"Can you tell her I came by and I'm sorry I missed her?"

Jesse left with assurances from Lena she would pass along the message. After going to the trading post to pick up her supplies, she made her way out of town.

∼

After a quick nap, Lena returned to Mabel's room. Abby was sleeping with her head on the bed beside her lifelong friend. She raised her head when the door squeaked, briefly disoriented as to place and time. "What time is it?" she asked, voice dry and raspy.

Pouring a glass of water from the ewer on the bedside table, Lena said, "Almost noon. Jesse came by to see you. Asked how Mabel was doing."

Abby jumped up, trying her best not to wake Mabel. "How long ago was he here?"

"Hold on now," Lena said, lightly pushing her friend back in the seat while at the same time pressing the glass of water in her hand. "Drink this. It was a while ago."

"Will you stay here with Mabel until I get back?"

"You know I will."

Abby checked herself in the mirror, arranging her hair before hurrying out the door. She knew she was probably too late, but hustled over to the hotel anyway.

Edith could see the disappointment on Abby's face when she told her Jesse had left. "He sure is a nice young man. Said he'd be back next year."

"I know, but a year is a long time." Disappointed, Abby went back to the saloon and resumed caring for Mabel.

∽

Jesse spent the rest of the summer preparing for the long winter on the mountain. In addition to the usual meat processing, hay bundling and wood chopping, she decided to take on a few new projects.

She took an axe to the wall separating the cabin from the lean-to. Swinging it dead center, she chopped out a doorway opening. After felling a few trees, she hewed them into planks and made a Dutch door, which she attached with four hand-carved hinges. On really cold days and nights, she could open the top half of the door so Buck could benefit from the heat of her fire. Plus, she wouldn't feel as alone as she had last winter when Buck was completely closed off from her. He'd be easier to feed this way, too.

She hewed more timber. This time she used the wood planks to enclose the lean-to and construct a large door. After she finished the shelter, she paused, hands on her hips, to admire her handiwork. Not only would the small barn keep Buck much warmer, it would also better protect her firewood from the elements. Finally satisfied, she gathered up her tools and headed inside the cabin, whistling as she went.

One late evening, while sitting in front of the fire, she came up with an idea for a project to help pass some time during the long winter. She had gotten quite good at whittling over the years. Now, as she stared at the nondescript piece of wood mounted on the stone face in front of her, a thought came to her. Carving the mantle was the perfect thing to do to keep her busy. It wasn't really a necessity, but she thought if she could keep her hands occupied, then maybe her mind wouldn't run away like it had last winter. That experience had been mind-numbing, and she was going to do her best to avoid going through that again.

The warmth of the fire made her mind drift. She thought of how much she had enjoyed her time in town. The sights and sounds of the saloon played through her head. A beautiful voice sang, the mere thought bringing a smile to her face.

Will I ever see her again? Jesse wondered as she dozed off to sleep.

CHAPTER FIFTEEN

1863

The subzero temperatures and heavy snowfall that winter were more extreme than any Jesse had experienced. Although she was more prepared than ever with her stockpile of wood, she was forced at one point to strap on snowshoes and venture into the deep snow to chop more. She burned through more firewood than she thought possible. The cold was relentless, unforgiving.

The Dutch door had been one of the most vital improvements she had made to the cabin. Had Buck not had access to the heat from her fire, he would have frozen to death.

She fed Buck extra hay to help regulate his temperature. With the hay supply dwindling and bag of feed long gone, she had to ration his bundles. A few handfuls of hay a day weren't nearly enough, so she battled through the elements to bring back strips of birch bark. She'd seen the deer eat them before. Hopefully, they would ease Buck's hunger.

Her own food supply diminished as well. She rationed herself to a miniscule amount of food every other day. Jesse did whatever she had to do to keep them alive through the most brutal winter she had ever encountered.

Jesse carved away at the mantel through the long snowbound

days. She talked aloud to Buck, whose head usually stuck through the opening of the double door, asking him for his opinions. To an outsider, she may have appeared mad. In reality, talking with the horse calmed her, and made her feel less alone. Stroke-by-stroke, each notch and groove was done with patience and precision until finally a scene emerged. A beautiful panorama showcased a central lake; framed by tall pines, elk, bear, and beavers which roamed its shoreline.

The unrelenting snowfall finally subsided. The sun attacked the drifts engulfing the cabin, and melted the sheet of ice covering the barn door.

Jesse stepped off the porch, weak and anemic from the sedentary months confined with little food. She stood with her face skyward, breathing in the fresh spring air, despite the fact the sunlight stung her pallid face.

Relief at being able to let Buck out of the dark barn faded when she saw the severity of his withered flanks. She took Buck's face in her hands, putting her own against his soft velvety nose. She inhaled deeply, relishing his smell.

With an arm around his neck, she said, "Oh, Buck, I'm so sorry. What do you say we go and find you some grass, boy?"

Both of them had shed a scary amount of weight over the winter. Buck recovered fairly quickly. It would take Jesse several months to regain all she had lost.

As the huckleberry blooms turned into small green berries and the half-moon returned, it was time once again for her to make the dreaded walk to the stream and slice off the three inches of new hair growth. She made quick work of it, wanting to be finished and to move on to other things. Jesse, her gaunt reflection less recognizable than ever before, watched her freshly shorn locks washing away in the current.

∼

Jesse and Buck made their way down the mountain for the third time, no longer needing the old markings in the tree bark to find the way. Mind free to contemplate other things, her thoughts turned to Abby, and whether or not she would see her again.

The first thing she did upon their arrival was head to Edith's hotel.

Edith smiled, trying to contain her alarm at Jesse's appearance. "Hey Jesse, welcome. I was hoping you'd come back. Looks like winter was a rough one for you."

"It's good to see you again, Edith. Worst winter of my life. I've never seen so much snow."

"Well, I'm glad you're all right. Let's go inside. I have something for you. Miss Abby left it for you a couple of weeks ago. She sure is a pretty little thing. I think she's sweet on you."

With a playful grin, she handed Jesse a folded piece of paper. As she took the note their hands clasped briefly. They seemed more like old friends than people getting to know each other.

Jesse went to the room. She sat on the bed and read the letter.

Jesse,

I hope this letter finds you well. I have thought about you often and have replayed our evening together over and over in my mind. I was told you came to see me the next morning and I feel terrible that I didn't get to see you. I have never met someone with a kinder soul than yours and would love to see you again, and learn more about you and your life. I have had many sleepless nights because I was so worried about you all alone out there in the harsh weather. I will be in town until the end of June, so please look me up when you get in. I hope to see you soon and I won't have any peace until I know you are safe.

Sincerely,
Abby

Jesse was conflicted. Her mind told her to go to the trading post, get her supplies, and head home; her heart, on the other hand, told her to run straight to The Foxtail and find Abby. She was drawn to the woman for reasons she couldn't understand.

She knew the right thing to do was leave Abby alone. Underneath the layers of clothing, she wasn't the person Abby thought she was. The last thing she wanted was to give Abby hope they could ever be more than friends.

The paper crumpled slightly when Jesse tensed, startled by a knock on the door.

Edith came in bearing a pitcher of water. "Here you go. Thought you might want to wash up before you see Abby." Edith winked.

"No, I don't have time for that. I'm heading out as soon as I take care of business in the morning."

There it was. Her answer was unforced and reflexive, made instantly and without thought. It wasn't what she wanted, but leaving without seeing Abby was the right thing to do.

"Well, that's a shame. I know she wanted to see you. Been coming by a lot lately to see if you were here." Edith set the pitcher down and exited, saying over her shoulder, "I just cooked a nice piece of venison. Come on out and get some."

The meal was awkward, with Jesse and Edith dancing around the Abby issue. When they finished, Jesse excused herself and returned to her room. It was a warm night and although risky, she decided to sleep without clothes. She had just started to drift off when there was a knock at the door.

"Jesse, you in there?"

Jesse leapt off the bed and frantically began wrapping her chest. In her emaciated state, it was barely necessary, but she did it anyway to be safe. "Yeah, Abby. Give me a minute!" Jesse called out. She hopped on one foot and then the other, scrambling about and trying to get her pants on.

Abby stood with her ear to the door, trying to figure out what was causing the commotion inside the room. Her imagination quickly got the better of her. Perhaps Jesse was not alone. As lurid images began forming in Abby's mind, Jesse opened the door.

Abby walked in, uninvited, and draped her arms around Jesse's neck. She squeezed tightly and glanced around the room.

"Jesse, I have been so worried about you. I thought for sure you would freeze to death out there. It looks like you haven't eaten in weeks."

"It's good to see you too, and I'm fine," said Jesse.

Breaking the embrace, Abby stepped back, looking Jesse directly in the eyes. "You're not fine at all. Your pants don't even fit anymore. You need to eat some—"

"I've been eating plenty. Just finished having a bite with Edith."

"I hear you're leaving in the morning. Don't you think you should stay in town and recover?"

Jesse found it hard to look directly into Abby's eyes. "I'll be fine. I have a lot to get done and need to get home." It sounded like a hollow excuse, even to Jesse's ears.

"Jesse, you're not going to get anything done if you don't take care of yourself first. You look so tired."

"I am, but I'll be better after a good night of sleep," Jesse said, stifling a yawn.

Abby's tone softened. She sounded vulnerable as she asked, "Can you at least stay one more day?"

Jesse had never felt so torn. "…I guess so."

"Good."

"But I have to leave day after tomorrow," Jesse said in a resolved tone, forcing herself to meet Abby's gaze.

"I understand. Since you're staying, can we spend the day together?"

Jesse felt the same longing she could hear in Abby's voice. "Yes, I'd like that. What did you have in mind?"

"You'll have to wait and see. I'll be back in the morning," Abby said, eyes sparkling. "I have something I want to show you."

"I'll see you in the morning, then." Despite her deep reservations, she was already looking forward to it.

They said goodnight and Jesse watched as Abby walked down the hall, not closing the door until she was out of sight. She leaned her back against the door and let out a sigh. Jesse had no idea how to sort through the feelings running through her.

∼

Jesse slept soundly, but anxiety flooded her mind the moment she woke up. It felt like a big day. It *was* a big day. Jesse got dressed and headed out. She ran into Edith.

"Morning, Jesse. How'd you sleep?"

"Just fine, thank you. How are you this morning, Edith?"

"Right as rain. Look, Jesse, I have to confess. I'm the one who told Abby you were here. I know I ought not be meddlin' in your affairs, but I couldn't let you leave without seeing her. Abby is a wonderful woman, and she deserves a good man. I can tell she really cares about you."

"I don't care that you told her. I care about her, too, but Abby and I are friends. Nothing more."

Before Edith could reply, Abby rode up on a beautiful white horse.

"Morning, you two!" she said from her saddle.

"Morning," Edith said.

"Morning, Abby." Jesse scratched the horse behind the ears.

"Jesse, this is Titan. You ready to ride?"

"Yeah. I'll go get Buck."

Once Jesse headed off to the barn, Abby leaned in the saddle, and whispered to Edith. "Thank you again for coming to tell me last night."

"Oh, now," Edith said, "you don't have to thank me. I know he's sweet on you, you just have to give him time to realize it."

Abby leaned back and shrugged her shoulders. "Well if he is, he sure is good at hiding it."

"Just be patient, dear. Love works in mysterious ways. Is that fried chicken I smell?" Edith sniffed the air.

"Yes it is. I'm going to try and see that he at least eats good while he's in town."

"I noticed the weight loss, too. Must have been one hell of a winter for him."

Jesse trotted Buck out of the barn. "Ready when you are. Where are we going?" Her eyes sparkled in the sunlight.

"You'll see, just try to keep up," Abby said. She gave Titan a nudge to the flanks. His hooves kicked up dust as she rode off.

Edith looked up a Jesse. "Well don't just sit there. Get goin'."

Jesse smiled down at her. She pulled her hat down lower to keep it from flying off and called out, "H'yaw!"

Buck had no problem catching up. The two rode out into the country, side-by-side. Abby's riding skills impressed Jesse. She had no problem getting Titan to leap over fallen trees or splash through streams. Conversation flowed easily during the ride, and even the quiet stretches were enjoyable. Jesse knew from the position of the sun the trip took them a couple of hours. It felt like minutes.

They dismounted, patted the dust off themselves, and secured the horses to graze. Abby asked Jesse to help her spread a blanket under a massive oak tree. The small clearing next to the river was absolutely spectacular, surrounded by lush vegetation. Across the river an enormous waterfall danced off the granite bluffs. The sounds seemed to serenade them.

"How's Mabel?" Jesse asked.

"She's fine. It was a long road, and for a while we weren't sure she was going to make it. She's tough, though. Women in her profession usually are. She did love the father. He said all the right things to her, and she fell for every word. She truly believed he loved her and wanted to marry her someday. Turns out he was just using her—just like I thought. When Mabel told him she was carrying his child, he left and hasn't been back."

"How could anyone abandon their own child?" Jesse shook her head.

"You'd be surprised. A lot of men don't want to be tied down with a wife and children."

"I can understand that. They can be a burden."

"What do you mean?" Abby felt a surge of heat go to her cheeks. *Maybe Jesse isn't the kind of man I thought he was. I should have known he was like the rest of them.*

Jesse noticed the stern expression on Abby's face. "I think that came out wrong. I shouldn't have said burden...it's just hard enough to support one's self, and having to support someone else and children too, well I couldn't imagine that responsibility. And then there are people like me. My life can be hostile at times. It's not fair to subject a wife and child to it. But if you're going to make a baby with someone, then I think you should be a man—take care of your responsibilities."

Abby felt her tension ease, but wanted to know what kind of person Jesse truly was. She asked, "So, if you were the one who got Mabel in trouble you wouldn't have abandoned her?"

The question struck Jesse funny, and she laughed out loud.

"I don't see why that's funny. To get a woman with child and then leave her—"

"That's not why I'm laughing. I'm sorry. It's just...well trust me when I say I will never get a woman with child."

"How can you be so certain of such things?"

"Abby, I may not know a lot of things but that is one thing I am sure of."

"But what if you did?"

Jesse cleared her throat and played along. "All right, if I did, I would be by her side through thick and thin. No matter what. We'd go through it together and raise one amazing child."

The words were like music to Abby's ears. *He is a good man.* A warmth spread through her body.

"What did Mabel do?" asked Jesse.

"She got introduced to this man. Said he could take care of her problem for her. He'd done it before."

"Done what before?"

"You know. Abortion."

"Oh, right," Jesse said. She had never heard that word before, but she continued listening in silence. Her facial expression gave away nothing.

"He hurt her really bad. The doctor says she might not be able to have children. You think you lead a hard life? Well, imagine how hard it is for a single woman with a child. Being all alone. What choice did she have? She can barely afford to take care of herself. There really is no place for a baby in a lifestyle like hers. Not saying I would have done the same thing, but Mabel's life is a lot different than mine. She has always dreamed she'd meet a man, fall in love, and start a family. I keep telling her that someday she'll find the right one. She is my oldest and dearest friend, and my heart just breaks for her."

What Mabel did troubled Jesse, but she recalled what Frieda had told her about how hard it was for a single woman to survive. Besides getting married, women didn't have too many options to support themselves.

"She's lucky to have a friend like you. I'm sure someday she'll find happiness," Jesse said, stretching out on the blanket. She wanted to change the subject. "Thanks for the food. It was great. Tell me about your travels. Did you get to sing a lot?"

"You're welcome. I did get to sing, but I stayed at The Foxtail and took care of Mabel. She was alone and in pain. Not to mention, she had a broken heart. I couldn't leave her. I always knew Earl was no good, but she just didn't want to hear it. She loved him, and that's all there was to it. The heart wants what it wants."

Abby pushed on, enjoying the intimacy. "I can understand that. When I would go out on stage I couldn't help but look around the room hoping to see you sitting there. I knew it was silly because I knew you wouldn't be. Still, I looked every time, just the same. I knew the night I met you that you were different somehow. There is just something about you. You can't tell me you don't feel something for me, because I see it when you look at me."

An uncomfortable silence hung between them before Jesse

responded. "It has nothing to do with how I feel about you. You're amazing and any man would be lucky to have you. I just know nothing can ever happen between us. Look, my life is hard and the places I go are no place for a woman like you." The words came out more harshly than Jesse had intended. She felt bad for being so curt. The last thing Jesse wanted was to upset Abby.

Abby didn't appear to be upset. Surprisingly, she looked amused. "Listen up, Jesse McGinnis. I'm not asking you to give up your life and settle down. I just want to spend time with you when you're in town. What's wrong with that?"

Jesse nodded. "I get what you're saying and I have no problem spending time together. I just want you to know nothing can ever happen between us. Abby, you have to trust me when I say I know I'm not the one for you."

Abby was not a conceited person, but she was puzzled by the comment. She had put up with advances by all types of men over the years and now, when she was finally interested in one of them, she was being rejected. This only added to the attraction.

"No, you don't know that." Abby had grown weary of men explaining what she did and didn't need in her life.

"My life is complicated and I wouldn't subject anyone else to it," Jesse said. "You deserve a full, happy life with a loving husband and children. But I do want us to be friends."

Abby sighed and shook her head. She was getting frustrated and a little annoyed. She was a strong, independent woman with a mind of her own. She knew exactly what she wanted. What she wanted more than anything at that moment, despite her frustration, was to kiss Jesse. She had spent a year daydreaming about their reunion and how wonderful it would be. Her yearning, and lack of control over the nature of their relationship only fueled her. She wanted even more.

I wonder what his lips taste like. Are they as soft as they look? Abby couldn't restrain herself. She moistened her lips with her tongue, leaned over, and pressed her mouth against Jesse's.

Jesse's world tilted the moment Abby's lips touched her own.

She placed her hand on the back of Abby's neck and returned the kiss.

Abby wanted nothing more than to give in and let the passion escalate unchecked. She moaned, hoping Jesse would make love to her right there under the large oak. Pressing her body firmly against Jesse's, she took Jesse's lower lip into her mouth and gently bit down, causing the grip around the back of her neck to tighten. Abby lowered her hand onto Jesse's thigh. The toned muscles beneath her fingertips motivated her more. Her hand wandered higher, making its way up until the provocative sensation brought Jesse to her senses.

Breaking the contact, Jesse said, breathlessly, "I'm really sorry Abs, we just can't. We really should be heading back now."

Abby opened her eyes and slowly pulled away. They shared such an incredible kiss, finally, and yet Jesse wanted to stop. It surprised her. She didn't know what to think or feel. She was confused and even a little embarrassed, but took consolation that Jesse felt close enough to call her Abs. Only one other person in her life was close enough to call her that—Mabel.

Abby stood slowly, determined to not let things end on a sour note. "How about we take a quick dip before we go back? It's hot and that water would feel pretty good."

"I'd rather not. But you can if you want," Jesse muttered.

"Fine, but if you change your mind, come join me."

Abby pulled out her hairpin. She shook her head, allowing her blonde locks to flow free. She turned away from Jesse, slipped out of her clothing, and covered her bosom with her arms.

Jesse couldn't help but notice how stunning Abby was as she strolled toward the water. The woman's skin was flawless.

Still covering her chest, Abby waded leisurely into the small pool created by years of erosion from the waterfall. Jesse forced herself to look away.

As Abby swam around, she called out, "Come in. It feels wonderful."

Jesse's face went scarlet red. Abby seemed unaware her breasts broke the surface. "Uh...no thanks."

"All right, but if you change your mind, come in. I promise I won't let you drown," Abby said, grinning, before she dunked her head underwater.

Jesse forced herself to look away again. She stood and examined her surroundings. Her gaze moved across the landscape and stopped on one particular tree. Her breath caught in her chest and she was struck with a strange feeling of déjà vu. She walked over for a closer look. The base of the tree had a teepee-shaped opening. She put her hand inside. Everything came back to her in a rush. She had been here, years before, on what had been the worst night of her life.

Jesse couldn't believe how small the opening was. In her mind it had been enormous. She rubbed her fingers along the inside of the opening, and found a sharp piece of wood. Her other hand went to the scar on her forehead.

Jesse stood transfixed. Abby's repeated invitations to join her faded into the background. There was no doubt in her mind this was the tree that had scarred her forehead. It seemed like so long ago. A lifetime, almost.

Jesse was shocked back to the present by a cold hand on her shoulder. She jumped, like a ten-year-old girl hiding from evil men and being caught.

"What are you looking at?"

The voice calmed her. This was no evil man. This was a beautiful woman, white dress clinging to her wet body, the thin fabric hiding nothing.

"Uh...nothing. I was...uh...just looking for tracks. It's a habit," Jesse said, stumbling over her words.

Jesse was still in shock as Abby took her by the hand and led her back to the blanket. Lying side-by-side and staring at the sky above, Abby pointed out clouds and shared what shape she thought each resembled. Their pinky fingers intertwined. It was a simple and innocent act, but both were aware of the heat it generated.

"Tell me about Barrel. I've never heard of it before. What's it like there?" asked Abby.

The overwhelming emotions and terrible guilt at deceiving Abby became too much for Jesse. She felt she had to share at least something true, no matter how small, or else she would burst.

"I don't really live in Barrel. I live up there," she said, her words gushing out. She pointed to Mount Perish.

Abby was baffled and confused as to why Jesse would lie to her about something like that. No one lived on Mount Perish.

Jesse said, "Years ago my parents discovered a secret crossing in the Devils Fork."

"A secret crossing?"

"Yes. But you can only cross in the summer, when the water level is low. Still, it's tricky to cross and if you lose your footing, you can get swept away. You can't tell anyone, ever. If people found out they would invade the mountain."

Abby considered it for a moment. She put her hand on Jesse's arm and said, "I promise not to tell anyone about your mountain, Jesse. So, were you born up there?"

"Um-hum," Jesse said, mumbling. *It really wasn't a lie,* she thought. *'Jesse McGinnis' really was born on Mount Perish.*

For the rest of the afternoon, Jesse enthralled Abby with her stories. She explained how her parents had built a tiny cabin home atop the mountain. Even though it was simple, the views were unparalleled.

I would love to see that someday, Abby thought.

As stunning as it was, though, Jesse told her the winters could be hell on earth. "Those are the worst. So long. There's nothing to do but think and whittle. Sometimes you think you might go mad."

Abby was in awe of Jesse's life. It took skill to survive such a harsh existence, especially alone. The more she heard, the more she wanted to see it for herself.

"I can't even imagine what the views must be like from that height," Abby said, wistful.

"It's absolutely beautiful, but it's also dangerous. You can die if you don't know what you're doing."

The sun was getting low. It was time to head back. Reluctantly, they packed up and mounted their horses, neither wanting the day to end. Jesse felt a small reprieve from her guilt, having told Abby one secret. It felt good to get it off her chest. She desperately wanted to tell her more, but decided some things were best left unsaid, for now. She liked being around Abby too much to jeopardize losing that.

Jesse talked the entire way back to town. The long ride seemed to fly by, even faster than the trip earlier. The two made plans to meet again later at the Tin Plate.

∽

Jesse arrived first. Anxious, she fretted over her appearance while she waited. She straightened her shirt a few times, and then bent down to brush off the dust she noticed on her pant leg.

A woman's shoe walked into view. Attached to it, Abby. Jesse jumped up to pull the chair out for Abby, nearly knocking both of them over in the process. Abby was more beautiful each time Jesse saw her.

"Thank you. You're so sweet," Abby said.

Jesse listened to Abby's stories of her summer. Neither of them mentioned Mount Perish. A lull in the dining room would allow people to overhear.

When Abby spoke of her last stop on the tour at Granite Falls this year, Jesse sat quietly. The town's name brought back demons, forcing her to face them head-on. It sounded like Granite Falls hadn't changed much from when she was a girl. The Rowdy Rabbit Saloon was still the busiest place in town.

"I've heard of that town," Jesse said. "You know there was a family slaughtered there years ago?"

"I've heard about that. They never found the youngest girl. No one knows what happened to her. Some say she ran off and died out in the wild, but I think whoever killed those people took that girl. It's an awful story and I don't like to think about what that poor child went through."

"Well, you should be careful when you go there. Always sounded like a place where you would find nothing but trouble." Jesse was careful to keep the tremble out of her voice.

"I'm always safe. Don't worry about me," Abby said, smiling.

"All right, enough about that. I want to hear more about you." Jesse desperately wanted to change the subject.

Abby had no shortage of stories. She recalled the events of the last year all through the meal. The pair had a wonderful evening sharing stories. Some were exciting; some were funny. It had been years since Jesse had so much fun. She couldn't have enjoyed herself more.

As usual, when they were together, time went by quickly. They were both shocked when they noticed it was nearing closing time.

Abby said, "You want to go to The Foxtail? I'll buy you a drink."

"I'd love to, but I need to get some sleep. I've got a long trip ahead of me."

"Can I come by in the morning and see you off?"

"I'd like that," Jesse said. "How 'bout we meet here in the morning?"

"That would be lovely."

Jesse escorted Abby to the saloon, and then returned to the hotel. She fell onto the bed. As tired as she was, she couldn't stop thinking. Thoughts swirled through her mind. She tried to make some sense of everything that had happened. She could still feel Abby's soft lips against her own; see her smooth skin gliding across the sparkling water. It made her feel funny inside. The feeling was new to her. She didn't understand this kind of attraction, especially for another woman.

They barely knew each other, but Abby was already taking a place in Jesse's heart. She fell asleep comforted she had let the woman in on one part of her life.

CHAPTER SIXTEEN

Accustomed to rising early, Jesse usually relished the hush of the predawn world around her. Now, a feeling grew in the pit of her stomach, gnawing at her like a hunger pain as she paced the darken room.

It had only been a few hours since she had last seen Abby. It felt more like days. Jesse was grateful when the first faint bands of sunlight crept across the floor. Unable to wait any longer, she grabbed her hat and made her way over to the Tin Plate. She didn't care how early she was.

Jesse was on her second cup of coffee by the time Abby arrived. She could tell Abby was as disappointed as she was about their time together coming to an end. More food was pushed around their plates than was eaten.

Jesse broke the awkward silence. "Abs, I don't like this anymore than you do."

Abby glanced up from her plate. "I want to see where you live."

"You'd really want to go up there?"

"Yes. But, I can't go with you now. I have to do this show in a couple weeks. It's a surprise birthday party for my boss, Boone, and I have to be there. People are coming in from all over to be there for it—but I could go with you next month." Abby leaned in. "Do you think you could come back and get me?"

Jesse was caught off guard. She hadn't thought Abby had any real interest in seeing her rugged lifestyle firsthand. She stammered as she said, "Um…I don't think…uh…I don't know if I can." She wiped her mouth on the napkin and laid it on the table. "I have a lot to get done. Have to be better stocked than I was last winter. That one just about killed us."

"I know you do, and I can help. Just think of how much the two of us could get done." Abby placed her hand on top of Jesse's. She was sure her idea was one that could not be refuted.

Jesse saw no way they could stay under the same roof. A one-room cabin provided no privacy. She gave the only answer she could. "I don't know. I can try to come back. If I do, it won't be until the next full moon."

"You know, I have a birthday coming up and I couldn't think of a better gift."

"When's your birthday?" Jesse asked.

"August 31st, and don't even think about asking how old I'll be. Let's just say I'm older than you, and we'll leave it at that."

"I'm older than I look. Might not be as far apart as you think. How old do you think I am anyway?"

Abby studied Jesse's boyish complexion before she answered. "I bet you're eighteen."

"See, told you. I'll be twenty next month," Jesse said with a grin.

"When?"

"July 4th."

"Hey, that's a great day to have a birthday—Independence Day."

"To me it's just another day. Don't really celebrate it anymore."

"Well, Jesse, maybe someday we'll be able to celebrate it together."

"I'd like that."

Edith, who had been preparing to leave and run an errand, paused when she saw Jesse and Abby together outside the hotel. She waited, giving them a moment alone.

Abby stared up into the most gorgeous green eyes she had ever seen. "Please be safe up there."

"I'm always safe. It's you I'm worried about down here. You be careful, especially when you go to Granite Falls."

"Don't worry about me. I never travel alone. Boone always has one of his men watching over us girls. Especially when we travel. It's his way of protecting his investment, so I'll be fine. I just wish I were going with you." Abby gave Jesse a peck on the cheek. A flush spread across Jesse's face. The bashful response to an innocent gesture surprised Abby. "Please try and come back next month."

"I'll try."

As Abby walked away, Jesse raised a hand, her final wave as heavy as her heart.

Edith had been watching from inside. It was hard to tell through body language what was going on between them. She knew how Abby felt. It was obvious in the woman's gestures. Her emotions practically oozed from her pores. Jesse, on the other hand, was a lot harder to read. There was something there. Yet, for whatever reason, it was being held back. She didn't know the cause of Jesse's reluctance, but she thought it best not to pry into their affairs anymore. In time, Jesse's feelings would make themselves known.

Meeting Jesse in the doorway, Edith said, "Hey Jesse, I'm going to the post to pick up some fabric. Be right back."

"Well, shall we?" Jesse said, offering her elbow.

Edith took hold of her escort, and the two made their way toward the trading post.

"You making some more shirts or pants to sell?" Jesse asked.

"Not this time. I got a new pattern and I'm going to make a dress. I ordered the prettiest periwinkle blue fabric!"

Felix greeted them warmly when they entered the Trading Post. "Hey there, Jesse. Miss Edith. Got your stuff right here." Felix pointed to a table next to the counter.

His stoic demeanor surprised Jesse. She knew he had feelings for Edith, yet his mannerisms gave nothing away. *Oh, he's good.*

Jesse loved the fabric the moment she saw it. It was the prettiest material she had ever seen. *I bet Jamie would have loved this fabric.* She smiled at the thought.

"It's perfect," Edith said. "I'm going to need some linen too."

"What's the linen for?" Jesse asked.

"I'm going to use it on the collar and cuffs."

"A dress that pretty deserves to be trimmed in silk," Jesse said, immediately regretting her words. She wondered if Edith found her comment strange.

Edith shook her head. "Silk is too expensive for my budget."

"Let me pay for it," said Jesse. "I have an idea."

"Fine. Felix, change that linen to silk."

Jesse carried the fabric for Edith. Strolling back to the hotel, Jesse blurted out, "I want you to make me a dress."

"What?" Edith raised an eyebrow.

"I mean, I want to hire you to make a dress for Abby. Her birthday is coming up in August and I thought you could make a dress for her. From me."

"Oh, Jesse, that's a wonderful idea. I'd love to make it." Edith clasped her hands under her chin.

"I'd like to leave a note for her, too. Would it be too much to ask for a piece of paper?"

"I think that would be lovely," Edith said, hand on Jesse's shoulder.

After penning a note, Jesse blew on the ink to help it dry. She folded it neatly and handed it to Edith, who promised to make sure Abby received both items on her birthday.

Jesse went to her room and packed up her belongings. Her

heart seemed to hang lower each time she performed the task, the lonely winter even less enticing. Packed up and ready, she joined Edith in the main room. "I'm all set, Edith. How much do I owe you for the dress?"

"Tell you what. You just pay Felix for the material, and I'll make it for free if you promise to bring me more of that special ointment of yours the next time you come." Edith gave her a wink.

"Deal. And thanks again for everything."

∼

Jesse made quick work of gathering her supplies at the trading post while Felix looked over her pelts. She was getting a later start than she had intended and wanted to be on her way before she wasted any more daylight. Something odd caught her eye on the way back to the counter. Intrigued, she stopped to get a better look. It was all one piece, with buttons up the front and a buttoned flap at the buttocks. The garment was perfect for her particular needs. She purchased two pairs as well as a scythe, in addition to her usual supplies.

∼

All Jesse could think about on the trip back was Abby. *She wants to come up the mountain!*

Jesse still couldn't believe it. She had worked hard on the homestead over the years and wanted nothing more than to show it to Abby. There were so many questions, though, so many pressing issues to address.

It would be nice to get to sit on the old porch again and have a real conversation. Is it possible to keep Abby from finding out the truth about me with both of us under the same roof? Going to the bathroom isn't that big of an issue since there's an outhouse, but is Abby going to find it strange a man relieves himself in an outhouse and not on a bush? *I could use an extra set of hands. What if Abby finds out the truth, though? How will she react? Will she never want to see me again?*

After weighing the pros and cons, she came to a decision by the time she reached the cabin.

∼

Jesse had plenty to keep her busy. Arms swinging, grass flying and falling all around her, it didn't take long for her to appreciate the new scythe. In just a short time she cut triple the amount of grass than she would have been able to with a machete. Aside from Buck, it was one of her best purchases to date. While the grass dried, she chopped wood.

Although she was able to keep her hands busy, she couldn't stop thinking about Abby. Knowing the full moon was approaching only made matters worse. She knew the best thing to do was to not go down after her. In reality, that's the only thing she wanted.

Two days after Jesse's twentieth birthday, she was tying up hay bundles in the meadow when she felt the hair on the nape of her neck rise. She stood, and slowly turned her head. Towering on its hind legs was the biggest grizzly she had ever seen. It was a good forty yards away, but Jesse was sure it had to be at least eight feet tall and close to fifteen hundred pounds.

It sniffed the air.

It smelled a meal.

Jesse glanced at her rifle she had carelessly left next to the ball of twine about thirty feet away—between her and the bear.

She knew from experience she could not out run the animal. Jesse stood completely still, hoping the bear wouldn't see her as a threat and lose interest. Terror froze her blood and her bones. Motionless, she willed the beast to leave.

The bear dropped to all fours. It swayed back and forth a couple of times, the motion emphasizing the sheer size of the animal. The massive threat swiped the ground with a claw before charging.

Jesse bolted straight at the formidable beast. The gun was her only hope. Some combination of adrenaline, luck, and the will to live carried her faster than she had ever run in her life. She slid on her knees and scooped the gun up with one hand.

In one smooth, quick motion, she brought the rifle up, arm on bent knee. She aimed. *One chance*, she told herself. Frieda had taught her years ago bears have small brains and hard skulls. To kill one, it was best to take a heart-lung shot.

This was not currently an option. Jesse held the shot for a split second. She waited until its head was lowered in exactly the right position and then fired, aiming a fraction of an inch above its muzzle. The bear hit the ground, the force so great grass and dirt shot out from beneath it. Due to momentum and his enormous size, he slid a good twenty feet before finally coming to a stop mere feet from her.

Jesse collapsed onto the ground. She forced herself to sit for several minutes, focusing on her own breathing until she could no longer feel her pulse thumping in her ears. *I can't believe I made that shot*, she thought, her shaky hands slowly releasing their grip on the rifle.

The animal was formidable even in death. Jesse knelt and picked up its huge paw. It was heavy, and twice the size of her head. She could have been decapitated with one easy swipe.

As usual she gave thanks to her father and brothers, but also to Frieda, who was now included in her hunting ritual. She took out her large knife and harvested more meat than she could have wished for. There would be no shortage of food this winter. After tanning the hide, she hung the large bearskin on the wall above her bed. The claws she placed in a tin.

∽

July passed. No matter how busy Jesse kept herself, her frustration intensified. She missed Frieda every day. Although the physical exertion took her mind off of Abby at times, nothing solved her confusion as to why she felt the way she did.

They were two women. Jesse didn't know a lot about this sort of thing, but she knew she wasn't supposed to feel the way she did. She could remember her mother telling her someday she would marry. She never considered it, but knew being with a man was the way it was supposed to be. Yet, when she recalled the feel of Abby's lips against hers, somehow it felt right. The more she tried to understand her feelings, the more confused she became. When she remembered Abby's naked body that day in the glade she couldn't deny, even from herself, she wanted more than anything to reach out and caress the flawless skin. The thought of Abby's breasts caused her face to burn red hot. No matter how hard she tried, she couldn't make the feelings go away.

~

Edith gathered the dress and made her way to The Foxtail in search of Abby. She hummed and waved at locals as she passed by. Mabel greeted her in the saloon before she continued up the stairs, wishing more than anything Jesse was here to deliver the gift instead.

She knocked softly. "It's Edith, dear. Can I come in?"

Opening the door wide, Abby asked, "Is he in town?" Before Edith could reply, Abby caught herself. "I'm so sorry. Where are my manners? Please come in."

"No, dear," Edith said, sympathetic to Abby's longing. "But he wanted me to give you this."

Edith placed a hand on Abby's shoulder as she handed over the dress and the note. "He made me promise that I would give these to you on your special day. Happy birthday."

Abby held the dress under her chin. "Oh my, this dress is gorgeous!"

"Please, you have to try it on. I can't wait to see how it looks on you, and I want to see if I got the fit right."

Abby stepped behind a screen and changed dresses. She could tell by Edith's expression when she stepped out that the fit was right. "Oh, Edith! It's perfect! I love it, and it's the prettiest dress I've ever had." Abby beamed and twirled in place.

"I have to say the fit is perfect. But I can't take credit for all of it. Jesse picked out the silk before he left town. And I have to say he was right. Dress wouldn't have been the same without it."

"I wish he were here. I miss him terribly."

"I know, dear," Edith said, "I'm sure he wishes he were here, too. I know he has feelings for you. I can see it in his eyes when he talks about you. If and when he stops by, I will let you know."

Edith gave her a hug and then quietly closed the door behind her, leaving the young woman the privacy to read the note.

Abs,
> Even though I can't be with you today, please know you are on my mind. Not just today, but every day. I hope you like the dress.
> Happy birthday,
> Jesse

Abby sat reading the note over and over. She was disappointed Jesse had not come back, and was overcome with emotion after having received such a thoughtful gift. The uncertainty of when or if she would ever see Jesse again was almost more than she could bear.

That night, miles away, Jesse lay on the bed and stared up at the old loft above her. "Happy birthday, Abs," she whispered into the darkness. She spoke only to shadows, but hoped the thought reached her nonetheless.

∼

Time seemed to crawl during the winter. Most days Jesse sat in front of the fire in her loose fitting one-piece garment, attempting to read a book even though her mind was elsewhere. It was hard for her to concentrate. By the middle of January, she was antsy to get back outdoors and get started on some chores.

One snowy day, Jesse turned three pages before she realized she had no recollection as to what she had read. She gave up and closed the book. She paced, restless. The axe propped up in the corner caught her eye. *Why not?*

Her curiosity got the better of her. She walked over to the bed and pulled the straw mattress off the log frame. She stood for a moment, looking at the puncheon log floor. She sat down and started prying up the floorboards with the sharp edge of the axe, trying her best not to damage the old, wood planks. One by one, she removed three floorboards. The dark hole revealed nothing.

Surely, Frieda wouldn't lie to me about gold. She started to reach into the shadowy void, but stopped when she felt a prickling in her scalp. She was a brave woman, but not a stupid one. For all she knew, this could have been home to a rattlesnake. She wasn't about to go through that ordeal again.

Frieda had been in an altered state of mind before she died. *Knowing Frieda, she probably set a trap in there and forgot to tell me.* Jesse grabbed a candle off the shelf and lit the wick in the fireplace. Cupping her hand around the flickering flame, she returned to the hole. Slowly, careful not to blow out the fire, she bent down. In the restless glow of light, the area beneath the floor glowed yellow. Her eyes went wide, mouth agape.

One. Two. Three. Four. Jesse counted until she reached seventeen. They varied in size and shape; the smallest was the size of an acorn and the largest was the size of a squirrel's head. She picked up the biggest one and bounced it in her hand to get a good feel for the weight.

If I can get a horse, tack, and a gun with a tiny nugget, I wonder what this thing would buy. She could only imagine. She stared down at all the shimmering metal for several minutes, until melted wax rolled across her fingers, breaking her hypnotic gaze.

"Ouch," Jesse said, mumbling under her breath. She blew out the candle, and then blew on her fingers until the sting started to subside. The extinguished candle emitted a wisp of smoke, which hung, lingering in front of her face. Jesse thought of Frieda, and how she could create the perfect smoke ring when she smoked her pipe. When Jesse was younger she would beg Frieda to make them. She loved to stick her arm gingerly through the ring to see how far she could reach her arm through it before the circle lost its shape. Now, Jesse thought it was silly, but at the time it amused her greatly. She remembered Frieda getting excited for her when she finally managed to get a perfect loop all the way up to her shoulder before it ruptured. The memory made her smile.

"Oh, Frieda, I miss you so much it hurts. You are my hero and I love you more than words can say. I can't believe you left all of this to me. You could have left this old, damp place and had a comfortable life, but you chose to stay here. You could have probably bought the whole town of Ely if you wanted…maybe even Granite Falls, too. I guess you knew what was best. This place was your home. I can understand that because it's my home too, and I can't imagine living anyplace else. I wish you were here right now. Thank you, and I promise to cherish everything you left me. I love you."

She decided it was best to leave the gold exactly where it was. *No better place to keep it safe,* she thought before returning the hunk of gold back to the same place she found it.

After reattaching the floorboards, Jesse placed the straw mattress back on the bed frame, and took a seat back in front of the fireplace. She rocked back and forth, unconsciously picking off the leftover bits of dried wax from her fingers as her thoughts shifted to Abby and whether or not they would see each other again. *Will she be there when I go back? Will she be mad at me for not coming to get her? Did she like the dress?*

Her boredom and thoughts nearly drove her crazy for the remaining winter months. Jesse was never more appreciative for the first signs of spring.

CHAPTER SEVENTEEN

Jesse poured her energy into her work as spring arrived, grateful for a reprieve from the cold and the ability to be outside again. Despite working from dawn to dusk every day, and crawling into bed exhausted each night, she still couldn't quiet the thoughts plaguing her. The turmoil over her feelings kept her awake at night, leaving her tired and listless most days. She struggled against an invisible adversary, pushing herself to the point where her mind could focus on nothing but the pain of aching muscles. Still, Jesse was powerless to keep all of these thoughts at bay. She relived moments with Abby, often wondering what it would be like if she were to visit the cabin. More than anything, she worried about the deception their relationship was built around.

Maybe it was because the winter had been mild, or her heart wasn't into it, but trapping season wasn't as successful as in years past. Jesse tallied up the harvested pelts, and counted a few less than the usual. Her profits and supplies would be impacted.

Money wasn't an issue. There was more gold hidden beneath the floorboards. Nonetheless, she came to the conclusion this year she might not get everything she wanted at the trading post. She would rather do without than have to depend on Frieda's gold.

Jesse woke smiling one morning after a beautiful dream. In it, she had spent the night in Ely, dressed in a beautiful gown, silken hair cascading down to her waist. Her smile faded and the dream drifted away like a wisp of smoke in the wind. She sat up in bed, realizing what day it was. Dreading the annual necessity, she skipped her usual cup of coffee. Sluggish, she headed straight to the stream to cut off the latest new growth of hair.

A couple clicks of Jesse's tongue were all it took to get Buck moving forward. While she was glad to finally be heading back, there was only a slight sense of relief. Jesse's mind continued to race, cluttered with all the possible scenarios she had concocted. The main source of her anxiety came from wondering whether or not Abby would be waiting for her. It was quite possible she had hurt Abby. Not returning last year had hurt her, too. *Will she even be in Ely? Is there a letter waiting for me?*

Those thoughts, and more, tortured her throughout the entire four-day journey.

∽

Edith smiled when she saw Jesse walk in. "It's so good to see you again."

"Good to see you too, Edith."

"I'm sorry but all my rooms are takin' for this evening. But I can reserve ya a room for tomorrow night."

It hadn't crossed Jesse's mind Edith might not have a room. "I see. You know any place else I could stay?"

"Well, they're building a new hotel down the street, but it won't be finished for several months. You can stay at The Foxtail, but you'll be payin' for more than just a room. You'd get a bedmate, too. Um…you're more than welcome to stay in the barn tonight, if you'd like. I'm sorry, I know it's not the best, but you're welcome to it."

"I'll take it," Jesse said without considering the other option.

She pulled the saddlebag off her shoulder and opened up the flap. "Here's the salve I promised you," Jesse said, handing over a tin.

"I was almost out. I don't know what's in it, but it does wonders. Thank you."

"You're welcome. I'm glad it helps. You have a letter for me?"

"No, I don't. Sorry. I haven't seen Abby in quite a while. Last summer she came by all the time wantin' to know if I'd seen you."

"There was no way I could get back here. I had too much to get done before it got cold." Jesse felt bad lying, but there was no getting around it.

"I did give her your gift," Edith said, smiling.

"Did she like it?"

"She did, but I could tell she wished you were the one giving it to her."

Jesse stood quietly, hanging her head, dejected.

"Just give it time," Edith said. "These things have a way of working themselves out."

If it were only that simple.

∼

After collecting her supplies and payment for her pelts, Jesse went back to the barn to get some much-needed rest. Several hours later she woke. Too restless to stay cooped up in the barn any longer, she walked out to the well. She wetted her hair, slicked back her bangs under the wide brimmed hat, and headed toward The Foxtail.

Jesse ordered a shot, and looked around for Abby. The sun had set and the place was already crowded. With nerves on edge, the rowdiness of the place was the last thing she needed. It made her uncomfortable and if she hadn't had a good reason, she wouldn't have been there.

Lena approached as Jesse received her shot. "She ain't here. She's down in Big Oak."

Jesse opened her mouth to respond. Before she could speak, Lena continued.

"Do you have any idea what a fool you are? It's so obvious she has feelings for you. If I were you, I'd get my ass down to Big Oak. If you leave now, you can catch her at The Drake."

"I don't even know where that is," Jesse said.

"Just follow the road south."

Jesse tipped her hat in thanks. She tossed a few coins on the bar, slammed back the shot, and hurried out the door. Back at the hotel, she saddled Buck, jumped on, and tore off down the dirt road.

The full moon lit the way. She rode fast and hard, despite her uncertainty about the trip. During the two-hour ride, she tried multiple times to convince herself to turn around and go back. This could only cause more heartache for the both of them. She continued southward, spurring Buck along at breakneck speed, fully aware of the pain that was sure to come.

The Drake was easy to find. It was the busiest place in Big Oak when Jesse arrived. From the sounds spilling out into the street, she could tell the place was in full swing. Jesse pushed through the door, took a seat at the long, mahogany bar, and ordered a shot. The place was even louder than The Foxtail with singing women, shuffling boots, and red-faced men arguing over poker games gone bad.

Three more rapidly downed shots calmed her nerves. The warm glow of alcohol relaxed her as it spread through her body. One of the scarlet ladies took a seat uncomfortably close to Jesse, hoping to make some money off of the new patron. Jesse didn't look up. She knew the swindle. She motioned the barkeep to bring them a round.

"Thank you, handsome," the harlot said.

"Welcome," Jesse said before gulping the shot. She slammed the glass down and turned to look at the woman. Jesse was stunned. This was no woman. This was a girl. Jesse guessed her to be around sixteen, if that. Her heart sank. Knowing this girl had to resort to this lifestyle at such a young age crushed Jesse's spirits.

The girl slammed back her shot. She coughed, acting as if it burned her throat. Jesse didn't fall for it. She knew it was tea, but she played along with the ruse.

"That's some strong stuff. You all right?"

"I'm fine," the girl said as she placed her hand on Jesse's leg. She leaned over and whispered in Jesse's ear. "So, handsome, would you like to take me upstairs? You know…I can make you feel good." Her hand climbed higher on Jesse's leg as she spoke.

Jesse grabbed the girl gently by the wrist and lifted her hand off of her leg. She held it. "What's your name?"

"Sarah."

"That's a beautiful name. That was my mother's name, too." Jesse reached in her pocket with her free hand. She pulled out some money and placed it in Sarah's hand. "I don't have a lot of money, but take this."

After looking at the money in her hand, her eyes met Jesse's. *Not once has a man given me money for nothin'*. "What's the catch, mister?"

"No catch. I wish I could give you more, but I need the rest to settle some business when I get back to Ely."

"What's your name?"

"Jesse."

Sarah stood up next to Jesse. "Well, Jesse, thank you," she said as she put her arm around Jesse in a crude hug.

Jesse felt so relaxed she paid no attention to the arm resting across her shoulders. "I wish I could do…"

When the piano man played the opening chords, Jesse turned toward the stage. As Abby made her way out, Jesse glanced over at Sarah. " I don't m-mean to be rude, but I came here to see this—b-but don't take off," she said, her words beginning to slur.

As Jesse and Sarah sat together at the bar, Mabel spotted them through the crowd. "How could he?" she said, mumbling under her breath. She knew how Abby felt about Jesse. Having the nerve to show up here after all this time was bad enough, but for Jesse to sit there with Sarah's arm draped like that was adding salt to the wound. She had the urge to walk across the room and slug Jesse in the gut. She held back, and instead, stood there glaring as she waited on Abby.

Abby finished her song to the usual explosion of applause and whistles. She took her bow and made her way toward the back of the saloon.

Sarah caught Mabel's scowl. She turned to Jesse and blurted out, "It was nice to meet you, but I have to go. I'll get in trouble if I'm not making money upstairs."

The girl hurried off before Jesse could speak. Jesse stood on wobbling legs, the result of too much alcohol on an empty stomach. She came close to making a spectacle of herself by falling flat on her face. Recovering somehow, she managed to regain her composure and stagger her way out front, grateful to breathe in the fresh, smoke-free air.

Jesse wanted, more than anything, to talk to Abby, but knew they would both be better off if she left. She fumbled to untie the reins, swaying on unsteady feet. A loud eruption of cheers came from inside the saloon. She paused with a foot in the stirrup, holding onto the saddle horn, waiting for the spinning to slow before hoisting herself up. Out of the corner of her eye, she caught sight of Abby making her way down the steps. The look on Abby's face told Jesse everything she needed to know.

Well, this isn't going to be good.

Jesse heard the sound echo down the street before she felt the sting of the slap. It was hard to save any kind of face balanced on one foot, the other lodged in the stirrup.

Abby fired off, "You never came back, and for all I knew something bad happened to you. I can't stand not knowing if you are dead or alive. I figured it would be easier to just let you go and pretend you were never coming back. What do you do? You show up here. Not only do you show up, you try to leave without even saying a word! Who does that?"

With both feet firmly planted once again, she let Abby rant. She felt Abby had every right to be upset with her. Even though the words stung, she stood and listened until she lost her balance and had to grab onto Buck to keep from falling.

Abby finally asked the obvious. "Are you drunk?"

How had she not noticed it before? The fumes alone could ignite should someone strike a match.

"Don't know! Never been d-drunk before. Believe me, Abs, this isn't easy on me either. I know it was wrong to come here, but I wanted to s-see you again. I should go."

Abby's heart softened a bit. No matter what, she couldn't stay mad at Jesse. "You are in no condition to ride back to Ely tonight. Listen, I have one more song to do. Will you please just wait in my room for me?"

"I don't think that's a good idea. Coming here was a mistake. I'm s-sorry."

"Jesse, please," Abby said, pleading.

"I suppose I could s-stay a while. Where's your room?" Jesse fumbled with the reins.

"Give me those," Abby said, smiling inwardly as she took the reins away from Jesse and tied Buck to the hitching post. "It's upstairs, first door on the right. Do you need help up the stairs?"

Jesse laughed. "Abs, don't you think if I can climb Mount—"

"Shhh," Abby said, interrupting as she put her fingers on Jesse's lips. She knew alcohol loosed lips. "Just go to my room. I'll be there shortly. And don't talk to anyone."

Jesse nodded, realizing what she almost blurted out. It was a sobering revelation. She staggered her way up the stairs and opened the door to Abby's room. She took methodical steps across the floor in an attempt to avoid stepping on anything. Finally at the bed, she took a seat and laid her hat to the side. *Good Lord, look at this place.* The condition of the room stunned her. It was in total disarray. There were clothes strewn about everywhere: on the bed and flung over a chair, not to mention those on the floor she had to dodge. Abby's vanity table held several fancy little bottles, some lying on their sides, all covered with face powder. The scene frustrated and confused her. Abby seemed like such an organized, put-together person. It didn't make sense.

The chaos made her uneasy. Jesse had become somewhat of a perfectionist over the years. Everything had a place, and she liked having everything neatly organized. For some reason, structure made her feel safe and calm. Without it, she felt out-of-control.

Ignoring the clutter the best she could, Jesse walked over to the full-length mirror. She combed her hair with her fingers. The messy room loomed behind her in the reflection. Then she spotted it. The dress, periwinkle blue, was as beautiful as she had imagined it would be. She retrieved the dress and returned to the mirror. She held it up to her body, letting it hang below her chin. She couldn't help but fantasize about how she might look in such a beautiful garment. *Don't do it. You'll get caught.* Besides, she was at least five inches taller and knew it wouldn't fit anyway.

Again she was distracted by the bedlam around her. Jesse put the dress back. She pushed some of the clothes out of the way and fell back onto the mattress. Grateful to have a solid surface beneath her while she waited, she mulled things over while listening to the sounds of Abby's voice drifting up through the wood planked floor.

That's it. Jesse couldn't take it anymore. She stood up and began folding the clothes, stacking them neatly at the head of the bed. The dresses went on hangers. She righted the overturned bottles on the vanity table, and continued straightening up until she heard Abby coming. Her approach was easy to make out as the catcalls of men followed her as she made her way up the stairs. "Jackasses," Jesse muttered under her breath. She took a seat on the bed next to her hat, head still spinning, and rubbed her hands together trying to clean off the face powder residue.

Abby walked in and locked the door behind her. She moved Jesse's hat aside and sat next to her on the bed. It was obvious, but Abby asked anyway. "Did you clean my room?"

"Thought I'd help you straighten up."

It bothered Abby, but she tried to downplay it. "You didn't have to do that. I am quite capable of cleaning up after myself. Look, you got my powder all over your lap." Abby started wiping it off Jesse's leg.

Jesse's body tensed involuntarily as soon as Abby began dabbing off the powder. She felt like a little girl again, being reprimanded by her mother when she had misbehaved. Then she was overcome with a warm sensation. It wasn't from the whiskey; it was having someone doting over her again. This simple act of kindness meant so much more to Jesse.

"Sorry, I didn't know it would upset you."

"It's fine," Abby said. With Jesse's body so tense, it was easy for her to feel the hard muscles underneath the pants. She smiled inwardly. "There, I got most of it off." Without waiting for a reply, Abby continued. "Jesse McGinnis, you make me crazy. I know we barely know each other, but I felt a connection with you from the moment we met. There is just something about you. I don't know what it is. I told myself months ago that I need to get over these feeling I have for you, and I was doing that. I even started seeing someone a few months ago."

Jesse's heart lurched at this unexpected news. "You're seeing someone? Are you in love with him?" Jesse asked, trying hard to hide how much it bothered her, searching Abby's eyes for the answers.

"I care about him. I never kept my feelings for you from him. We talked about it a lot. Things just started to happen and over the past few months, I let myself get close to him—then you showed up tonight. I thought I was falling for him, but when I saw you again…" Abby's voice trailed off as she searched for the right words. "You have this invisible hold on me. You have since the first time I saw you. I honestly feel there could be so much more between us if you would just give us a try."

"I do care about you, don't ever doubt that, but I have nothing more to offer you than my friendship."

"You know, I can still feel your lips on mine," Abby said. "You can't deny you felt something when we kissed. Why can't you give us a chance?"

Momentarily speechless, Jesse's heart skipped as the memory of that kiss pulsed hot through her veins. Never had she known true regret until she heard the words falling from her mouth. "You deserve a normal life with someone who can make you happy, and I promise you I am not that person. I do want and appreciate your friendship, though, and I hope I don't ever lose that."

Abby could tell by the set of Jesse's mouth nothing would be gained by discussing it further. Although she didn't understand, she knew she wouldn't be able to change Jesse's mind, despite knowing they desperately wanted each other.

Jesse stood, retrieved her hat and said, "I'm gonna go."

"Jesse, please. We haven't seen each other for a year. Besides, you have had way too much to drink tonight—just spend the night here."

"What about him? What will he think if I stay here?"

"He's out of town until tomorrow evening. Besides, you and I are just friends, right? So what's the harm? Stay here tonight and sober up."

Abby had a point. Jesse relented. "Thanks for letting me stay," she said, plopping down in the chair and kicking off her boots. "I'll sleep here."

"You don't have to sleep in the chair. We can share the bed. You and I both know nothing will happen."

Too tired to argue, Jesse stood up. Abby tossed the pile of neatly folded clothes off the bed and onto the chair. Jesse looked at the pile and hid her annoyance as she climbed back onto the bed. She leaned against the headboard.

Abby slipped behind her dressing screen, draping her dress and then a laced corset over the top. She reemerged wearing nothing but a sheer silk robe. She then lay next to Jesse. "I'm sorry I slapped you. I had no right to do that. My emotions just got the better of me."

"I'm sorry, too. I shouldn't have tried to leave without talking to you. I was afraid I would just make things worse. What do you say we forget the whole thing?"

"Let's. Thank you so much for the wonderful birthday gift. It's beautiful. Edith did a wonderful job. She told me you picked out the silk. Somehow it made turning twenty-five not feel so bleak."

"I'm so glad you like it," Jesse said.

"I love it. You know, I really do try to understand your lifestyle, even if I don't act like it. It's just hard when I've never seen what you go through." Abby rolled over, placing her leg over the top of Jesse's.

Jesse could tell the move was inadvertent. It unnerved her a bit, but she decided not to draw attention to it. She took hold of Abby's hand as it found its way to her chest. In an attempt to stop Abby's fingers from exploring further, Jesse held it in place. Abby was none the wiser as to why she did it.

Jesse caressed Abby's forehead with her free hand. "Tell me about this man you've been seeing."

"You seriously want to talk about that right now?"

"Yes…well, no. But I think we need to talk about it at some point, don't you?"

Abby sighed. "I've known Sam for about two years. He's Boone's business partner. No one knows we've been seeing each other. Mabel doesn't even know. We are keeping it private."

"Why?" Jesse asked.

"I don't know. I guess we wanted to wait and see if it was going to work out between us."

"Do you travel together doing shows?"

"Rarely. He is usually gone on business. Him and Boone own several saloons together."

"Do you see yourself finally settling down?"

"I don't know. I'm so confused. I thought I was falling for him, but when I saw you again…I just don't know."

"I shouldn't have come here. I should have stayed away."

"Don't say that. I'm glad you're here. I like being with you. I wish you would just give us a chance. Maybe you're right and we shouldn't be together, but what if we are meant to be. How will we ever know if we don't give us a try?"

"Abs, I wish I was the one for you."

"How do you know you're not? I'm not asking you to give up your life on the mountain and settle down with me."

"That's it. My life is far away and yours is down here. It would never work."

"I guess. Maybe you're right. We are from two different worlds. I wish we weren't."

"Me too, but at least we can be good friends. I really want that. Is that something you can live with, or would it be better if I leave in the morning and we never see each other again? I don't want to come between you and Sam."

"I definitely want you in my life. Regardless. I care about you. If Sam and I are meant to be, then it will happen for us."

"All right. It's been a long day. Let's talk more in the morning," Jesse said, stifling a yawn.

Abby got up. "You probably should sleep off the whiskey anyway." She extinguished the two kerosene lamps in the room and then curled up next to Jesse again. "You sleep well, Jesse."

"You too, Abs. Goodnight."

"Goodnight."

Jesse lightly massaged her fingers across Abby's temple, sending her straight to sleep, head in the crook of Jesse's shoulder.

Jesse turned her head, unable to stop herself from inhaling the lovely fragrance of Abby's hair. Soon her fingers began to tingle and she lowered the sleeping limb. It fell on Abby's bare thigh, pushing through the folds of the robe. Jesse couldn't resist. She grazed the skin ever so slightly, and it was as soft as she imagined it would be. Abby stirred and Jesse pulled her hand guiltily away.

How can I be attracted to another woman? I've never heard of such a thing. But it feels so right being with Abby. What would it be like to touch each other? To really touch each other? No more secrets. No more lies.

The thought of how much she would like it frightened her

enough that she considered sneaking out of the room right then, never to see Abby again. It was all too much to deal with.

After such a long day of riding, stress, and whiskey, Jesse simply couldn't think anymore. She gave in to her fatigue, drifting off to sleep with Abby nestled beside her.

∼

Abby woke the next morning lying in Jesse's arms, relieved it hadn't been a dream. She gave herself a few extra minutes to enjoy the moment before crawling out of bed. After slipping into a dress, she hastily ran her fingers through her hair. She tiptoed from the room, careful not to make a sound.

Downstairs, Mabel was waiting on the coffee to brew. "So, did you finally make a man out of him?" she asked with an ornery grin.

"It's not like that. I don't think he would be with any woman unless he was married."

"Oh, hun, there ain't no man on earth who don't want it, married or not. Especially from one that looks like you."

"Believe me, I've tried. He says he just wants to be my friend."

Mabel shook her head in disbelief. "Take him a cup of coffee and when you get back to the room, strip off all your clothes and say come and get it." They both chuckled at the comment.

Abby went back to the room with two cups of coffee and a shot of whiskey. Quietly, she placed the drinks on the bedside table, pushed the clothes off the chair, and took a seat. Abby studied Jesse as she slept, recalling what it felt like when their lips touched. She could tell, even fully clothed, that Jesse's body was solid muscle. She admired Jesse's hands, fantasized about how it would feel to have them travel over her body, exploring each curve and hollow.

Jesse began to stir, pulling Abby from her musings. She kissed the crescent-shaped scar on Jesse's forehead. "Good morning. How are you feeling?" she asked.

This was the first time Jesse could recall being sad to see the sun come up. Even though things hadn't turned out the way either had truly hoped, their night together had been wonderful all the same, and they hated to see it end. Jesse sat on the edge of the bed, elbows on her knees, her pounding head in her hands. "I've been better. Got a terrible headache and I'm so thirsty." She rolled her tongue in her mouth, trying to produce some saliva. "You got any water?"

Abby handed her the shot glass.

"Whiskey? Thank you, but no thanks," Jesse said, grimacing.

"I know it's the last thing you want right now, but you have to trust me on this one. The hair of the dog is just what you need."

"The hair of the what?"

Laughing, Abby pushed the shot glass closer to Jesse's mouth. "Just drink it. I promise it will make you feel much better." Jesse didn't want it, but she trusted Abby. She threw back the shot, wincing as it burned all the way down.

"Hopefully you'll start feeling better soon," Abby said, exchanging the shot glass for a cup of coffee.

"Thanks. You can be sure of one thing. It will be a long time before I ever have another shot. I guess I'm not a drinker."

"Well, that's not a bad thing. Trust me. I've dealt with my share of drunks, my father being the biggest," Abby said. Not wanting the memories of her childhood to ruin the moment, she changed the subject. "Someday, I would still like to see where you live. I can only imagine how beautiful it must be up there."

Jesse would never know if it was the instant courage of the alcohol, jealousy, or the yearning to spend more time with Abby. For whatever reason, she blurted out, "Come with me and I'll take you up the mountain. You can't stay long because I'll have to get you back before the river becomes impassable."

"I'd love to go with you, but I'm not sure I can leave right now," Abby said, stunned by the invitation.

"I know. It's sudden."

"Let me think about it. I would love to go, but I'm not sure now is the time."

"I'm going back to Ely. You know I can't stay long and if you decide not to come, I'll understand."

They finished their coffee and walked downstairs. As Jesse untied Buck, Abby, unable to resist, wrapped her arms around Jesse for one final hug. With the reins in one hand, Jesse let her free arm slide neatly up Abby's back.

"Remember, I will only be in Ely for two days, then I have to go." She broke the embrace and settled onto the saddle.

Abby reached up and placed her hand on Jesse's leg. "I know. I can't give you an answer right now. Let me think about it."

"If you can't make it, there's always next year."

"Well, if I don't see you before you leave, you be careful up there," Abby said.

"I will, Abs. I'll see you when I see you. Bye for now."

"Goodbye, Jesse."

Abby stood and watched Jesse ride away, waiting until she could no longer make out the horse or rider before walking back into the saloon. When she did make her entrance, she was greeted by the oohs and aahs of her friends.

"We know what you did. Shame! Shame!"

If they only knew.

CHAPTER EIGHTEEN

Since there was no need for haste, Jesse kept Buck at a smooth trot as she made the ride back to Ely. Despite Abby's assurances of the cure-all, she still wasn't feeling well. Even with her hat pulled down low, the glaring sun still managed to sting her sensitive, bloodshot eyes. A massive headache had started to throb. Without warning, Jesse leaned to the side and vomited, a spontaneous reflex. She pulled back on the reins, dismounted, and doubled over at the side of the road. Hands on her knees, she continued to purge on a small juniper bush until the urge had passed.

She lifted her brim soaked hat, wiped the sweat from her brow, and spat a few sour remnants into the dirt. Scanning the area, she searched for a nearby water source—she saw nothing. Flies had already begun to swarm the acidic mass before she swung up in the saddle.

Several more times along the way she had to stop and dismount. Eventually, there was nothing to heave except dry guts, fighting for escape with every retch. Pain racked her abdomen and bile stung her throat. She was parched. Not a drop of saliva wet her dry and tacky mouth. Dehydration burned her stomach and squeezed her skull. She obsessed about finding something, anything to drink.

Now, with a sense of urgency, she increased Buck's speed. She never slowed, even when she passed fellow travelers on the road. Just a quick nod as she galloped past, leaving a trail of dust in her wake.

Jesse had never been more grateful to see the hotel come into view. She leapt off Buck before he stopped. The arrival invigorated her, giving her the strength to run to the well. She cranked the wooden handle feverishly. She couldn't wait. Jesse swore to herself, grabbed the rope, and yanked the bucket up by hand. Never in her life could she remember being so thirsty.

Jesse plunged the ladle in the bucket and gulped down the cool water. Mouthful after mouthful she swallowed until her stomach roiled. She paused, ladle forgotten. The water she had taken in wanted back out. Hands on her stomach, body still, she managed to keep it down. When the urge had passed, she continued to drink until she felt her stomach might burst.

Edith could tell something was amiss before she reached the well. She'd been letting rooms out to men for a long time. One look at Jesse told her everything she needed to know. Not as bad off as some she'd seen, but even so, it surprised her to see Jesse that way. She knew what Jesse was experiencing was doing more good than anything she could ever say. Edith decided to skip the lecture. "I was wondering what happened to you last night. Thought you might've ended up sleeping at The Foxtail."

Jesse wiped the dripping water from her chin with the palm of her hand. She grumbled, voice raspy, "Never again will I drink whiskey." She took off her hat and used her wet hand to slick the bangs off her forehead, and then put her hat back on. "I rode down to Big Oak to see Abby."

"How'd that go?"

"Not too good at first, but things are better now."

"Glad to hear that," Edith said. "I got your room ready. Why don't you finish up and come inside? I baked some fresh cornbread this morning and from the looks of you, I think you could use some food in your belly."

After taking one last drink, Jesse joined Edith inside. Already full on water, and still nauseated, Jesse could barely bring herself to eat. She made herself sit at that table and eat two small pieces of cornbread before heading to her room.

With what little strength she had left, she kicked off her boots and collapsed onto the bed. It was a significant upgrade from the barn, but she couldn't enjoy it. She cursed herself again as she lay there with her arm shielding her eyes, entertaining the worst headache she had ever had.

Several hours later, wonderful aromas woke her before she opened her eyes. She rose slowly. Emptiness gnawed at her stomach as she sat on the edge of the bed. The water and sleep had done her a world of good, and she was relieved to find her head actually felt much better. She slipped on her boots and made her way toward the kitchen in search of the tantalizing smell.

"I was wondering when I'd see you. You looked pretty rough this morning," Edith said. "Have a seat and I'll fix us a bowl."

"I'll be right back," Jesse said, fidgeting. She hurried outside, in desperate need of the outhouse. When she returned, Edith was seated at the table. Jesse licked her dried, cracked lips as she looked at the steaming bowl of ham and beans.

"So, is this a good time to ask what's going on with you two?" Edith handed Jesse a slab of buttered cornbread.

"She might show up here in a day or two. If so, she's going to Barrel with me—to help me get some things done. She's not sure if she can get away right now. Edith, this looks delicious."

"Well, thank you. There is plenty more if you'd like, but you might want to go easy on your gut right now."

A wagon pulled up to the barn, making enough noise to draw their attention. They looked out the window.

Jesse asked, "What's Felix doing?"

"Oh, he's droppin' off some lumber for me. I want to get started on adding another stall in the barn."

"Is Felix going to build it for you?"

"Heavens no. God gave me two perfectly-capable hands."

"Look, I'm going to be staying for a couple days. Let me build it for you," Jesse said.

"Well, that would be awful nice of you, but I can manage."

"I want to do it. You'd be doing me a favor. I'd rather keep busy while I'm here."

"Well, if you insist, I'm not going to turn down good help." Edith reached across the table and patted Jesse's hand. "I need to show Felix where I want those boards," she said, standing up from the table.

Jesse scooted out her chair. When she went to stand, Edith placed a hand on her shoulder and guided her back in the seat. "You just finish up your soup beans."

Edith went outside. Felix jumped down and stood next to her. They leaned on the edge of the wagon, looking at the planks of wood.

"Afternoon, Sunshine," said Felix. "Do you realize I've been asking you for almost two years now? Woman, when are you going to say yes?" He nudged her with his elbow.

"Felix, we have talked about this. I'm just not ready for that kind of commitment. Besides, why do something that could ruin what we have?"

"All right, I know better than to argue with a woman who has her mind made up. I might be later than usual tonight. I've got a late delivery coming in."

"I'll be here." She gave his arm a tender squeeze.

It was a struggle for Edith to move on after her husband's sudden passing. They had been married for sixteen years when Isaac came down with tetanus after stepping on a nail. She truly loved him, but she had always lived under his control. He made all the decisions and she obeyed. Not that he ever mistreated her, but a wife knows her place. After his passing she slowly began to realize how much she enjoyed her freedom. She could do whatever she wanted, whenever she wanted. She had started a new business, on her own, and it was doing well. Even though she loved Felix, she had no desire to live under anyone's thumb again. She cherished her independence.

Felix started unloading the boards. "I'll start working on it this weekend," he said.

"Actually, Jesse is going to build it for me."

"No reason to pay someone. I'll do it."

"He doesn't want paid. Just wants a project to do while he's in town."

"Well, that's nice of him."

"Sure is. He's a nice young man." Edith smiled.

Jesse made her way outside and helped Felix and Edith unload and stack the remaining boards. Edith explained where she wanted the stall erected, and not one to waste daylight, Jesse set right to work. She was thankful to have a project to focus on. If she kept her mind on the task at hand, maybe she could stop thinking so much about the young girl she met at The Drake who had to give her body to paying customers. Jesse always knew she had been blessed to have been taken in by Frieda, but seeing young Sarah was an epiphany. She realized that could have been her. And then there were thoughts of Abby. The idea of sharing a small cabin with her for an extended period of time concerned her greatly.

∼

Time passed swiftly as the stall took shape. In two days, the blink of an eye, the stall was completed.

Jesse slept in much longer than usual. Groggy, she splashed water on her face from the bowl on the bureau. Still warm from her night's sleep, she shivered as rivulets ran down her back.

She was sad Abby had not shown, but she also felt relieved knowing it was probably for the best. Pushing the thoughts away, she got dressed and began packing for the trip home. She startled when someone rapped at the door. Jesse smiled when she heard the voice.

"Jesse, you up?" Edith asked. "Got something for you."

Since finishing the stall, Jesse had been thanked so profusely she was beginning to think no one had ever done something kind for Edith. She opened the door, ready to tell Edith no more thanks were necessary. Her words vanished, utterly forgotten, when she saw Abby standing next to Edith.

After Abby stepped into the room, Edith gave Jesse a conspiratorial wink before closing the door.

"I didn't think you were coming," Jesse said. "Are you sure you're up for this? It's not going to be easy—you are coming, right?"

"Yes. And I'm more than ready!" Abby said, eyes sparkling.

"What did you tell Sam?"

"I told him I'd be back next month. I don't think he was happy about it, but this is something I really want to do. Of course, I never told him *exactly* where I was going. Just said I was going with you to Barrel to help you get some things done this summer. We will be back next month, right?"

"Yeah. Is he mad you're going with me?" Jesse raised an eyebrow.

"Maybe a little, but it's not like he is going to come here and shoot you for taking me away. I told him it's just a friend helping out a friend. Enough about Sam. I heard you made quite an impression on Sarah. She said you were the perfect gentleman. I expected no less. It was sweet of you to give her money."

"I can't get her out of my mind. She is so young. What is she, sixteen?"

"Fourteen actually." Abby could tell by Jesse's expression she was stunned by the revelation. She shook her head. "Sad to say, I've seen younger ones than that working in some of the saloons."

"The whole thing makes me sick to my stomach. Those poor girls—"

"Strange thing, she said you told her your mother was named Sarah, too. I thought you said it was Frieda?"

Jesse had been so upset by Sarah's youth she hadn't realized she'd made a huge slip of the tongue. She sputtered, "Um...I just said it...it was getting awkward."

Abby cleared her throat. "You mean when she asked you to go upstairs?"

"Yes, exactly. I didn't want to hurt her feelings by declining her offer. Didn't know what to say, so I tried to lighten the conversation and it came out."

"I can understand that. A lot of men would have rushed her up the stairs. You're so different, such a caring person. That's a rarity these days."

I'm definitely not like most men. Jesse smiled inwardly at the thought. "Thanks for the compliment, but it's only because I was lucky enough to have wonderful people in my life to look up to. I'm the person I am today because of them." Jesse wanted to shift the conversation before something else slipped from her lips. "Are you ready to go? Did you pack some warm clothes?"

"I did."

"Thick socks?"

"Just my stockings."

Jesse knew first-hand how cold it gets up on the mountain at night, even in summer. "Those won't do. Your feet will freeze in those...Felix sells socks. We can swing by and get you a pair. You're going to need 'em. Are you hungry?"

"Yeah."

"Me, too. Let's grab a bite at the Tin Plate before we go? It will be the last decent meal for a few days."

Abby agreed.

They caught up on the last two days while they ate, and then headed to the trading post. They were met with the familiar sound of the jingling bell over the door as they entered.

"Hello, Jesse. Miss Abby."

"Afternoon, Felix," Jesse said.

"I just need a pair of socks," Abby said, picking them up off the shelf.

"Anything else?" asked Felix.

"No, this will do it." Abby placed the money on the counter.

Odd to see those two together, Felix thought as the pair left the store. It wasn't because he thought they were an odd-looking couple. He was somewhat surprised Abby was with a man, any man, for that matter. It was a well-known fact around town she paid no mind to any fella. If anyone would know this, it was Felix. Men liked to talk when they came in. He had heard it all. Not one eligible bachelor in town had been lucky enough to spend time with her—Lord knows they'd all tried.

Back at the hotel, when Abby put her socks into her saddlebags, Jesse noticed two neatly folded up dresses lying inside. "You did bring pants, didn't you?"

Abby looked at her like she had three heads. "Jesse, women don't wear pants."

"All you packed were dresses?"

"Yes. Why?"

"Doing the things that we're gonna do…well, I don't think wearing a dress will be too accommodating, that's all."

"Well, what am I supposed to wear, my unmentionables?"

Jesse chuckled as she imagined Abby cutting grass in her bloomers. "Don't worry. It'll be fine."

Edith knocked on the open door before entering. "Take this with you," she said, handing Abby a burlap sack. "I made some food for your trip. Can't expect you two to live on jerky and water, for goodness sake."

"That is so sweet of you. Thank you," Abby said, taking the bag by the drawstring.

"You two be careful out there and I'll see you next month."

"Thanks for everything," Jesse said, smiling warmly.

Edith watched and waved as the pair rode away, delighted things seemed to be going their way.

Darkness had descended upon them by the time they reached the river's edge. The moon was full in the sky and the silvery light easily lit the surface of the Devil's Fork.

Abby's voice rose slightly as she clutched tightly to the saddlehorn and turned to Jesse. "You can't be serious! We aren't crossing here, are we?"

"We are. Do you trust me?"

"Well," Abby said, "I thought I did. Now, I think you might be crazy."

"Just do what I say and everything will be fine. I promise."

Abby had her doubts, but she had no choice. If she wanted to continue, she had to trust Jesse completely.

Jesse jumped down, removed her boots and socks, and stuffed them into the saddlebag. She helped Abby down from Titan and switched reins with her. "You hold onto Buck. I want to see how your horse reacts. We might have to take him back to Ely and leave him at the corral," Jesse said.

"I'm sure he'll be fine. He's been in deep water before."

"Deep and raging are two different things. I hope you're right. I'll see how he does. If I have any doubts, we are taking him back to town."

Jesse led Titan down the embankment. Titan's ears flickered as they approached the river. At the water's edge, she stopped to gauge his response. Titan just stood there as she spoke quietly, gently stroking his neck and withers. *All right, if he starts to panic I'm taking him back to Ely,* she thought as she led him forward, placing his legs in the water. Jesse's doubts about Titan soon vanished. He barely flinched when the strong current hit his legs.

Abby stared in disbelief, mouth slack, as a reassured Jesse made her way across. It was almost biblical. If she hadn't seen it with her own eyes, she never would have believed it.

Jesse secured Titan to a tree branch on the opposite bank, and made her way back to Abby. "I'm glad that's over. I wasn't—"

"I can't believe you did that," Abby said, breathless. "How did you do that?"

"I've done this a few times. I'll explain later. You ready?" Jesse asked, motioning for Abby to get on Buck.

Abby placed her hand on Jesse's shoulder, for reassurance more than anything, before sliding her foot into the stirrup.

"Abs, are you sure you want to do this? I understand if you're too scared. We can go back to Ely."

Abby didn't want Jesse to see how scared she was, nor did she want to miss her opportunity to go up the mountain. She took a deep breath and hoisted herself up in the saddle. "Ready when you are," Abby said in the most confident tone she could muster. "What do I do?"

"You just sit there and I'll take you across."

Jesse grabbed Abby's trembling hand and placed it around Buck's reins atop the saddle horn. "You just hold on and don't let go."

"Oh, I'll hold on. Don't you worry about that, Jesse McGinnis."

Jesse took slow and shuffling steps, taking more caution than ever before knowing Abby's life was in her hands. In Jesse's mind, the crossing seemed to take forever. In reality, it lasted only minutes. Once safely on Mount Perish, Jesse let out a long sigh of relief, feeling like she could breath again.

Abby couldn't believe they had actually made it across. Over the years, she'd listened to the warnings, and had heard about the death toll associated with the river. She stared at the roaring water: dark, writhing, and alive. The river terrified her.

Jesse understood the fixation. She felt the same way when she crossed for the first time. "Abs, we need to get going," she said, putting on her boots.

The sound of Jesse's voice startled Abby, pulling her gaze away from the violent power of nature.

As they rode, Jesse explained the secret of the river crossing, Abby still in awe.

They soon bedded down for the night. Jesse and Abby huddled close, wrapped together under a deer hide for warmth. The sounds of crickets serenaded them to sleep; immeasurable points of light piercing the blanket of night sky overhead.

Up early the next morning, Jesse untied Edith's burlap sack of food from the tree. She hung it the night before to keep it safe from unwanted critters and bears. She untied the drawstring. Inside were biscuits, a hunk of smoked ham, and a sack of coffee with a note tied to it. She unfolded the piece of paper and mouthed the words as she read.

Jesse,
Thank you for all your hard work.
Much appreciated.
Edith

She was moved by Edith's kind gesture, and realized just how much the friendship meant to her.

∾

Jesse spent the next three days showing Abby the important landmarks, including the trees with the special markings. The higher they rode, the more breathtaking the views. The scenery amazed Abby. The mountain was a different place seen up close than from afar.

Abby's euphoria affected Jesse, and she was able to fully feel her own emotions once again. She took the time to appreciate the magnificence of their surroundings. Every evening, they watched the setting sun, sharing food and talking late into the night about their lives.

On day four, they came upon the large mountain lake. Its crystal-clear water was the most gorgeous hues of blue Abby had ever seen. They dismounted to let the horses drink and graze. They stood at the water's edge, looking out over the placid body of water, enjoying the beauty in silence.

Jesse reached down and picked up a flat stone. She rubbed her thumb across its smooth face before tossing it side-armed across the glassy surface. Seven times the stone skipped before sinking from sight. "This is my favorite place," Jesse said, breaking the silence.

"I can see why." Abby picked up her own stone. "It's breathtaking." She tossed the stone. It hit the water with a hard kerplunk and sank out of sight.

Jesse smiled, selected another stone, and handed it to Abby. Standing behind her, she placed her hand over Abby's and mimicked the sidearm motion necessary to skip a rock. Abby gave it a toss. They smiled at each other when it skipped four times.

With the horses rested, they headed out. They were getting close now and both were anxious to reach the cabin.

As they came around the final bend, the cabin appeared out of nowhere. To Abby, it seemed to sprout up in a small clearing hidden in the pines. The trickling of a stream echoed off the trees. She was moved by the serenity of the place, and understood in an instant why Jesse loved it here. She inhaled deeply, breathing in the strong, pine scent. It took her a minute to realize what was so confusing to her senses. Gone was the overwhelming stench of too many men crammed into a tight space full of cigar smoke.

After securing the horses in the paddock, Jesse led Abby to the cabin. Abby stood inside the threshold as Jesse opened the shutters to allow in some light. Abby was able to see the cabin in its entirety. The hay stacked up against one wall caught her off guard, but everything else was as she expected—nice and organized—everything in its place.

Abby caught sight of the mantle straight ahead. She walked over to the fireplace and ran her fingers across the surface of the wood, amazed by the fine detail.

"Doing that passed a lot of time and kept me from going crazy," Jesse said.

"This is the most beautiful mantel I have ever seen! I can't believe you did that." Smiling, Abby continued to look around, noticing the small carvings placed throughout the cabin. "Did you do all of these?"

"Just that one," Jesse said, grimacing. She blushed from embarrassment as she pointed to the lopsided deer propped against a tin on the table.

Jesse was horrified when Abby picked it up to have a closer look. She blurted out, "I did that one years ago. It was my first. I should have chucked it in the fire a long time ago."

Abby smiled inwardly. "It's cute, but I can tell you have improved over the years. If this was your first, where are all the others you've done?"

"Never thought they were good enough to keep. Burned 'em."

"I bet they weren't that bad."

"They were awful compared to the ones my folks made," Jesse said, swinging her finger out at Frieda and Nathaniel's carvings.

Abby didn't believe it. Someone without talent couldn't make a mantel like that. Sensing Jesse's discomfort, she placed the deer back on the table. It fell over as soon as she released her hand.

"I'll fix it," Jesse said. "Stupid thing can't even stand upright."

"It really isn't that bad for your first one. I couldn't make one half that good." Wanting to change the subject for Jesse's sake, Abby continued. "That must have been one huge bear," she said, pointing at the wall above the bed.

Retrieving a tin off the shelf, Jesse removed the lid and dumped the bear claws on the table. "It was the biggest grizzly I have ever seen. Living up here can be deadly. You have to be careful. That's why you have to always keep a gun with you."

Motioning to the loft, Abby asked, "What's up there?"

"That's where I'm going to sleep while you're here."

The two tended to the horses and unpacked. After they had finished, Jesse reached for her rifle. "Will you start a fire? I'm going to go get us something to eat."

"I will. A hot meal sounds wonderful."

Jesse laid her pistol on the table. She secured the door behind her before heading into the woods.

The light from the fire played off Abby's delicate features. Alone, she took in the cabin in the flickering flame. The bed caught her eye. A fantasy unfolded of the two of them together. The images were so vivid. In her mind, Jesse came back from hunting, bolted straight for her, and kissed her passionately. Without a word, Jesse picked her up and carried her to the bed. Slowly, Jesse began undressing her, kissing every inch of her newly exposed flesh before gently laying her back. Just as dream Jesse started to undress, the real Jesse opened the door. Abby was jolted back to reality.

Jesse had already skinned and cleaned a rabbit. She was surprised to find Abby more red-faced and sweaty than herself. "You look hot. Why don't you have a seat out on the porch? I'll take it from here," said Jesse.

Abby said nothing, smiling as she took a seat on one of the old stump chairs out front. Jesse tossed the rabbit into a cast iron skillet and placed it on the grill suspended over the fire. She joined Abby outside, and gave her a quick tour before it got too dark.

The evening air was remarkably cool for June. Abby huddled in front of the fire as Jesse removed the iron skillet and doled out portions onto tin plates. Jesse had told her how serious the weather was up here, but actually feeling it made it real. The hot meat did little to fight the chill. *If it were this cold in June*, Abby wondered, *how did a person survive a winter in this place?*

"I'll wash the dishes," Jesse said, rising from the table. "I need to take them down to the stream. Gotta put the horses in the barn for the night, too."

"Let me help you." Abby gathered the plates and forks. "I'm ready when you are."

"Abs, I got this. You don't have to go."

"I didn't come up here so you could wait on me hand and foot. I want to contribute and be a part of your life. I'm going."

At the stream, Abby held the pistol while Jesse washed the dishes. Jesse began, "The water feels pretty warm this—"

Something splashed loudly downstream. Abby lifted the pistol and aimed, the weapon much too close to Jesse's head for her liking.

Jesse grabbed the barrel and pushed it away. "It was probably a fish jumping. Abby, you have to be careful where you point that thing. I thought you were going to shoot me," Jesse said, her tone serious.

"I'm sorry. It scared me."

"That's all right. I can understand your fear. There are lots of things out here, so you always have to be aware. You did the right thing, just be mindful of where you point."

"I will, and sorry I scared you."

"No harm done. We're awful far away from any help, so be careful while you're here." Jesse stacked plates and forks in the skillet, and they returned to the cabin and went inside.

"I don't know about you, but I'm going to have to excuse myself. I have to go," Jesse said, placing another log on the fire.

"I was thinking the same thing."

"Well, by all means, you go first. I'll go with you if you're scared."

"I'll be just fine, Jesse." Abby picked the pistol up off the table on her way toward the door. She was scared to death. Feigning courage, she hurried to the outhouse and back as fast as she could.

"Do you want to take a bath?" Jesse asked when she got back.

Abby raised an eyebrow. "That would be wonderful. I'm sure I still have dust on me from Big Oak."

"The water didn't feel too cold tonight."

Abby couldn't believe it. Even if it were dark outside, she hoped to at least catch a glimpse of Jesse. "Ready when you are, Jesse."

"Let's go." Jesse held the chamois and soap. "And grab my pistol, will ya?"

The warm glow of the moon lit their way. Jesse sat the soap and chamois on a rock close to the bank. "Give me the pistol. You go on in."

"Why can't we go together?"

"That wouldn't be right. And no need to stand here and argue over it, so you just go on in. I'll sit here and make sure you're safe. I promise I won't look." Jesse sat down on a large boulder, and turned away.

Abby didn't respond. She undressed and grabbed the soap. The water was much too cold for her liking, so she made quick work of it. She dried off with the soft piece of tanned hide and slipped into her clothes. "All right, Jesse. I'm finished. Your turn." Her teeth started to chatter.

"Let me take you inside to get warm. No reason for you to freeze out here."

"I'm fine. I can hold the gun while you bathe." Her teeth clacked together harder this time.

"Abs, I do this all the time. I'm used to it. Let me get you inside before you catch your death out here."

"All right." Abby was too cold to stand and debate it. Once inside, Abby hustled to the fireplace, rubbing her shoulders and trying to get warm.

"I'll be right back. Gun's right there if you'd need it." Jesse placed the pistol on the table. She grabbed her rifle, and closed the door behind her.

As soon as the door shut, Abby sprang into action. She had planned this all evening. Dashing over to the bed, she hurried out of her dress and into her nightgown. It was long and white, but thin enough to see through in the right light. If things went her way, she wouldn't be sleeping in it tonight. Her feet were cold. She considered putting on the thick socks, but she didn't think it would enhance the look she was going for.

Jesse went a little farther downstream to bathe. It was easy to maneuver in the darkness, the terrain familiar. She bathed in peace, knowing there was no way Abby would be able to see her in all her glory. As Jesse washed her hair, she smiled inwardly, feeling relieved the new bathing ritual would not reveal her secret.

By the time Jesse returned, Abby had scooted one of the bedside tables in front of the fire. She held a deck of cards. Jesse stared, caught off guard by Abby's change of attire. It took a moment to find her voice. "Well, it's been a long day and you must be tired. We should probably get some sleep."

"Come over here. Let's play cards."

"I don't know how."

"You're kidding me," Abby said.

"No, I'm not. I've never had a reason to learn."

"Well, why don't you get comfortable and I'll teach you." *Maybe he'll at least unbutton his shirt.*

Jesse had seen people playing poker in the saloons. Even if she knew how to play, she lacked the courage to join in. She took off her outer shirt and laid it over one of the chairs by the table. Jesse pushed up the sleeves of her long underwear and sat opposite Abby, eager to learn how to play.

Abby was a good teacher, but Jesse still found it difficult to concentrate. Abby sat with one foot on the floor and the other in the rocker, her chin resting on her bent knee. Each time Abby leaned forward to place her cards on the table, the opening of the shirt revealed the ample cleavage beneath.

A fine bead of sweat formed on Jesse's upper lip. Abby's exposed skin and the heat from the fire were too much. "Abs, we should get to bed. It's been a long day and life up here starts pretty early." Jesse pulled on her damp neckline.

"I was just having so much fun."

"Me too, but it's getting late."

Jesse stoked the fire one last time, told Abby goodnight, and climbed the ladder leading to the loft.

Lying in bed was torture for Abby. Jesse was so close, and yet so far away. She had tried her best to get Jesse stirred up. All she had gotten for her trouble was to end up in bed alone and frustrated. Still wide-awake, she closed her eyes. She focused on the sound of her own breathing, hoping for sleep to come quickly.

Jesse, too, was frustrated. She stared at the roof above her until she fell asleep, just as disappointed as the beautiful woman below her.

CHAPTER NINETEEN

Jesse woke with a start in the still cabin. In desperate need of the outhouse, she hurried to slip on a pair of pants over her long underwear. She treaded lightly as she descended the ladder, but stopped when she glanced toward the bed and saw Abby asleep on her side, a bare leg sticking out from under the blanket. *She's even pretty when she's sleeping.* Shaking her head, she forced herself out of the reverie and spotted Abby's clothes lying on the floor. She picked them up and gently placed them at the foot of the bed before she continued on her way.

After washing up in the stream, Jesse returned to find Abby dressed and stoking the embers in the fireplace. "Good morning. I hope I didn't wake you," Jesse said.

"Morning. You didn't. Thought you might want some coffee."

"You read my mind. I'll take over if you need to go out."

Handing the poker to Jesse, their hands touched and, although brief, sent a shiver through both of them.

When Abby returned from the stream, Jesse was digging through a trunk. "I don't want you to ruin your nice dresses. My old buckskins should fit you just fine, but you'll have to wear one of my shirts." Jesse pointed to the shirt she had placed on the bed and handed her weathered buckskin pants that she had outgrown. "Sorry they aren't as fancy as what you're used to."

"Jesse, I don't need fancy."

"These should fit you, too." Jesse held up a pair of tall moccasin boots she'd outgrown. "Put all this on and I'll meet you out front."

As soon as Jesse closed the door, Abby undressed and put on the tanned pants that were a little long for her petite frame. When she put on Jesse's shirt, her hands disappeared in the sleeves. She had to roll them up a couple times so the cuffs were resting around her wrists. Lifting the shirt from her chest to her face, she inhaled, relishing the scent. There was just something about the way Jesse smelled. Not like most men; something more tantalizing, something sweet. She couldn't figure out what it was, but she was most certainly attracted to it.

She finished off the look by slipping on Jesse's boots. Abby looked down, taking in the whole ensemble. *Well, this look is attractive.* Not wanting Jesse to see her in this rugged attire, she considered changing back into her dress. After debating with herself she exhaled a long breath, blowing her bangs off her forehead, and walked outside. "Well, what do you think? And don't laugh." Her tone was flat.

"What's there to laugh at? They're just clothes. Those fit all right?" Jesse pointed to the boots.

"Just a hair too big, but they're comfortable. I've never dressed like this before. Feels kind of strange."

"You'll get used to it." Jesse handed Abby a cup of coffee.

"Oh, thank you. I can really use it this morning."

"How'd you sleep?"

"Had trouble falling asleep. You know...new setting and all."

"I can understand that," said Jesse. "Had trouble falling asleep myself. Think I'm just not used to having company," she said with a nervous smile.

Both could sense a slight tension. Each of them chalked it up to spending their first night in the cabin together.

"I can't believe the view you have here," Abby said. "I would sit out here every morning if I lived here."

"I think I take it for granted. I used to feel the same way. Now, I'm usually too busy working and don't take the time to enjoy it anymore."

"Speaking of work, I promised to help. So, what are we doing today?"

"We should start cutting grass. It has to dry before we can bundle it. I need to make sure I have plenty for Buck this winter."

"I see you keep it in the cabin. Have you ever thought of building a separate shelter to store the hay, so you don't have to keep it inside?" Abby hoped the statement wasn't offensive.

Jesse shook her head. "I've never thought about it. But I like the way you think—let's do it," she said.

"Do what?"

"Build a shelter for the hay. We have everything we need right here," Jesse replied, excitement creeping into her voice. "We can build it up against the cabin."

Abby had never used a hammer in her life. She listened as Jesse explained the process.

"If we build it up against the cabin, we only need to build three walls, a roof, and a door. Sorta like a closed-in lean-to. I'll be right back." Jesse hurried inside.

Abby set down her empty cup, ready to prove she could handle anything. She was a little apprehensive when Jesse reappeared, axe in her hand, a gleeful expression on her face.

"You ready?" Jesse said, pushing up her sleeves.

"Yes." Abby smiled through her anxiety, with no clue as to what she had gotten herself into.

Occasionally, Jesse let Abby have a swing of the axe. It took Abby most of the morning to find a good rhythm. The high altitude, coupled with her inexperience, made her lose her breath quickly. She was grateful Jesse didn't call attention to it. It was exhausting work, but at least Jesse allowed her to share the hard physical labor. Most men would never let a woman try.

Abby found herself unable to tear her gaze away from Jesse's strong back, and the way the muscles in Jesse's forearms bunched and flexed with each swing of the axe. *Even his sweat smells sweet.*

By early afternoon, Jesse felt they had felled enough trees to complete the structure. On the short walk home, Jesse noticed Abby looking at her hand. She stopped in her tracks. "Oh, Abs, let me see!" She cradled Abby's hand in her own. A seeping blister had opened up in her palm. Jesse had been so caught up in the work and enjoying her company she'd overlooked her inexperience with manual labor.

Back at the cabin, Jesse sat Abby at the table and retrieved an old tin from the shelf. Frieda had used this same salve on her many times over the years. She knew firsthand how much it helped.

Abby watched, appreciative of Jesse's tender touch as the soothing balm was carefully applied over her broken skin.

Jesse said, "Well, I think we should take it easy for the rest of the day. Let me get you something to eat."

"That sounds good, but let me help."

"No. You sit there. You've done enough work for today."

∼

Jesse decided to spend the rest of the afternoon doing something less physically demanding, but equally important. "Do you know how to shoot a rifle?"

"I've shot one before, but it was years ago."

Jesse grabbed the rifle and asked Abby to come outside. "Wait here. I'll be right back." Jesse walked about thirty feet out, stood a few pieces of firewood up on end, and returned next to her. "I know your hands are sore, so I'm just going to show you the basics."

Abby listened as Jesse continued. "Now, the first thing you need to learn is how to load it..." After explaining the process, Jesse lifted the rifle to demonstrate.

"Can I give it a try?" Abby asked before Jesse took aim. "I want to shoot it."

"But, your hands are—"

Abby interrupted, "Jesse, they're feeling much better. I'm fine."

"You sure?"

"Yes." Abby placed her hand on Jesse's arm. "I'm sure."

"All right, then," Jesse said, handing the loaded rifle over to Abby. She wrapped her arms around Abby from behind. As Jesse helped lift the barrel of the rifle, she said, "Close your eye and use the other one to line up the sight. The sight is the little nub on the end of the barrel. Aim that nub toward the log. Once you're lined up, take your shot." Jesse released her grip on the gun, and stepped back.

Abby focused on the target and squeezed the trigger. The loud blast ricocheted, worrying birds from their perches. A plume of smoke was the only evidence of the shot.

"Hey, not bad," Jesse said. "You were just off to the left a bit. Try it again."

It took Abby several attempts to knock over the rest of the logs. She was proud of herself, and could tell Jesse was proud of her too.

Jesse told her about some close calls she had had on the mountain. She was relieved knowing Abby could hit a predator if she had to—at least in theory. It was one thing to hit some pieces of wood, another altogether to hit an angry animal with mortal fear running through your blood.

Realizing how late it was getting, Jesse asked, "Do you like to fish?"

"Uh, I've never actually done it myself. Why?" *Please for the love of God, please, I don't want to go fishing right now!*

"This is the best time of day to go. Well, now or at first light. Wanna go?"

Abby was shocked Jesse could have the energy to even think

of fishing. "It's been a long day. How about you go get us something to eat and I'll cook us up a nice meal this evening?"

Jesse could tell by Abby's strained smile she had pushed too hard on the first day. "You go on in, and I'll be back shortly. My pistol is hanging by the door. If you need me just fire and I'll come running."

They dined on the delicious grouse Abby prepared. The food and the fresh air wore Abby out and she couldn't wait to crawl into bed.

"I'm going to the stream to wash the dishes. Maybe we can play some cards when I get back," Jesse said.

"Sounds good. Do you need my help?"

"No. You stay here and I'll be right back."

Abby collapsed onto the bed as soon as Jesse shut the door. By the time Jesse returned, she was sound asleep.

Jesse covered her with a blanket. "Goodnight, Abs," she whispered.

∼

Abby was still sleeping soundly when Jesse gently shook her awake in the morning. "Time to get up," Jesse whispered.

Abby looked up at Jesse through squinting, sleep-blurred eyes. She couldn't believe Jesse was already dressed and ready for the day. Abby's lifestyle usually kept her up late into the night, and she never was much of a morning person.

"I've got coffee on. Come outside when you're ready. The fish are sure to be biting this morning." Jesse couldn't hide the excitement in her voice.

"I'll be out shortly." Abby's voice was gravelly. She rolled out of bed, still tired and sore.

After finishing her cup of coffee, Abby excused herself and walked toward the outhouse.

Jesse couldn't help but see how stiffly Abby was moving. *A relaxing morning of fishing is just what she needs.* She was standing with fishing pole in hand when Abby returned. "Let's go catch some food this morning." She handed Abby the fishing pole, grabbed her rifle, and the two set off toward the stream.

They came to a place where the stream widened into a pool of clear water. Rocks of all sizes scattered the pebbly bed, and low hanging branches reached across covering it in shade like a protective curtain. "This is a great fishing hole," Jesse said. "Fish love to hang out here."

"What are we using for bait?"

"Worms. We gotta get some."

"What do you mean, we?"

"Set down the pole and come with me." Jesse grinned. She turned over a large rock and said, "Grab it."

Abby stood frozen, eyes wide with disgust at the slimy earthworm. Her hesitation gave the worm plenty of time to burrow back into the soft soil.

Jesse chuckled. "You're going to have to be quicker than that next time." She put her hands on another rock. "You ready?"

Abby shook her hands in the air as if shaking off invisible mud. She took in a deep breath. Yesterday, she had been impressed with the way Jesse assumed she could do anything a man could do. She now began to rethink that opinion. She would be fine if Jesse thought she was too dainty to handle slimy worms. Sighing, she gathered her resolve. "No, not really...but, go ahead."

Jesse turned over the rock and Abby quickly yanked the worm out of its hole. She was so repulsed by its cold squishy texture she inadvertently flung it through the air.

Jesse laughed and let go of the rock. She ran to fetch the squiggling worm. "That was funny. You know they don't bite, right?"

"What a terrible thought. I didn't even think of it biting me. They are so awful!" Abby squirmed as she spoke.

"Well, at least you did it. I don't mind doing it, so I'll get the worms from now on," Jesse said, still snickering.

"Thank you. I'm not sure I could touch another one." Abby

smiled, grateful she wouldn't have to do that again. They went back to the fishing hole and took a seat on a large boulder.

"Don't forget to jerk when you feel a tug on your line," Jesse said.

Abby nodded and then placed her hand on the back of her neck.

Noticing a pained look on her face, Jesse asked, "Is you neck sore."

"It's just stiff this morning"

Jesse got up and sat behind Abby. She began massaging the sore muscles in her neck and upper back.

Abby was in ecstasy, and honestly didn't care if they sat there all day. Jesse's strong hands felt incredible as they worked out the knots in her muscles. She hoped the fish wouldn't bite. Unfortunately, it didn't take long before she had one on her line.

Jumping up, abruptly ending the massage, Jesse hurried to pull the fish out of the water. She held it up by the gills. "It's a nice one, Abs."

Abby caught two more by the time the sun made its full appearance along the horizon. Although smaller than the first one, Jesse declared them keepers. They had plenty for now.

"I'll clean 'em," Jesse said, pulling out her knife. "Best to clean fish downstream. Keeps the scent away from the cabin. Better to have bears coming here to check out the smell."

Abby and Jesse enjoyed fresh fish for their morning meal.

"Well, that was wonderful." Abby scooted back from the table, coffee cup in hand.

"Hard to beat fresh fish. Why don't you go lay down on the bed? I've got something for you."

Abby went to the bed without saying a word, wondering what Jesse had in mind.

"Roll over on your stomach," Jesse said, walking over to the shelf next to the bed.

Abby's heart raced when she felt Jesse raise her shirt; her pulse drumming so loudly she thought for sure Jesse could hear it.

Jesse opened a tin and stuck her fingers in the thick ointment. She cleared the lump growing in her throat. "This will help your back," she said as she smeared the soothing salve all over Abby's flawless skin.

"That feels so good, Jesse. Mmm." She relished the strong hands massaging her. Never had anyone attended to her like this before. She hoped Jesse would never stop.

"That should do it," Jesse said, lowering her shirt.

Disheartened the treatment was over so soon, Abby sat up and took hold of Jesse's hand. "That was so sweet. Thank you. It feels better already."

"You're welcome. I need to get busy. Got a lot to get done today." Jesse pulled her hand away. "I'm going to cut some grass and get it drying. You should stay here and rest."

"I'm coming with you."

"All right, but grab that so you have something to sit on." Jesse pointed at an old blanket.

Abby talked as Jesse cut grass with the scythe, both grateful for the company.

When Jesse finally finished mowing for the day, she said, "I'm going to go start moving some of those trees back to the cabin."

"All right, but I didn't come here to watch you work. I'm going to help."

Jesse offered Abby her hand. "You can help," she said, pulling Abby to her feet.

They went and got Buck and some equipment from the barn. Jesse tied the rope around a tree and connected it to Buck's yoke. Wanting to make Abby feel needed, but not wanting her to damage her hands further, she let her guide Buck toward the cabin.

They worked until they started losing daylight. After having a bite to eat, both fell asleep quickly, too exhausted for anything else.

Jesse climbed down the ladder in the morning and gently

shook Abby by the shoulder. "Morning, Abs. I'll make some coffee and meet you on the porch."

"Be out in a minute," Abby said, her voice barely above a whisper.

Jesse smiled as Abby took a seat on the old stump chair next to her. "I forgot I still had them. I wish I would of thought of them sooner." She handed Abby a pair of well-worn rawhide gloves that Frieda had made for her when she was a young girl. "I know they look rough, but they'll protect your hands."

"Thanks." Abby prodded the stiff leather.

"How's your back this morning?"

"Why, I had forgotten all about it. Whatever that stuff was did the trick." She regretted the words the moment they left her mouth, costing her the opportunity for another massage from Jesse. She would welcome Jesse's hands on her in any situation.

∼

"Dammit!" Jesse yelled.

Abby turned in time to see Jesse throw the hammer. She approached the ladder and looked up. "Did you get your thumb?"

"Yes. I hate when I do that."

Abby chuckled.

"And just what is so funny?" Jesse asked.

Having seen plenty of men with tempers over the years, she couldn't help but be amused by Jesse's. "I don't mean to laugh. I know it's not funny. But I've never heard you curse."

"Sorry, I didn't mean to swear."

Abby laughed even harder. It amazed her Jesse felt the need to apologize for using such a mild curse word.

"Now what's so funny? I could use a laugh."

"It's just…well, your little tantrum was adorable."

"Ha, ha." Jesse grinned as she climbed down the ladder.

"Let me see it," Abby said, taking Jesse's hand. She stopped laughing. "Oh."

"Oh, what?"

"Blood is already pooling underneath your nail. That must hurt like the dickens."

"Well, it doesn't feel good that's for sure."

Abby kissed the thumb lightly. "Maybe we should quit for the day."

"I've had worse." Jesse caught Abby's gaze. "It's fine." She pulled her hand away, picked up the hammer, and climbed back up the ladder.

"Like it or not you're going to let me tend to it later," Abby called up to her.

"If you say so." Jesse smiled down at her before she started hammering again. "By the way, I think you look lovely in my clothes."

Abby knew that probably wasn't the case, but enjoyed the compliment all the same.

∽

The pair fell into a smooth and easy pattern. Their friendship grew stronger. The more time they spent together, the more their desire for one another deepened. On nights when they had the energy, Abby helped Jesse perfect her poker skills. They went straight to bed other nights, too exhausted to even hold a hand of cards. Abby fell asleep each night wishing Jesse would stop fighting the temptation and join her in bed. Jesse fell asleep each night wondering how empty her life would be on top of Mount Perish once Abby was gone.

As Jesse came down the ladder one morning, she was surprised to find Abby already seated out on the porch, sipping a steaming cup of coffee.

"Morning, Abs. You're up early. How about we take it easy today?"

Abby raised an eyebrow. "What did you have in mind?"

"Let's go hunting."

"So long as there are no worms involved."

After a quick bite, they got ready for the hunt. Jesse strapped on the holster, slid the knife into its sheath, and grabbed the rifle. She led the way through the woods, impressing upon Abby the need for silence.

They stopped and hunkered down at a small cliff overlooking a clearing. Time passed in complete silence. The longer Abby sat quietly, the more her thoughts consumed her. She had never met someone as wonderful, tender, and kind as Jesse. Abby felt the time was right to disclose her darkest secret. Unable to face Jesse, she stared at the ground. "I was married once."

Jesse was speechless, stunned by the revelation.

"We lived in Missouri, and things were good at first. I was sixteen and Silas was twenty-five. I was his second wife—his first passed away from an illness, or so he said. Si was a different person when we were courting. Once I became his wife, he thought he owned me. Never in my wildest dreams did I know a man could be so evil. He changed into a monster the day we got married. I guess he thought he should put me in my place from the start. He didn't like what I had made for dinner. When I asked him what was wrong with it he hit me in the mouth, and stormed out. When he came back that night, I was in bed pretending to be asleep, hoping things would just blow over and be better in the morning. Without warning, he yanked me by the hair, turned me over to face him and told me it was his wedding night. I could tell from his breath he had gotten into the whiskey."

Jesse set down her rifle and put an arm around Abby, pulling her close to protect her from the past.

"He had his way with me that night, kissing me so hard my lip started bleeding again. He hurt me so bad—I just wanted to die. I could barely move the next day, but he had no pity on me. I wanted to run out the door but he was on me again. I've never felt such pain in my life."

Jesse's own blood began to boil. *How could a man be so mean to his wife, especially Abby?* She had the instant urge to kill him with her bare hands.

Abby continued. "He would get violent over the smallest things. If one thing was out of place, he would take it out on me. It was like a game to him. I think he would move stuff just to see if I would put it back where it belonged. If I didn't…well, he'd make sure I did." She looked at Jesse. "I noticed you're like that too."

"I'm nothing like him." Jesse's body stiffened.

Abby turned Jesse's face to meet her own. "You're not, I just meant that I noticed you like things put in their place." Abby dropped her gaze. "I learned quickly how to live with him without setting off his temper. Every day is a living hell when you live with someone like that. There was no way I could leave him. I knew he would search until he found me if I did. There was no doubt about that. He told me repeatedly he would kill me if I ever tried to leave him. My only blessing was I never had to carry his child. Of course he blamed me, saying I was no good at anything and couldn't even make a baby."

Abby placed her hand on Jesse's leg. "I had no way out. I had no money and nowhere to go. I had taken his abuse for three years and then it came to me one night after a beating. The next morning he woke up and you know…which always made me sick to my stomach, but I knew better than to deny him. After he finished, he said he was going to go down to the river and do some fishing. I told him I would bring him some food later and we could have a nice picnic. I couldn't wait for him to leave so I could wash away any trace of him off my body. I always did."

Abby's body shuddered as she thought of her husband's touch. She felt Jesse pull her closer. "That afternoon I went to the river. As we ate, I looked around to make sure we were alone. I walked over to the river and looked down. I asked him to come tell me what kind of fish I was seeing. He stomped over, looked in, and asked me what the hell I was talking about."

Abby paused. She took a few deep breaths before she continued, voice shaking. "While he was bent over, I hit him in the head with a rock and pushed him in. I knew he couldn't swim and I would be rid of him once and for all. I dropped a bottle of whiskey on the ground next to his pole and went home. The next morning, I went to town and asked if anyone had seen him. Some men went to search, and I went back to the house and waited for the news. They never did find his body. I often wondered if his first wife actually died of illness or if he had beaten her to death."

Jesse wiped the tears from Abby's cheek; sad Abby had to relive the pain, but deeply touched to have been entrusted with something so personal.

"I've never told anyone…not even Mabel. Everyone thinks he got drunk and drowned in the river."

Jesse put her hand on Abby's cheek, turned her head, and looked into her eyes. "I would have done the same thing if I were you. He could have killed you." Guilt welled up at the thought of her own secret, and Jesse wondered if Abby would think her a monster if she knew the truth. Perhaps now was the time to tell her.

Jesse swallowed hard. "There's some—"

Abby gasped. "Look."

"I see him." Jesse handed the rifle to Abby. She wrapped her arms around Abby, helping her take aim at what she believed to be a sixteen-point buck. "Easy, Abs," she whispered. "Aim just behind his shoulder."

Feeling the warm breath on her cheek, Abby wanted more than anything to drop the rifle and turn for a kiss. She also wanted to impress Jesse. She focused, blinking hard before she aimed and fired.

The deer dropped to the ground. Jesse took the rifle from her tight grip, set the gun aside, and helped Abby to her feet. "You did it. That was a clean shot. I can't believe it was your first time!"

Leading Abby down, unsure how she would react to seeing the dead animal up close, Jesse said, "You don't have to watch this if you don't want to."

Abby didn't want to appear weak. She still felt she had something to prove. She took the knife out of the sheath, and said, "Tell me what I need to do."

Jesse smiled. She was surprised by Abby's willingness to tackle the process. Then again, she was coming to realize how strong of a woman Abigail Flanagan truly was. Following Jesse's instructions, Abby managed to gut her first deer. Jesse hoisted the carcass over her shoulders.

As they walked back, Jesse explained the tanning process. "…that's why we need the brain. You have to mash it up really good and mix it with your pee. Then smear it all over the hide and let it dry."

"Oh, good Lord."

Jesse laughed.

∽

They spent the rest of their time together finishing up the shelter, chopping and stacking firewood, and bundling up the hay. When the shelter was completed, they filled it with hay. When all of it was removed from the cabin, Abby spent the rest of the day scrubbing the wood floor. She was pleased Jesse wouldn't have to live with the dusty hay stacked inside.

On their last day together, with no work left to do, they decided to go for a walk. Feeling bold, Abby took a chance and grabbed hold of Jesse's hand. She liked the way her hand felt tucked safely inside, and smiled inwardly whenever she felt Jesse's thumb caress her fingers as they strolled. After stopping to snack on berries, Abby was surprised when Jesse took hold of her hand. As they continued walking hand in hand, both did their best to hide the inner turmoil they felt, knowing the inevitable was only hours away.

Jesse led the way back to the cabin as twilight descended. They packed quickly, wanting to make the most of their remaining time together. Jesse went outside to start a fire.

Wrapped in a blanket with her back against a log, Jesse watched the flames grow, flickering in the breeze. Her eyes were focused on the fire, but her mind was elsewhere. *She's leaving in the morning. How will life ever be the same once she is gone?*

"I thought it might be nice to spend our last evening under the stars," Jesse said, smiling, as Abby approached. She pulled the blanket aside and motioned for Abby to join her.

Abby rested her head in the curve of Jesse's neck, overcome with a feeling so far removed from anything she had ever felt, she wasn't sure what to call it. She sensed a change in Jesse's breathing, felt a quickening in the rise and fall of the chest beneath her. She knew Jesse was attracted to her—could see it in those green eyes—but she couldn't figure why Jesse was reluctant to further their relationship. Thinking naiveté might be the reason, Abby asked, "Have you ever been with a woman?"

"...Um...no. No, I never have."

"It's all right, Jesse. I will show you what to do. You don't have to be scared to touch me."

Jesse exhaled. "It's not that I'm scared to be with you like that. We just can't."

"Is it because you're scared what happened to Mabel will happen to me? There are ways we can prevent that from happening, you know."

Before Jesse could respond, Abby placed a hand on her leg. With the Northern lights playing out above them, hearts beating in sync, their passion could be restrained no longer.

Hesitant at first, Abby's hand continued, trailing higher until she felt Jesse remove her arm from beneath her. Expecting another lecture on why they couldn't be together, Abby was surprised when Jesse sat up, removed her hairpin, and placed it on the log.

Jesse had wanted to run her fingers through Abby's hair since that day at the waterfall. She had been too scared to do it then. She was still scared, but her desire eclipsed her fear.

Abby lay back on the blanket and the movement caused her gown to ride up, exposing the bare thighs beneath. She stared into

Jesse's eyes, heart racing, feeling more aroused than she ever thought possible.

Jesse placed her hand on the soft skin of Abby's bent knee. She leaned down and kissed her lips lightly, teasingly, and pulled away quickly. Slowly, she slid her hand up the smooth thigh before clasping Abby's hands in her own. She raised Abby's hands above her head and held them in place.

Abby lifted her head, searching frantically for the lips just out of her reach.

Finally, confidently, Jesse kissed her again, their tongues coming together for the first time. Releasing Abby's hands, Jesse ran her fingers down Abby's arms, caressing the soft skin, making Abby quiver.

Abby wrapped her arms around Jesse's neck, pulling her close, and whispered in her ear. "Make love to me," Abby pleaded, her voice trembling.

Panic flared, bringing Jesse to her senses. "Abs. We need to stop."

Confusion flickered across Abby's fire-lit features. "What? What do you mean? I want you now more than ever."

"If we don't stop now, I won't be able to." Jesse's eyes bore deeply into Abby's. Their intensity mirrored her feelings perfectly.

"We don't have to stop. I want you. I want to touch you."

Jesse's intense gaze fell guiltily away. "I'm sorry. I shouldn't have done that."

"Don't apologize. I want you. I've always wanted you. I know you have to be wanting—"

Jesse shook her head. "I am, but it wouldn't be right. We already went farther than we should have. I'm sorry."

"You really want to stop? Now?" Abby was even more confused.

"Yes," Jesse heard herself say. What she truly wanted was to strip out of her clothes and let Abby touch every inch of her.

Abby took a tremulous breath, trying to accept what Jesse was saying. "Well, if that's what you really want. But please don't be sorry for anything that just happened." Unsure of what more she could say and not wanting things to turn awkward, Abby didn't force the issue.

They lay together under the blanket staring at the night sky, both thinking about what just happened—and wanting what didn't. Abby finally broke the silence as she clasped Jesse's hand. "I don't want to leave tomorrow."

Jesse squeezed back. "I don't want you to leave. But since you've helped me get so much done, how 'bout I stay in town a couple days when we get back? I'd love to come hear you sing."

"I'd love that," Abby said, grateful for any time they could share.

Jesse stood, helped Abby to her feet, and led her to the cabin on still-trembling legs.

Abby climbed into bed, surprised when Jesse took a seat next to her and kicked off her boots. Jesse slid off her pants and joined her under the covers. Abby was disappointed the one-piece underwear stayed in place, but still happy to fall asleep in Jesse's arms.

Jesse and Abby finally snuggled together in the same bed on their last night together on the mountain.

CHAPTER TWENTY

Abby woke in the same position she had fallen asleep in. She felt it as soon as she opened her eyes, but she still looked down to be sure. Jesse's arm was around her waist, and she couldn't help but smile. She placed her arm over Jesse's, relishing in the warm cuddle for as long as she could. She could stay like this all day. Jesse's body twitched. The muscular forearm slid out from under her hand. The sudden absence was like a cold breeze.

"Abs, wake up. We need to get ready."

"Don't get up." Abby jumped out of bed. The old puncheon log floor creaked as she hurried across the room and retrieved a package from her saddlebag. Beaming, she returned to the bed, lay on her stomach, and handed it to Jesse.

"What is it?" Jesse sat up.

"You'll have to open it and see." Abby's smile widened.

Jesse pulled the end of the long red bow and ripped off the fancy wrapping paper.

Abby sat up and placed her hand on Jesse's leg. "Well, do you like it?" Excitement radiated in her voice.

Jesse didn't speak.

"The man in Big Oak said it was the best of the best."

Jesse ran her fingers over the ornately carved, walnut handle. "I love it," she said, sliding the long, shiny blade out of its sheath.

"Happy birthday, Jesse!"

Still holding the knife, Jesse put her free arm around Abby. "I can't believe you remembered. I didn't even know it was today. Thank you." Her gaze shifted back to the knife. She lightly tapped her finger against the blade, admiring the sharpness. "I really do love it, but you didn't have to get me anything."

"Hey, it's not every day you turn twenty-one. I'm glad you like it. I almost bought you a pocket watch instead. But my gut said you'd like this better."

Jesse leaned over and nudged Abby's shoulder with her own. "I'm glad you went with your gut."

∽

Even though it was a special day, a sense of sadness still loomed in the air. After eating, they took their seats out on the old stump chairs, coffee cups in hand. With chirping birds and running water from the nearby stream playing in the background, they sat silently enjoying their surroundings; watching as two squirrels battled over an acorn on their last morning together atop Mount Perish.

Jesse broke the silence. "I need to get the horses ready."

"Give me your cup, and I'll do the dishes," Abby said, reaching out her hand. Jesse went to the paddock while Abby straightened up inside. She took comfort in knowing Jesse would at least have a clean cabin to come home to.

Jesse got the horses saddled and ready before returning to the cabin. She noticed immediately Abby had tidied up the place. Then it struck her. She bit her bottom lip, her hand on her stomach. It wasn't because things were put in places where they didn't belong. It was because Abby felt she had to do it.

Jesse understood in that moment why Abby liked things somewhat disorganized. She was fighting back, in her way, against the husband and institution that had held her prisoner for so long. Jesse cleared the lump from her throat. "You didn't need to do that."

"Do what?"

"Straighten up in here. I'm not like your—you just didn't need to do that."

"You are nothing like him. Not even close. For him it was all about control. I want to do things for you. There's a big difference." Abby caught crumbs in a cupped hand as she wiped down the table from the morning meal. She looked up at Jesse. "I'm really going to miss being here with you."

"I'm going to miss having you around. It won't be the same without you."

"Well, maybe you'll invite me back some day." Abby tossed the crumbs out the open door.

"I'd like that very much. Thank you for all your help. Are you ready to go?" Jesse didn't want to delay the inevitable any longer.

"You are more than welcome, and I suppose so," Abby said. She took one last, longing look around, trying to commit every detail to memory.

Jesse helped Abby mount Titan. Swinging up onto her own horse, she asked, "Hey, Abs, want to play a game on the way down?"

"What'd you have in mind?"

"You take the lead. Let's see if you can find the way. Just for fun."

"All right. I bet I can do it," said Abby, confident.

"Remember to look for the landmarks I showed you on the way here. Tell you what, if you get all the way down without needing my help, I'll buy you dinner at the Tin Plate."

"You got yourself a deal, and if I can't do it, then dinner is on me."

"You're on."

Jesse hoped the little game would help take their minds off of last night. A palpable tension had been growing between them all morning, but neither was ready or willing to bring it up. They both knew they should discuss it. Somehow, not talking about it made it more provocative.

The trail became too narrow for them to ride side-by-side. Jesse's mind drifted. She could hear Abby chatting away about what a wonderful time she'd had, and how she couldn't wait to come back. Jesse saw and heard everything. Her mind was somewhere else altogether: back beside the fire, beneath a starry night sky, Abby more beautiful than ever, exposed and vulnerable beneath her. The recollection, along with the sight of Abby feet ahead of her, the swaying motion of her hips matching the movement of the horse, was enough to drive Jesse crazy.

She forced herself to snap out of it. "It's so easy to get lost out here. Just one wrong turn could be deadly. You have to pay attention to every little detail."

"I can't imagine getting lost out here, all alone," Abby said. It was a terrifying thought, but she wasn't concerned since Jesse was by her side.

Having made the trip so many times, Jesse tried to break the monotony. "Abs, will you sing me one of your songs?"

"What would you like me to sing?"

"I don't care. You pick."

With no barriers, Abby's voice carried unimpeded. Still emotional from last night's encounter, Jesse was rocked to her core. A passion she had never imagined overcame her. Should Abby have turned at that moment, she would have seen Jesse moved to tears.

Abby struggled several times along the way to figure out the correct course. Jesse held her tongue, confident her silence would give Abby the time she needed. Once again, Jesse was impressed with Abby's bold determination.

∽

Dusk had become their favorite time of day. It gave them intimate time together. They would curl up under the deerskin, and talk late into the night, enjoying each other's company and warmth.

Every morning, Abby would relish Jesse's body spooning hers as she woke. She would lay completely still, not because she didn't want to wake Jesse, but because she loved lying there in the embrace. Besides, Jesse was up long before Abby, and she too chose to lay there without moving a muscle. Holding Abby was one of the best feelings Jesse had ever known.

∼

By the river crossing, before they rode into Ely on their last day, Abby stood next to Titan as Jesse began to saddle the horse. Abby pulled out one of her dresses from the saddlebag and began to change her clothes. Jesse stood on the other side of the horse, listening as Abby spoke.

"It's kind of strange," Abby said, slipping her dress over her head, "wearing a dress makes me feel pretty again. Not that I didn't like wearing your clothes. I couldn't have imagined doing all that work in this." She glanced down at her dress.

"Abs, you never stopped being pretty. I'm just glad I never got rid of 'em."

"You hold on to these. I'll want them back the next time you invite me up."

They finally rode into Ely late in the afternoon. "I know you're probably hungry," Abby said, "but I really could use a rest."

"I'm more tired than hungry myself. How about we meet up later at the Tin Plate? I owe you a dinner. Say, around seven?"

Abby leaned in her saddle and placed her hand on Jesse's leg. "That would be lovely. I'll see you then."

They parted ways. Abby headed to The Foxtail and Jesse to the hotel.

Riding up to the barn, Jesse was greeted by Edith. "Hey, Jesse. Where's Abby?"

"She's at the saloon."

"Well, you look exhausted. Why don't you go get some rest and we can catch up later?" Edith took hold of Buck's reins.

"All right. Can you do me a favor? I'm meeting Abby at seven for dinner, so please don't let me oversleep."

Edith nodded. "I'll put Buck in the stall. You go on in, same room as usual. I'll wake you later."

"Thanks, Edith." As Edith led Buck into the barn, Jesse went straight to her room. She fell asleep as soon as her head hit the pillow.

Jesse woke to Edith knocking on her door. She'd only slept a couple hours, but was eager to get to the Tin Plate. *I can't imagine how my life will ever be the same when I get home. To go month after month without seeing her—it seems like an eternity.* Spending another year alone on top of the mountain concerned Jesse greatly. Part of her wished she had never met Abby. Life would have been much easier without all these new emotions.

Jesse washed up quickly and headed to the Tin Plate. She saw Abby through the window, already seated. Jesse paused only long enough to remove her hat before taking a seat. "Did you see Sam?" Jesse asked guilelessly, the question weighing heavily on her mind.

Abby looked a little startled. "Uh. No. He...uh. He's in New York on business. Should be back next week."

"Oh. I'm sorry. I'm sure you've missed him," Jesse said, though she felt somewhat relieved.

"Are you being sarcastic?" Abby's eyes narrowed.

Now it was Jesse's turn to be surprised. "No. Why should I be?"

"I just thought you might be a little jealous. Well. Are you?" Abby's tone was sharper than usual, perhaps a little challenging.

"Maybe I am. A little," Jesse said, far more jealous than she was willing to admit.

Abby sighed and seemed to deflate a little bit. "Well, don't be. I'm not going to be seeing him anymore. Being with you made me realize he is not the one for me. Not that I'm giving up on love. I just know that he doesn't come close to making me feel the way I do when I'm around you. If I can't be with you, then I want to find someone who can make me feel that way. Wouldn't be fair to him if I couldn't return his feelings." Abby paused. She looked deep into Jesse's eyes. "Jesse, I have had the time of my life with you. I'm really going to miss you."

"I can't tell you how much I enjoyed you being there. It won't be the same without you." Some of Jesse's despair crept out, unbidden, in her voice.

Abby noticed. She sat straight up and changed the subject. "Hey. I have some good news and some bad news. You still want to come watch me sing tomorrow night?"

"Definitely," Jesse said before hearing the bad news.

"Well, I know you're probably not going to like this, but we'd have to go to Granite Falls. Lemuel and the girls are there now, and they won't be coming back to Ely until late next week."

"Lemuel?"

Abby nodded. "The pianist who plays for me. I know you're probably tired of riding. We'd have to leave tomorrow afternoon if we want to make it to Granite Falls tomorrow night. We can spend the night there. Or we can just stay here. We don't have to go."

Jesse heard herself speak, her own voice far away. "I want to go. I'd go anywhere to hear you." Of all the places Abby could sing, why did it have to be in Granite Falls? Her breath caught. If she hadn't already committed to go, she would have found an excuse to get out of it. Maybe it wouldn't be as bad as she feared. Besides, what happened in Granite Falls was a long time ago. Surely she had to be better equipped to deal with it as an adult.

A soft hand covered her own on the table, startling Jesse from her wandering thoughts. "Hey, is everything all right?" Abby asked, worry in her voice.

"Uh, yeah. Sorry." Jesse grinned somewhat sheepishly. "I guess I'm more tired than I realized."

"Look, you have been taking care of me, so now let me take care of you. I'm going to pack us a picnic tomorrow. We can stop at the waterfall since it's not far from Granite Falls. We can have a quiet dinner, just the two of us. You get a good night's sleep, and tomorrow we'll get a fresh start."

Don't be stupid. You have nothing to worry about. But if she asks you to look at a fish in the river, get the hell out of there. Jesse smiled inwardly as the thought crept into her mind. "I'll be ready."

After saying goodnight, the two went their separate ways again, both wishing they were heading to the same room.

∼

After a restless night, Jesse decided she might as well get up and face what lay ahead. After all these years, she was going to her hometown. She saddled Buck, speaking to him softly, trying to quiet her growing anxiety. This calming ritual between horse and rider did nothing to soothe the ages-old wound about to be ripped wide open.

Abby hoped Jesse's silence during the two and a half hour ride to the waterfall was due to fatigue.

Jesse was grateful Abby didn't pressure her into talking.

As they ate, it was obvious something was bothering Jesse. Abby had to know what it was. "Jesse, what's wrong? It's like you're here, but you're not."

"I'm sorry. Nothing is wrong. I just feel a little off."

"I hope you aren't coming down with something."

"No. I'll be fine," Jesse said to assure her. "Don't worry."

"All right. But you let me know if I can do anything."

"I will." Jesse desperately wanted to change the subject. "That was very good. You're quite the cook."

"I'm glad you liked it. Why don't you come lay here beside me and relax."

They stretched out on the blanket, hand in hand, watching as the billowy clouds did their lazy dance across the sky.

"That one looks like a duck," Abby said, pointing, trying to rouse Jesse from her stupor with their familiar game.

Jesse lay silent, overwhelmed with thoughts of Granite Falls.

Abby did her best to get Jesse's attention with the game, or at least to jolt her out of the mood she had fallen into. She couldn't get through. Defeated, Abby stood. "Well, we should get going," she said. "I need to be there soon so I can start getting ready."

~

Once in Granite Falls, Jesse's anxiety grew to an all-time high. She dismounted behind the Rowdy Rabbit and helped Abby down from her horse.

"We can keep the horses in here for the night," Abby said, leading Titan into the barn.

Jesse stood still, rooted in place.

Abby asked, "Aren't you coming?"

"If it's all right with you, I think I'm going to check out the town while you're getting ready."

Abby could tell by Jesse's expression the ride had done nothing to bridge the distance growing between them. She hoped a look around would lighten Jesse's mood.

"That's fine, but just don't be too long. When I sing tonight, I will be singing just for you, Jesse McGinnis."

Jesse nodded, helped put Titan in a stall, and waited until Abby was inside the saloon before riding away. She made her way slowly through the town. She was surprised to find some businesses still looked the same, even after all those years. The storefront of Carlson's General Store was exactly as she remembered, save for the writing on the window, now declaring it Granite Falls Mercantile.

Doc Tilson was unmistakable, sitting on his porch, hat slightly back, cigar held loosely between the second and third fingers of his left hand. Both tipped their hats at each other as she passed. Although some things remained the same, many others had changed considerably over the intervening years. Quite a few new buildings dotted the skyline. In fact, the town had changed so much it was not at all like the one she had etched in her memory.

Good sense told her to stay away from the old homestead. During the ride from Ely to Granite Falls she had fought an inner battle, finally coming to the conclusion nothing good could come from visiting her childhood home. Now, curiosity was getting the better of her. She rode out of town, an internal compass taking over as if she had made the trip yesterday. The closer she got to her old home, the faster her pulse raced.

Her knotted stomach clenched tighter still as they got closer. "Whoa, boy," she said, slowing Buck to a trot.

She scanned the horizon. Something was wrong. It took her a minute to realize what it was. Remnants of the stone fireplace still stood, but there was no house for it to warm. She struggled to process the information. She wasn't sure why, because she knew there had been a fire. It was a shock to ride up to such a familiar place and not see her house. The roof of the old barn had caved in from years of neglect.

An unexpected, almost unbearable pain shot through her when she saw the tall oak in the yard. She jumped from her horse and walked over to the tree, using it to steady herself as a new wave of emotion washed over her. With her slender fingers clinging to the rough bark, she could almost hear the laughter floating down from the branches above. *How many hours did Toby and I spend climbing this tree?* She smiled at the memory.

When she regained some of her composure, she walked over to the spot where the house used to stand. It was nothing but rubble now. Charred pieces of wood peeked out from grass, struggling to grow in scraggly patches. The flood of memories overwhelmed her. She saw her mother's sweet face, inevitably followed, as usual, by the sounds of her screams. Jesse dropped to her knees and vomited violently, over and over, until there was nothing left to purge.

Wiping her mouth with the back of her hand, she took a long, slow breath and rose to her feet, once more in control of her emotions. She walked the short distance to the creek to rinse her mouth. It used to take her so long to carry buckets of water from the creek to the house. The memory brought on a fresh round of tears. For a moment, she was ten years old again.

Jesse was rooted in place by memories so vivid she felt she could reach out and touch them. She could visualize her entire family, moving around the old homestead, right in front of her. It all broke through. She allowed the little girl inside of her to cry until there were no more tears to shed.

Jesse didn't want to be this person she had become. She was proud of her family, who she was, where she came from. She was sick of hiding her true identity. *I'm telling her tonight. If she never wants to see me again, well, I'll have to learn to live with it. I've lived through worse. No more lies.*

Mind made up, she took one last drink from the creek and splashed water on her face. Jessica Pratt walked the old path one last time from the creek to what was once her home. She shivered in the fading sunlight. Whether it was from the loss of the sun's warmth or from the stress of being there again, she couldn't stop. Jesse donned the buckskin coat from her saddlebag and hoisted herself onto Buck.

With a quick, "Let's go, boy", she headed back to Abby without a backwards glance.

CHAPTER TWENTY-ONE

Night had fallen by the time Jesse made it back to Granite Falls. Later than she had intended, she hurried to tie Buck up out front of the Rowdy Rabbit. The lack of song emanating from the place worried her. *Did I miss it?*

A commotion down the street caught her attention and kept her from hustling inside. A group of boys were picking on a man who clearly lacked the mental ability to defend himself. One of the boys tripped the man, causing him to fall to the ground. They swarmed around their fallen victim, chanting "Ta-ta-ta-ta-tard."

Maybe Granite Falls hadn't changed as much as she had thought. Jesse walked toward the delinquents, brow furrowed and pistol drawn. "Get away from him!" she shouted.

Her voice and the sight of the gun sent them scattering in every direction. Jesse helped the man to his feet. As she patted the dirt off his back, she asked, "Are you all right?"

"I'm…all…r-r-right," he said, stuttering. His speech was slow, every syllable demanding a focused effort. Even this small conversation seemed hard for him. He was disheveled. Even in the darkness, a large jagged scar stood out, bold on the right side of his forehead. The years had done little to change his features. Jesse looked up into his eyes. She knew without a doubt they were the same eyes she had spent so many hours staring at as a child. There he was, in the flesh.

Real.

Live.

Jesse she could scarcely believe what she was seeing. In a tiny, trembling voice Jesse whispered, "Toby?"

"I Toby."

Jesse felt faint, and she wasn't sure how she managed to stay standing. Her strength had fled her body. She floated in the street. She found no sign of recognition in her brother's familiar face. She thought he was gone, but now she realized what his life may have been like since she'd last seen him—since that day.

Jesse cleared her throat. "Hi, Toby, my name is Jesse. It's nice to meet you."

Toby smiled. "Hi, J-J-Jesse."

"What happened to your head, Toby?"

Toby rubbed his fingers along the scar, but gave no reply. He either didn't know, or lacked the words to explain it. Taking Toby gently by the arm, she led him back toward the saloon. They stopped next to Buck.

"This is Buck. Will you do me a favor? Will you watch him for a minute? I'll be right back."

"I st-st-stay," Toby said, rubbing Buck's forehead.

Jesse hurried inside. She found Abby in the back of the saloon. "Where is your room?"

"Well, hi to you, too."

"Sorry," Jesse said, face flushed. "Don't mean to be rude."

Abby felt a tinge of guilt for not noticing immediately how disoriented Jesse was. "Upstairs, second door on the left. Why? And where have you been?" she asked with a tone of alarm in her voice.

"I can't explain it right now."

"All right, but don't run off. I'm going on soon." Abby searched Jesse's face for answers. She found nothing, but didn't press.

"I won't miss it, promise."

Jesse went back to Toby. She still couldn't believe her older brother had been here in Granite Falls all this time. She had seen his lifeless body with her own eyes. She had believed, without a doubt, he had died that day.

"Toby, can you come inside with me?"

He nodded and followed her inside and up the stairs.

Back in Abby's room, Jesse gave him instructions. "I need you to stay here, and don't come out until I come for you."

It hit her like a punch to the stomach, the words crushing as soon as they came out. That was the last thing Toby had said to her all those years ago. Jesse grabbed hold of the bureau for support in a world suddenly off kilter. "I'll be back. Don't leave," she finished as she headed for the door on wobbling legs.

"I st-st-stay."

Abby was making her way onto the stage to the usual wave of cheers as Jesse came down the stairs. She wedged her way into a spot at the crowded bar, antsy for Abby to be finished. Jesse tried to focus on Abby. She was so consumed with elation at having found Toby she was totally oblivious to the singing she loved so much.

Toby was grown now. It was a strange thing to wrap her mind around. In her imagination, he had remained the little boy she had teased for having puny muscles. At twenty-four, Toby was now taller than Daniel had been. Mentally, he seemed childlike, but his outward appearance told a different story altogether. Toby Pratt had grown up to be a tall, blond, and handsome man.

"Shut the hell up!"

The voice came from behind her. Jesse stopped breathing momentarily as the hair on her scalp tingled. She braced herself against the bar as she slowly turned. There, a few feet from her, was the Devil himself—the scrawny blond-haired man who had been atop her sister that day in the barn. Sitting directly across from him was the man who stood outside her house that night and watched it burn.

Jesse pushed her way through the crowd, barely making it to the street before retching. She bent with her hands on her knees, dry heaving, her stomach empty after her trip to the old homestead. Fear she hadn't known since she was a young girl came rushing back. She cursed herself for letting it affect her so profoundly.

"Did you see them? Why, they're nothing. Weak and pathetic." The voice was familiar. Jesse recognized it instantly. Frieda. It was as if the woman was standing right beside her. "Don't you be frightened by them anymore."

Something inside Jesse shifted. Fear melted away, replaced by anger. Jaw clenched and white-knuckled, the rage slowly built until it consumed her like kindling into an inferno. She wanted nothing more than to walk back inside and shoot the bastards where they sat. She reached for her pistol and ran her finger along the trigger.

Then, it hit her. Abby and Toby were also inside. If something were to happen to either of them, she would never be able to live with herself.

Jesse took a deep breath, took her hand off of the gun, and gathered her wrath into her balled up fists. She had a moment of clarity as the crowd once again exploded in cheers. She knew what had to be done.

Jesse pushed her way through the crowd and hurried toward the back in search of Abby. Grabbing her by the arm a little more forcibly than she intended, Jesse said, "I need to talk to you. Now."

Jesse's force and tone left no doubt in Abby's mind she was serious. Jesse held her grip as she escorted Abby out back, behind the saloon. Jesse had never acted like this.

"What's wrong?" Abby asked. "I saw you walk out. Is everything all right?"

Jesse released her grip. "Look. I know you don't owe me anything, and I have no right to ask this of you, but I need you to do something for me."

Without hesitation, Abby said, "What do you want me to do?"

"Do you remember when we talked about the family who was killed here years ago?"

"Yes. Why?"

"Well, two of the guys who did it are sitting in there. Can you get those two out by the waterfall? I'll be watching the whole time to make sure nothing happens to you. Will you do that for me?"

Abby paused, blindsided by the request. She wasn't sure exactly how to react, but she did know one thing: she trusted Jesse to do what was right. "How do you know they are the ones?"

"I can't tell you right now how I know, but I do know. Without a doubt." Jesse swallowed the lump stuck in her throat and took a calming breath, trying to maintain her composure. "If you don't want to do it, I understand. I'll figure out a way to do it myself."

"You know I'll do whatever I can to help you. Just please, tell me what's going on."

"I can't right now, but I will, I promise."

"Which ones are they?" asked Abby, as she heard her name being announced back inside.

"They're the ones sitting at the table close to the bar. One is blond and thin, and the fat guy across from him has black hair." Grabbing Abby by the shoulders, Jesse continued, "I just found out that someone else survived that night, Toby Pratt, and right now he is up in your room. He is kind of…simple, and needs my protection. Look, if something should go wrong tonight, I need you to look after him for me."

"Jesse, tell—" Abby started, only to be silenced when Jesse urgently placed a finger on her lips.

"Abs, there's something else." Jesse put her face next to Abby's and whispered in her ear, "Under the bed up at the cabin, dead center, there is more gold than you could possibly need. Just pull up the floorboards, and you and Toby will never have to worry about money." Pulling away, Jesse stared into Abby's eyes. "Promise me you will look after Toby."

"If, God forbid, something should happen to you, I will. I promise," Abby said, eyes wide, voice faltering.

Jesse hated the fear she saw in Abby's eyes. She was scared, too, but she had to do this. She took Abby's face in her hands. Her lips brushed lightly over Abby's, a whisper, then harder, an intensity driving her as if she would never get to see Abby again.

Jesse broke the embrace. "Everything will be fine," she said.

"I don't know what you're planning, but please be careful."

"I will."

Abby retook the stage, eyeing the crowd as she started to sing. The men were easy to spot. Even the looks of them gave her an uneasy feeling about what was to come. After her final bow, Abby went directly to the bar. She ordered three shots of whiskey. No tea in the shot glass this time. She was going to need the liquid courage.

She walked over to the table where the two men were seated. Placing a shot glass in front of each man, she held up hers and said, "Drinks on me, boys."

The scrawny blond-haired goon sat with his mouth hanging open, surprised such a beautiful woman would speak to him. The black haired man was a little more vocal, though not much more intelligible. "Hell yeah, darlin'!" was the brightest he could think to say. Abby was repulsed the moment he opened his rotten maw.

Tapping their glasses together, the three downed their shots in one swift gulp. Abby gritted her teeth as she removed the hat off the man with black hair. She ran her fingers through the greasy, unkempt mess. *I'd rather be picking up worms.*

She untangled her fingers from the rats nest and announced, "I'll be right back, boys."

"Awe, come on now. Where you goin' honey?"

"Don't you fret, handsome. We're just getting started."

Abby made her way back to the bar in search of a bottle of whiskey, disgusted by the obvious arousal of the brothers.

"Watch out for those two," the barkeep said, handing her the bottle. "They're nothing but trouble."

Abby gave him a wink. "Thank you. I'll be fine, Floyd. Don't worry."

Abby brought the bottle back to the table. "Hey, you boys want to get out of here and help me with this?"

Both men looked at each other and smiled wide. Needing no additional prodding, the two vile men stood, more than ready to join her. "I'll get my horse and meet you fellas out front," Abby said.

The brothers rushed out the door. They were ready and waiting by the time Abby came riding around from the back. Handing the bottle to the blond, she said, "Here you go, handsome."

Using his nasty teeth, he pulled the cork, and took a big gulp. The black haired man introduced himself as Jake. Pointing to the bottle-bearing blond he said, "That's my brother, Clay."

"Well, I'm Abigail, and it's my pleasure to meet you boys. Follow me and try to keep up."

Abby nudged Titan and he took off in a full gallop. The two men rode behind, doing their best to match her pace. Jesse followed from a distance, careful not to give herself away, but close enough so she could keep an ever-watchful eye on Abby.

Once they reached the secluded spot in the woods, both men jumped down, shoving each other in an attempt to be the one to help Abby dismount. Jake, always the winner, grabbed Abby by the waist and plucked her from the saddle. Acting the part of a helpless woman, Abby thanked him profusely and complimented his strong arms.

If Jake and Clay were aroused before, they were doubly so now. The brothers passed the bottle back and forth, desire reeking from them in rotten waves. Their clothes, too tight for anyone's comfort, did little to hide their excitement. They grabbed at themselves, oblivious or uncaring about the unease it caused Abby. Taking big swigs of the whiskey, they continued passing the bottle until it was empty.

Seated between the pair, Abby forced a smile and prayed for

Jesse to show up soon. A volatile marriage and countless nights in the saloons had taught her the signs. Things were about to get out of her control. *Jesse, where are you?*

"Now that is one fine tit!" Jake said, reaching into Abby's dress. He placed her trembling hand on his crotch. "Why don't you go ahead and undo 'em? I got somethin' real special just for you. You know you want to see it."

Clay started grinning as he always did when his older brother played this game. He unfastened his trousers and began fondling himself.

Mouth poised and ready, inches from Abby's chest, Jake was totally unprepared for the pistol that crashed into the back of his skull. He slumped forward, eyes rolled back. Clay jumped to his feet, fumbling for the pistol buried somewhere in the trousers wrapped around his ankles.

"Don't even think about it!" Jesse shouted.

One hand covering her chest, Abby used her other to remove Clay's pistol from its holster. She readjusted herself as she handed the gun to Jesse, asking, "What do you want me to do?"

"I want you to ride back to town." Jesse didn't take her eyes off Clay, who stood with both his hands in the air. He'd held the pose since the moment he saw Jesse's pistol pointed at him.

Abby stood frozen in place as if she hadn't heard Jesse speak. Jesse raised her voice. "I need you to leave. Go back to town. Now. If something happens to me tonight, remember what I told you. Now go!"

"I don't want to leave you here with them. Let me help you," Abby said, pleading.

"Please just go. If you care about me at all you will leave. I will see you soon. Please, go."

Fighting against everything inside of her, Abby got back on her horse. She reluctantly left Jesse in the woods with the loathsome men.

Jesse removed Jake's pistol from its holster and tossed it to the side. She motioned with her gun for Clay to take a position on his knees next to his brother. His erection had long since fled, hidden like a frightened turtle. As exposed as he was, she felt no remorse for him whatsoever.

Jake rubbed his head as consciousness returned. "I'm going to kill the son of a—" The sight of the gun leveled at his head made his mouth stop working.

"Get on your knees or I'll just go ahead and shoot you now," Jesse said.

With both men now facing her, she could tell they were clueless as to why this was happening. "You don't know me, but I know you. I also know what you did. I saw what you did to that girl in the barn. I saw you kill all of them." Jesse's voice rose as she spoke. "I saw you burn down their house and then take a piss on it without a care in the world. I saw everything!"

Unmoved, Clay replied, "We didn't kill that boy. Didn't even touch him. But, oh yeah, that was a good piece of ass I had in the barn."

The grin on his face filled Jesse with such a murderous rage she was unsure how she kept her feet on the ground.

Jake jabbed his elbow into Clay's ribs. "Shut the hell up!" He wasn't an intelligent man by any means, but even he was smart enough not to provoke someone who was pointing a pistol at his head.

Years of emotions simmered inside of Jesse. The sight of the men responsible for her family's deaths made it all boil, and a murderous rage spilled over. Jesse lowered the barrel and fired, shooting Clay directly in his flaccid penis. "That's for my sister!" she shouted.

Staring down at the bloody mess that used to be his genitals, Clay wailed in agony. He doubled over. Jesse ignored his howls and fired again, shooting directly into the top of his head. Clay crumpled and collapsed to the ground. "And that one's from me you piece of shit!" she yelled, wishing more than anything she could have shot that smug grin of his right from his ugly face.

Using the back of his hand, Jake flung away bits of his brother's blood and brain matter that had splattered his face. His demeanor was causal; it could have been nothing more than phlegm. He put his hand behind his back as he spoke, calm and collected. "Ya shouldn't done that."

Jesse caught a glimpse of him making a sudden move, and both guns fired. Neither knew who fired first.

∼

Nearly a half-mile down the trail, Abby flinched again as she heard another gunshot ring out. *Did that one hit Jesse? Was that the one to take Jesse from me forever?* Everything inside of her wanted to turn around and ride back, but she had made a promise to Jesse and she intended to see it through.

∼

Still on his knees, Jake dropped his gun. Panic covered his face as he reached up and squeezed his throat. He gurgled, eyes wide, blood squirting out from between his fingers. He locked his gaze on Jesse, fear obvious in his eyes. He surely would have begged for his life could he speak. A thick stream of blood poured out of his mouth. His body swayed. He extended a pleading arm toward Jesse, blood dripping off his hand, thick like oil.

Jesse dropped to her knees and clutched her side. Eyes focused straight ahead. She heard Jake's body; struggling, gurgling, and gasping. She saw the whites of his eyes before he fell over on his face. She remained frozen, sitting on her heels, pressing her fist tight against her side. Her other hand held a death grip on the pistol, ready to shoot him again if need be. She continued her steadfast gaze, listening as Jake's dying body continued to struggle. Then, there was silence.

Jesse knew she had been shot, but the gravity of the situation only hit when her hand came away covered with blood. She needed to get back to Granite Falls before it was too late. Her hand trembled as she slid her pistol back into the holster. The toes of her boots dragged the ground as she stumbled to Buck.

Blood was warm on her cold skin as she mounted. Already lightheaded, too weak to sit up, she now rode hunched over. She held on tight as Buck moseyed along.

Unguided, Buck wandered aimlessly until finally he came to the Devil's Fork. He paused to munch on some grass, and then headed south. The direction led to the familiar crossing that would take them home. It was the opposite direction of Granite Falls, taking Jesse farther away from the help she desperately needed.

Her vision faded. Unable to hold on any longer, Jesse crashed to the ground, her face landing on a patch of pine needles.

∼

Abby jumped down from Titan, and went straight to her room at the Rowdy Rabbit. A young man sat alone, quietly playing with a deck of cards.

"Hi, Toby. My name is Abby. I'm a friend of Jesse's."

"Hi." Toby looked up and smiled.

Abby could immediately tell the man was innocent and child-like, as Jesse described. There was also something familiar about him, but she couldn't place it. "It's so nice to meet you," Abby said, sitting down next to Toby. "Want to play a game?"

"What do you want to p-p-p-play?" Toby's eyes grew wide.

"How about blackjack?"

"Never played t-t-that before. How about old m-maid?"

"I like that game. Let's play." Abby rifled through the deck and removed the ace of clubs.

Toby sat intently, his mind focused on the game.

Abby's thoughts were elsewhere. She watched the door, praying for Jesse to walk through it any second. *He should have been back by now. What if he is out there bleeding to death?*

She had no idea if Jesse was dead or alive. Either way, she

needed to find out. "Toby, can we finish this game later? We need to go."

"All right." Toby smiled and laid his cards on the floor.

The two rode double, heading toward the waterfall. Abby was thankful for clear skies and a full moon to light the way. She slowed when they neared the spot in the woods where she had last seen Jesse. "Toby, we have to be really quiet now." Abby set an example with a soft and low tone. She brought Titan to a stop and the pair dismounted. Handing over the reins, she whispered, "I need you to stay here and be very quiet."

"I st-stay, shhh."

After hearing the gunshots, Abby had no idea what she was about to come upon. In her gut she knew it was going to be gruesome. Bullets didn't tickle. She didn't want Toby to see such things. She didn't want to see them herself. She was terrified to look. Having no other choice, Abby had to see if Jesse was alive.

She came upon Jake's body, his face covered with blood. A few feet away lay Clay, face down in the dirt, pants still bunched around his ankles. Abby turned away from the bloody scene, fighting the urge to vomit. With a pounding heart she looked around, frantically. Her pulse slowed when she found no sign of Jesse or Buck. *I didn't pass him on my way here. He must have gone back to Edith's.*

Abby ran to Toby, and the pair quickly made their way back to Ely. Had they rode next to the river instead of taking the dirt road, they would have found Jesse, unconscious and bleeding.

∼

They barely came to a stop before Abby jumped down and ran into the hotel.

"Edith, is he here? Is Jesse here?" Abby yelled. She was distraught.

Edith came rushing out of her bedroom, rubbing sleep from her eyes. "Abby is that you? Let me get some light in here."

Two other doors opened down the hall. Edith said, "It's fine fellas, go on back to your rooms." She looked at Abby. "No, dear. I haven't seen him since the two of you rode off. Why? What's going on?"

Abby's heart and shoulders sank. Edith took her hand and led her to the kitchen with Toby following silently behind. Edith guided Abby to the table and pointed to a chair. "Have a seat." Pulling out a second chair, she motioned for Toby. "Young man, why don't you have a seat here?"

"I T-Toby."

"Well, it's nice to meet you, Toby." Reaching into the back of a cupboard, she pulled out her secret stash of moonshine and began pouring shots. For Toby, who seemed as uneasy as Abby, she poured a finger full. "All right," Edith said, "tell me what's going on."

Abby couldn't blurt out Jesse had killed two men. Instead, she said, "It's bad. I wasn't there, so I don't know everything for sure. I heard he got into a nasty fight tonight. I don't know if he is hurt, or worse. I don't know where he is. I can't just sit here and do nothing. I need to go find him."

For the life of her, Abby couldn't figure out where Jesse might be. *He didn't go back to Granite Falls. He wasn't at the waterfall. He wasn't here. He just killed two men. Where is he?* Then it came her. Jesse had to know killing was a hanging offense and must have fled back up the mountain. *If I leave now, I can catch up to him when he stops for the night. I have to hurry.* Abby asked, "Edith, I need to ask for a favor. Can you watch Toby for a few minutes? I have to run and grab some things and I'll be right back."

"Where are you going?"

"I think Jesse went back to Barrel. I have to find out. I have to try and find him."

"Why don't you wait 'til it's light out?"

"No, it's a long trip and I have to leave now. I'll be fine. I know the way."

"Do you want Toby to stay here? He's more than welcome to stay with me for a while."

Abby considered it until she remembered how scary Mount Perish could be—down right terrifying. Not knowing if she would be able to catch up to Jesse, she didn't want to risk traveling up the mountain alone.

"No, he's going with me. We'll be fine."

"All right, but let me fix you up some food to take. I just hope you know what you're doing."

"That would be so kind. Thank you."

Abby ran to The Foxtail and quickly tossed a few things into her saddlebags. Before she walked out the door, she was mindful to grab a lantern. Her mind was spinning. *Did he go back up the mountain? Is he hurt? What if I can't catch up to him? Can I make the trip up the mountain without Jesse?* All she knew for certain was that Jesse wasn't where she was or had been. Going back up the mountain was the only logical plan of action.

~

Back at the hotel, it dawned on Abby; she didn't own a gun. She was well aware of the dangers on Mount Perish. God knows Jesse had drilled it into her while she was there. She thought of the bearskin that hung in Jesse's cabin as she asked, "Edith I'm going to need one more favor. Do you have a rifle I can borrow?"

"A rifle? Dear, of course you can. But, are you sure you know what you're getting into?"

"Yes, I probably won't even need it, but I'd feel a whole lot better having it with me, just in case. Thank you so much for everything."

"No need to thank me. Just find him. I'll pray for all of you. Be careful out there." Edith went to her bedroom to get her rifle. If Edith had known where Abby was really headed, she wouldn't have let her out of her sight.

Abby and Toby mounted the horse. Edith handed the rifle up

to Toby.

"I g-g-good with r-r-rifle," he said. It was a declaration which surprised Abby.

"That's good, dear. Now, you hang on tight to that," Edith said.

Abby gave Titan a kick to the flanks. Just like that, the two were off, speeding toward the river, racing against the rising sun.

∼

Pushing Titan, they reached the river crossing before the sun came up. Abby jumped down, kicked off her boots and stockings, and then shoved them into her saddlebags. "Toby, I need you to stay here for a minute."

Abby walked to the edge of the embankment and stared down at the fast moving water. She thought, at first, she might do a trial run by putting her feet in to see how it felt. After seeing the water up close, she decided against it. Her fear would probably take over and panic would set in. She didn't want to chicken out. She quickly tried to recall every detail Jesse had ever told her about crossing. It occurred to her she would have to make one major adjustment. She slipped her dress over her head and shoved it into her saddlebag. The pull of the water on the dress might be enough to sweep her off of her feet. Nothing about crossing in her corset would be lady like, but she had no other option.

"Toby, you stay up there and hold on tight. Don't let go. Understand?"

Toby nodded and grabbed hold of the saddle horn, a look of fear on his face.

"It's going to be fine, Toby," Abby said. She took a deep breath, took hold of Titan's bridle, and stepped into the water. "Just keep holding on."

She managed to find the ledge with her right leg. Whispering a silent prayer, Abby slowly stepped forward. Chancing a backwards glance, she caught sight of Toby's wide, terrified eyes.

"Toby," she said, "this is going to be fun. Just hold on tight, and no matter what, don't let go." Abby took another step, putting her into the deep water. "Ready, Toby?"

"R-r-r-ready!"

Slowly, one cautious step at a time, Abby made her way across the mighty river. She shuffled her bare feet the way Jesse told her to. She could almost hear Jesse's voice telling her to make sure she had good footing before taking the next step. Her knuckles were white from holding the bridle as she led Titan and Toby painstakingly across.

When she made it to the opposite shore, she wanted nothing more than to collapse. Relieved and exhausted, she felt more spent than ever before.

Toby seemed to enjoy the trip. "Let's do it again."

"Not today, Toby. Not today," Abby said, putting on her clothes. "We have to go find Jesse."

Abby and Toby rode for a few hours, hoping they might run into Jesse along the way. She knew Jesse's routine; Jesse only traveled during the day.

∼

The sun had now been up for several hours and there was still no sign of Jesse. Abby had a sinking feeling. It occurred to her while she was traveling up the mountain, Jesse might still be on the other side of the Devil's Fork. She couldn't turn back now. She had to keep going.

Abby prayed Jesse didn't try to ride directly to the cabin without stopping. If that was the case, she would be forced to make the journey entirely on her own. She had no idea if she was capable of that. The challenges of coming down the mountain previously were a different matter altogether. It was easy to be confident with Jesse by her side. Now, she was responsible for not only her own life but Toby's as well.

Oh, Jesse, where are you?

CHAPTER TWENTY-TWO

Jesse opened her eyes, blinked hard against the sunlight filtering down to the forest floor. Through the shadows cast by the towering pines, she stared at the dark lump next to the dying fire. As she focused, it morphed into her pistol. Lingering smoke from the embers fighting to stay alive floated on the breeze.

Disoriented, she struggled to recall how she had gotten to this unfamiliar and desolate place in the woods. The world spun and she placed her hands on the ground for support. Sitting up was an effort. The slight movement sent pain surging through her body. The small rush of adrenaline brought clarity, the events of the previous night swimming into stunning focus.

On the ground, alone and lost, she put a hand to the damp shirt clinging to her back. She knew it would come away red even before her bloodshot eyes saw the evidence. Her flank felt like it was on fire. She lifted her shirt and looked down at her charred flesh. *At least it stopped bleeding*.

Jesse focused on the few remaining embers, their glow almost hypnotic, as she contemplated her situation. She didn't have the strength to gather the wood and without fire there was no way to cauterize the exit wound on her back. Not that it mattered now, anyway. What she went through the first time was unbearable. She wasn't sure she had the nerve to do it again. Her best chance for survival was to get out of the woods and find help before it was too late.

The metallic scent of blood hung thick in the air. Buck reacted on pure animal instinct. Eyes wide, flags of black on white, he stood guard over his gravely wounded companion.

After holstering her pistol, she pulled herself to her feet using a stirrup. The effort took more blood than she had to spare. The world turned and grew dimmer, less distinct. She clenched her teeth and summoned all the strength she could muster. Somehow, she hoisted herself onto the saddle without losing consciousness. The simple endeavor was now excruciating. Warm blood trickled down her back.

There was a good chance of passing out. She knew it. She groped blindly through her saddlebag and pulled out a piece of rope. Head spinning and fingers shaking, she did what she could to secure herself to the saddle. She stared at the knot, pulled it, and checked it. She couldn't remember if she tied it right or how it was supposed to look. It was just going to have to do. There was no way she could do it again.

She gave Buck a tap to the flanks. So weak, she wasn't sure he even felt it until he started walking. She rode slumped in the saddle. Even at his slowed pace, the agony of each step was almost more than she could take.

Pain soon overwhelmed her. She slipped mercifully into unconsciousness. The horse wandered without guidance along the banks of the Devil's Fork in the waning sunlight.

~

Buck finally came to a stop. His master offered no guidance. He struck at the ground with his front hoof. The whinnying and head-tossing finally elicited a response from Jesse. She opened her eyes. Even in the dark, she recognized the moonlit crossing immediately.

"Good boy, but we aren't going home this time." Her voice faded as she spoke. "This is as far as I go, my friend." With trembling, bloodstained hands, she loosened the rope and slid down from the horse. She was too weak to stand; gravity took her. The already fuzzy world took another step away from her, taking some of her breath with it. She was so tired—more tired than ever before. All she wanted to do was sleep.

The men who murdered her family had finally paid for their crimes. This gave her peace. Toby was safe with Abby. With the gold hidden in the cabin, they would have a comfortable life. They'd never have to struggle for anything again. This would be the end for Jesse and she could accept that.

A vision of Abby floated before her eyes, bringing a smile to her lips. "I loved you from the moment I saw you, Abigail Flanagan. I always have. Always will," she whispered. Her eyes fluttered and finally closed as she surrendered to the darkness

Several miles up the mountain, Abby closed her eyes. She didn't want to, but they'd been open since the night before. She desperately needed sleep, if only for a few minutes. It had taken everything she had to get this far. She had nothing left.

Thank God Toby is here, she thought. He secured Titan for the night; she didn't have the energy for that. After the horse was secure, Abby and Toby lay together on the frigid ground. They shared a blanket. Toby fell asleep almost instantly and snored loudly beside her. She understood Toby didn't like to talk much, and his mental capacity wasn't what it should be. Still, she was grateful to have a man his size next to her.

Abby burrowed closer to Toby, thankful for his body heat. She was exhausted but powerless to quiet the storm raging through her mind. *Did I do the right thing? Is Jesse on the mountain or still on the other side of the river?*

She had come too far to turn back now. Good or bad, she'd see where this path led. A wolf howled in the distance and she nestled even closer to Toby. Her tired eyes didn't want to close anymore.

Toby stirred. His snoring stopped briefly and then continued as if he was accustomed to sleeping in such a scary place. Abby was miserable. She remembered telling Jesse about her trip to California on the stagecoach, and how she couldn't imagine anything more awful. *And all because I was uncomfortable, cramped in a small space and covered in dust with some smelly men. That trip was nothing compared to this.*

At least during that trip she had been safe and warm. Now, she was cold and afraid, lying in the middle of the forest like a piece of live bait. Her eyelids grew heavier and she couldn't fight her fatigue any longer. Even as the howls closed in around them, Abby fell asleep, whispering into the night sky, "I'm coming, Jesse."

∼

The sun lit the sky when Abby woke. She slept longer than she wanted to and was anxious to be up and moving again. Her body cried for more rest. She could spare it none. Her joints cracked loud enough to make her flinch as she stood, her body unused to sleeping on the cold forest floor.

"Let's get going, Toby," she said, gently shaking the sleeping man by the shoulder. His size was that of a man, but his moan of protest that of a boy. As she shook him again, Abby had to remind herself to be patient. Toby may not understand everything that was happening.

Once roused, he was up and moving. The sudden wake-up did nothing to diminish his energy. "Can I t-t-take the reins. I may st-st-stutter, but I'm not stupid. I c-c-can handle a horse. Can shoot, too."

"I don't think you're stupid," Abby said. She handed him the reins. "We just need to make sure we follow the right path or we'll get lost."

The ride was tempered by familiarity. They soon reached the first marked tree. "Want to play a game? Sorta like hide and seek?" Abby asked.

Toby smiled and nodded.

"There are several trees that have markings like this. Can you help me find them?"

"I'm good at t-this game." Toby's smile widened. "I can find 'em." He had a keen eye. Whenever he saw one of the special trees, he jumped in the saddle and called out, "There's one."

"You won. But I bet I find the next one before you." She never failed at enticing him to look for the next carving. They continued riding throughout the day with Abby resting her head against Toby's back.

"There's one," he called out, startling her again. It was for the best. She couldn't afford to fall asleep, despite her worsening fatigue. She played along with Toby, watching out and reaffirming they were continuing in the right direction.

As the purple gray of twilight filled the sky, Abby took the reins from Toby. She decided to keep going even though she knew Jesse would tell her she was being reckless. There was no way she was going to spend another night sleeping on the hard ground, forest noises all around her.

Some of the tree markings were much harder to spot in certain areas. Towering trees obscured the moonlight, forcing her to dismount throughout the night for a closer look. Each time, she stumbled into the underbrush with the lantern, verifying they were still on the correct path.

Toby didn't complain, but she knew this couldn't be any more pleasant for him than it was for her. As soon as she mounted, he wrapped his arms around her waist, lay his head on her shoulder, and struggled to get comfortable. He was exhausted and the novelty of looking for trees had long faded. She, too, was beyond tired. Abby caught herself falling forward in the saddle several times. She sang softly, trying to stay awake. Toby sometimes hummed along behind her.

They reached the mountain lake by dawn, giving her a renewed sense of hope. They were on the right path, getting closer. The final stretch to the cabin was fast and easy. Even though Abby made the journey in record time, she felt as if she'd been traveling forever.

Abby called Jesse's name as she ran toward the cabin. Her heart sank the instant she opened the cabin door; Jesse wasn't there and hadn't been since they left together. The cabin had the same empty, unoccupied feel it had when she first visited. She dropped into the chair by the fireplace and cried into her hands.

Toby placed the rifle on the table and went to Abby. He patted her on the back. "It's all r-r-right."

Remembering her promise to Jesse, Abby wiped her eyes and stood. "Toby, why don't you have a seat at the table and I'll get you something to eat," she said. She offered him a large piece of jerky from Jesse's supply. The dried meat seemed to mollify him, giving Abby a chance to let her mind run through several different scenarios. None of them ended well. *Jesse, where are you?*

Toby finished the snack. His eyelids were so heavy he could barely keep them open.

"Why don't you go lay down and get some sleep?" Abby said.

Toby said nothing. He walked to the bed and fell asleep quickly.

The blanket beneath Toby brought back memories of the incredible night she and Jesse shared under the stars. A fresh round of tears flowed freely. She sat at the table, distraught, weighing her options. She knew what she had to do. The thought of having to head straight back down the mountain was overwhelming, but she had no choice.

If Jesse wasn't here, then they would have to keep looking. She decided when Toby woke, they would start the trip back down. Abby wouldn't stop looking until she found Jesse, dead or alive.

I'm just going to rest my eyes for a minute. She rested her head on the table and closed her eyes.

Abby woke with a start when she heard a noise out on the front porch. She jumped up, knocking the chair over in her haste to get to the door. *Jesse's here, thank God.*

She flung the door wide open. Her mouth dropped and her stomach sank. She stepped back. *Oh, God. Indians.* It never crossed her mind she would need protection. Jesse had told her repeatedly no one knew about this place. No one knew how to cross the river.

She was totally defenseless, no rifle within reach. Fear took hold. She knew what these men were capable of. Her first thought was to protect Toby. Before she could move, the men in front of her stepped aside, revealing a third man approaching the cabin. He carried Jesse's limp body.

Forgetting her fear, Abby pushed past the men on the porch. She rushed to Jesse, lying cold, blue, and motionless in the stranger's arms. *He's dead!* Invisible hands choked Abby, rendering her speechless. When she finally found her voice again, she cried out, "What happened?"

Toby watched in silence as the man carried the lifeless body into the cabin. He gently lay Jesse on the bed. An old native man followed, skin so aged by the sun it seemed to be made of leather. His hair was pure white and held in place at the back of his head by a leather thong. He said nothing, nor did the three beautiful native women who trailed behind him.

One of the women grabbed Abby softly by the arm. "Come, let him give medicine," she said, motioning for both Abby and Toby to follow her outside. The woman closed the door behind them.

The two women who remained in the cabin stripped Jesse of her clothes. The old man tended to the infected wounds. Jesse was barely alive. They would do everything they could to save her, though the situation was grave.

Outside, Abby approached the man who carried Jesse to the cabin. "What happened?" she said, pleading with him again.

"Me Kaga. My people keep eye on river between trees. If white man cross, we know if 'em walk this side of river. My people see you cross. Running Bear track you. Follow up mountain. White Feather see Burning Bush laying other side of river. White Feather get Burning Bush. Little Deer run to village. Get help for Burning Bush. Burning Bush shot. We go. Help White Feather bring Burning Bush to white man home. Tribe friend to Burning Bush."

Why did I leave Jesse with those two? I should have stayed. Abby tried to process the information. She understood they called Jesse 'Burning Bush', but she was surprised to learn they considered Jesse a friend. Not once had Jesse mentioned an association with them.

Abby asked, "You're friends with Jess—I mean, Burning Bush?"

"It long story," Kaga said. "You sit, I tell. Many, many moons ago, we go Dothka village to talk white man problem. Meet white couple. Lost son. Dothka welcomed white couple. 'Em good people. My tribe make trade with white couple. We bring 'em up mountain. They teach my tribe white man talk. Must know white man talk. We know 'em come someday. Good trade for tribe. We build white man shelter with white couple," he says, pointing to the cabin. "Nathaniel was name. Wife of white man, taught tribe white man talk. Great Spirit come for Nathaniel. Tribe keep eye on Frieda. She good to us. We good to her. We friend to Frieda. She sad for many moons. White woman have no people on mountain."

"But she had Jess—Burning Bush. I don't understand," Abby said, brow pinched in confusion.

"Many moons ago, Lonato hunt bear, see white girl with hair of fire in woods. Lonato track bear. Bear track girl. Bear want to eat girl. Lonato kill bear. Lonato bring girl to Frieda. Same skin go together. Frieda no more sad. Tribe talk to Frieda. Best we no tell girl about tribe. If white man come for girl, girl tell 'bout tribe. Tribe secret on mountain. Tribe no trust white man. Tribe always on mountain. Tribe live other side. Frieda need tribe she put eagle feather in hole in tree in meadow. We watch. Always keep eye on Frieda and girl. Frieda take good care of girl. Girl grow. Great Spirit come for Frieda. Tribe keep eye on girl with hair of fire."

A woman opened the door and asked for more water. A young man took the bucket of bloody water and poured it out on the ground before fetching fresh water from the stream.

"What happened to the girl?" Abby asked, looking back at Kaga, her mind still unable to put all the pieces together.

Kaga pointed to the cabin and said, "There Burning Bush. After Great Spirit come for Frieda, Burning Bush cut hair of fire. Leave mountain."

For a moment, Abby was lost. A vice tightened around her chest as she understood. *Jesse was the little girl in the woods!* Blood rushed from Abby's face and she felt like she might be sick. She squeezed her eyes shut as she tried to understand.

Jesse was the little girl from Granite Falls who went missing after her family was murdered. The possibility tore at her heart. She didn't want it to be true but the circumstances were starting to add up. Abby understood why Jesse wanted those two men out in the woods. Why Toby was so important. Why Jesse shied away from her insistent advances.

Abby's vision blurred. It was too much to take in all at once. Her head felt light and her body had started to shake. Kaga noticed Abby's condition, perhaps due to a change in her color. He grabbed her by the shoulders to steady her. His lips moved silently. The only thing audible was the sound of her own blood pumping through her ears. It took a moment to come to her senses. She nodded to assure Kaga she was in control once more.

Abby had been distantly aware of the voices coming from inside the cabin. Now, the rhythmic chanting ended and a woman motioned for her to come inside. Abby entered the cabin with trepidation. Jesse was on the bed, covered with blankets. The old man standing next to the bed finally spoke. "Now up to Great Spirit."

Abby nodded her appreciation. He left without another word.

A woman sat silently on the bed, wiping Jesse's face with a cool rag. Abby kept her distance, choosing to stand in the doorway.

Outside, the women prepared a freshly killed deer. The men tended to a large fire out by the stream. *It's obvious these people care about her*, Abby thought. Not yet ready to face Jesse, she went outside and took a seat by the fire. Her mind was somewhere else as she watched the women prepare food.

As dusk turned to shadow, the native people sang and danced around the blazing fire. After taking their turns tending to Jesse, the women also joined in the dancing. Abby didn't understand their chants, but found their movements and harmonies beautiful.

Toby, who had spent most of the night sitting quietly, jumped to his feet. He did his best to imitate the native dance. Even though her heart was broken, Abby smiled as he clumsily hopped from one foot to the other around the fire, his own chants mixing in with the chorus.

A woman grabbed Abby by the arm and tried to get her to stand. "You dance, Great Spirit come. Heal Burning Bush," she said. Abby had no desire to partake in their dance, but understood their belief. Somehow, the dancing would call the Great Spirit to save Jesse. She stood and accepted the invitation, and although challenging at first, it wasn't long before she found her rhythm. Toby and the others looked on, smiling, as Abby lost herself in the dance. It was only temporary, but she let herself forget about the pain tearing her up inside.

After dancing and feasting late into the night, the natives settled in various spots around the fading fire. Abby asked Toby if he wanted to come inside, but he preferred to sleep under the stars with his new friends.

Abby paused for a moment, her back against the weathered door. Her emotions were turbulent, barely held in check as she approached the bed where Jesse's restless body lay. She floated across the cabin as if in a nightmare. She replaced the rag on Jesse's burning forehead. She wondered if it was the fever causing

Jesse's restlessness, or if it was something more deeply rooted that haunted her.

The emotional onslaught was relentless. She was relieved Jesse was alive yet angry with her for the deception. Abby felt violated. Confusion painted everything. *It has all been a lie. Since the first day we met, nothing but a lie. How could I have been so stupid?*

Abby's mind wandered back to the evening they spent by the fire. She had no idea another woman could make her feel that way. She had never been attracted to a woman before, never thought about it.

She took a seat on one of the old wooden chairs near the fireplace. Staring at the flames, her mind raced. There were so many times she should have known Jesse was a woman: Jesse's modesty; the reluctance to be intimate; why she was never allowed to touch her.

The man she loved more than anything in the world wasn't a man at all. Abby's anger turned to grief. All she had wanted was to be with Jesse, and now those hopes and dreams had been destroyed. Abby was left with nothing. Silent tears rolled off her flushed cheeks and landed soundlessly in her lap. So caught up in her angst, she didn't hear the door open. She jumped when a hand settled lightly on her shoulder.

It was the native woman who had persuaded her to dance earlier. "My name is Aponi. Don't cry. Burning Bush doing better. I think Great Spirit will save her."

"I hope so."

"Did you know Frieda, too?" the woman asked.

"No, I never got to meet her, but I've heard a lot about her. Did you know her?"

"Oh, yes. Frieda was a great woman. Kind spirit. She was my teacher long ago. I used to come here when I was a child. We'd sit out front and she would teach us. Sometimes she would come to our village and teach us."

"I notice you speak my language quite well."

"Some of us speak your language better than others. Older

people in my tribe had a harder time learning the new language back then. They were, how you say, old dogs no tricks. It was easier for us younger ones to learn it, and we have continued to teach our children your language over the years. It's important that they learn it too."

Can't teach an old dog new tricks. Abby smiled inwardly at Aponi's misinterpretation. "Do you live far away?"

"Not far. Half a day's walk, if you know the way. You should come to village." Aponi smiled.

"I'd like that. I'm sure Jesse would like to see your village, too."

"Jesse? That's Burning Bush's white man name?"

"Yes it is. Well, that's what I've always called her."

"You and Jesse are welcome at our village. You in love with Jesse?"

The question stunned Abby. *Why would she think that?* The idea disarmed her. If asked the question hours earlier, the answer would have been yes, without a doubt. A lot had changed, though, in a short time. Abby was unsure what she felt.

"Honestly, I don't know what I feel anymore."

"I saw you when we brought her here. You really care about her. I call it love."

"Well, I do care about her. Don't wish her any harm. But things aren't always as they seem."

"What do you mean?"

"I don't know if I can even say it out loud." Abby felt her face burn, knew she was turning bright red.

"You can tell to me. Maybe I can help."

Abby took in a deep breath. The words came out in a rush. "I'm not sure why, but Jesse pretended to be a man. I don't know why she would do that. I fell in love with a man, not a woman. I don't even know who that person is." Abby pointed an accusing finger at Jesse.

Aponi scooted her chair closer and said, "Sometimes some women love women and some men love men. Some women dress like men and some men dress like women. Not all men like to hunt for meat. Some like to pick berries. Not all women like to pick berries but like to hunt for meat. We call them Ashatas."

"Ashatas? What does it mean?"

"They have more than one spirit. The Great Spirit chose them to be special." Aponi paused, maintaining eye contact. Finally, she nodded once and spoke again. "I have to go now. You sleep. I'll see you tomorrow."

"I'll try, and thank you."

Abby spent the long night tending to Jesse, her mind reeling as she tried to come to terms with the chaos that was now her life.

CHAPTER TWENTY-THREE

All throughout the night, Jesse tossed, calling out in her frail voice. Abby, overwrought about Jesse's fragile condition, tamped down her own tumultuous thoughts, and focused solely on caring for the woman still clinging to life.

In the early morning hours, Abby noticed a slight change in Jesse's color. Her cheeks, so ashen and corpse-like, gained back a hint of pink. "That's a good sign. Thank God," she whispered. Abby lay her head on the bed. She was beyond tired. Sleep took her quickly.

"Abby, wake up." A distant voice, muffled as if underwater, tugged at the back of her consciousness. "Abby". She felt her body move. "Abby, w-w-wake up." She jumped up, ignoring the hand on her shoulder, panicked thinking Jesse was gone. Jesse's cheeks still had color, rendering Abby's fears premature. Abby thanked God again. She shifted her gaze on Toby.

"S-s-s-sorry I w-w-woke you. I'm gonna go huntin' w-with 'em." Toby pointed over his shoulder at two men standing in the doorway. "I d-d-didn't want you t-to worry."

"Don't be sorry. I'm glad you let me know. Thank you."

"I'll b-be back later."

"All right. Be careful." Abby gave Toby's arm a gentle squeeze.

"I will." As Toby left the cabin, two women came in to relieve Abby and took over tending to Jesse.

Abby thanked them and went outside. She stepped onto the porch, hands on the small of her back, shivering in the cool morning air. She was exhausted, but grateful for the break. She had not been alone in days, and she needed some time alone to think. Abby started walking, and found herself at the spot where Jesse had taken her fishing. The rock where they sat together seemed like the perfect place to rest. She sat and stared into the current.

Inside the cabin, Jesse stirred. Squinting, she tried to get her eyes to focus on the blurred figures of the two women standing over her. After a few seconds, she recognized her surroundings. She was in her own home, in her own bed. She had no recollection of getting there. Her last memory was collapsing to the ground by the river. The end, or so she'd thought.

The women explained to her how she was found at the bottom of the mountain and carried home so her wounds could be treated. The severity of her injuries came rushing back. She flipped the blankets in a panic, expecting to see festering damage, a death sentence. Her heart went light when she saw how well it was healing.

Toby! It came back to her in an instant. Her brother was still alive. Toby was with Abby.

Abby, I have to get to Abby. Jesse tried to sit up, sending pain shooting through her body. She was in no condition to go anywhere. There was no way to get word to Abby, who must have been frantic.

Jesse looked up at the figures standing by the bed. She had no idea who they were or where they had come from. The only obvious thing about them was they had been caring for her. In a voice raspy and thin from disuse, she asked for her clothes, explaining she needed to go outside. They helped her dress. Although movement was painful, the trio made their way slowly to the outhouse.

"That's Lonato," one of the women informed Jesse, pointing out a tall, older man. "He found you in the woods and brought you here long ago."

"No," Jesse said. "Frieda did."

The two other women exchanged a knowing glance. As the women helped Jesse back to the cabin, they asked Kaga and Lonato to come inside. Kaga pulled a chair next to the bed and repeated the same story he told Abby the day before.

Jesse couldn't believe it at first. It didn't line up with what she'd always believed, for years, living up on the mountain. The more she repeated the facts Kaga gave her, the more she realized it all added up. Frieda hadn't wanted anyone to know about the native village on top of Mount Perish, not even her, ensuring their clandestine existence.

It all made sense now. When Nathaniel and Frieda were with the Dothka tribe, they agreed to go to California and teach these kindly people the English language. In turn, they were free to live on the beautiful portion of land atop Mount Perish.

Taking Lonato's strong hand in her weakened one, Jesse said, "Thank you for saving my life. I'm not sure how to repay you for all that you've done for me. If I can ever do anything for you, just ask, and consider it done."

"You go off mountain. Did you tell white man about tribe?" Lonato asked.

"No. I didn't even know you lived up here. Frieda never told me about you or your tribe."

"Frieda keep word. No tell about Tribe. Tribe want you no tell about tribe."

"I swear on my life. I will never tell anyone."

Lonato nodded. "You come to village soon. Want to talk about white men. We go now. You rest."

They went outside, leaving Jesse alone with the two women. One of them approached the bed and gave her a cup of liquid, which she drank without question. It wasn't the coffee she wanted and half expected. Her face contorted, the acrid taste overwhelming her senses. She should have expected as much. It tasted like something Frieda would have given her.

Jesse's thoughts shifted back to Abby and Toby. Abby must have been worried. She wanted more than anything to get back to them. There was no way she could make the trip now. Her wounds may have been healing, but she was still a long way from being able to make that journey again. Jesse lay back down, trying to find a comfortable position in the old, familiar bed. Her mind raced, in no condition for sleep. Jesse was oblivious to the women talking quietly amongst themselves at the table. Their conversation nothing more than chatter in the background—until she heard it. She wasn't sure she heard right.

"Abby. You know Abby?" Jesse called out.

"Yes," one of the women said. "Abby and Toby outside."

Relief they were there and safe quickly turned to horror when Jesse realized her worst nightmare had come true. Abby knew. She had to. Jesse's racing thoughts ground to a cloudy halt. She felt heavy. Perhaps there was strong medicine in the drink they had given her, or perhaps it was the utter shock of understanding Abby must now know the truth.

Her vision blurred. As sleep claimed her, her final thoughts were gratitude to have found her long lost brother, and grief in knowing she had undoubtedly lost Abby forever.

At the fishing hole, Abby still didn't know what to feel. She was relieved Jesse was alive, but she was also angry, hurt, and felt like a fool. *How could I have been so blind?* She sat, lost in a world that had been turned upside down.

From the corner of her eye, Abby saw Aponi approaching. She was not alone. "I went to my village after talking with you. I want you to meet Honovi and Onawa. They love each other greatly. Live in same teepee. Honovi is woman who likes hunt meat not berries."

Honovi was of average height, well-built, and muscular. Prominent cheekbones defined her face. She was quite stunning. Her hair, long and black, shined in the sunlight. She was dressed in the same traditional clothing Abby had seen the native men wearing around their waists. Her long hair covered her bare chest. Onawa, slim and graceful in a beaded leather tunic, was as beautiful. Colored beads adorned her long black hair, tied back with a leather strap.

Abby said, "It's nice to meet you." She treaded lightly. She was afraid to offend anyone, but very curious about their relationship. "So, you two are like a couple?"

"Yes. For many moons," Honovi said in her husky voice. "Me always loved Onawa. Since small, always knew Onawa one for me."

Onawa looked up at Honovi. It was obvious from the gaze of their locked eyes how much they loved each other. Abby had never met two women in love, but the couple didn't seem odd. In fact, they seemed perfectly natural together.

Aponi smiled. "They're two women who love each other. Theirs is a great love. Jesse can do anything a man can do, yes? So why does it matter if Jesse likes to hunt for meat instead of picking berries. Love is love. What you feel for Jesse. I say it's love."

"I appreciate what you're trying to do. And it's been a pleasure meeting you two. I just need time to figure it all out. Thank you, though."

"You'll know what to do, just follow your heart. We leave you now," Aponi said. They turned and walked away, leaving Abby to contemplate her feelings.

Abby watched a leaf float by, carried along on the surface of the water. She felt as if she, too, was being carried along with no control over where things were going. She returned to the cabin to find Toby sitting on the grass, trying to teach some of the tribe how to play cards. She could tell by their faces they had no idea what they were doing. For all she knew, Toby had no idea either, but it was keeping him occupied, smiling, and content.

As she approached the cabin, one of the women came outside

to tell her Jesse had awoken. Abby took Toby inside and sat him on the bed next to Jesse.

"Toby, this is your sister," Abby said.

"Hi, Toby, it's me. Jessica."

"B-B-Berry?" Toby said, confusion twisting his brow.

"Yes!" Tears pooled in Jesse's eyes. It had been years since someone had called her Berry. Although it felt good to hear it again, it made her chest tight. She was beyond happy to have him here. The full weight of everything the two of them had lost threatened to take her breath away. She focused on his face and controlled her breathing. Toby tugged on her short locks, his face unable to hide his confusion.

"I had to cut if off," Jesse said. "Don't worry, it'll grow back."

Abby stood in the doorway, watching as the siblings shared their first hug after years of separation. The reunion made her realize how precious life was. How Jesse could have been ripped from her life in an instant. All it took was one hug; one unbreakable-familial bond to give her hope that everything might turn out all right after all. With a renewed sense of understanding, she turned and left the cabin.

"They're g-g-gone. Thought you gone too. What happened?" Toby asked.

"Don't you remember?" she asked, brushing his bangs out of the way. The scar didn't look as hideous as it had when she first saw it, but it still hurt her to look at.

"No. Woke up—everyb-b-body gone."

Jesse knew full well what happened. Telling Toby the graphic details would do him no good. It was better to let that day lie in the shadows. The truth was too hard to live with. Jesse knew this first hand, having lived with it eleven years.

"It was a bad accident. They're all together in heaven. Someday you and I will see them again." She leaned up and kissed the scar, still in shock her brother made it out alive that night. She wasn't sure what happened to him that day and would probably never know. The important thing was that he was alive and they were together again.

Jesse couldn't get over how much Toby resembled Daniel. He was so tall and handsome, but his mind still functioned like the boy she remembered. No matter what, she would take care of her big brother from this day forward. Jesse sat on the side of the bed, wincing from the effort. Toby helped her to her feet. She stood with her arm on his shoulder, testing her legs to make sure they were strong enough to hold her weight without assistance.

The two women sitting at the table spoke in their native tongue. Unbeknownst to them, Jesse could understand everything they were saying. They abruptly stopped talking as she approached, standing to help her walk.

"Eo dik e settay."

Their mouths dropped open when their words came from the white woman's tongue. Jesse had never understood why Frieda insisted she learn the strange language. Now, that too made sense.

Toby asked, "What did you s-s-say?"

"I told them I'm fine, good medicine."

After being on her feet for a few minutes, it was clear that recovery was within her grasp. She'd need to regain her strength soon if she wanted any hope of getting prepared for winter. Standing in the doorway, Jesse happened upon a scene she was not at all expecting—native men and women everywhere, some busy smoking meat, some busy cleaning berries. Jesse was unable to hunt, so they made sure she had enough food to last while she was on the mend. She would be forever grateful to them, and had no idea how to start paying back a debt like this.

Abby worked right alongside them. The mere sight of her was enough to break Jesse's heart. She turned her head away, hiding the pain on her face from Abby. After keeping her secret for so long, she thought she would be able to hide her emotions better. She could not. She had hurt Abby deeply and probably destroyed their relationship. The thought was too much, too painful. She walked back inside, leaving the work to those strong enough to do it.

Abby continued to think about the couple she met, and the things Aponi said. The more she thought about it, the more she understood. At least, she thought she did. Jesse had told her several times they could never be together as man and wife. She pursued Jesse, not the other way around. It wasn't all Jesse's fault. She needed to start accepting her part of the blame.

It occurred to her in that moment Jesse probably had good cause for posing as a man. Jesse wasn't frivolous, and didn't seem to do things without having a good reason. There was only one way to find out, but Abby wasn't ready to have that conversation yet.

∼

Jesse stepped out onto the porch the next afternoon. A darkening sky and gusty winds greeted her. A storm approached. She could tell by the activity her new friends were in a hurry to be on their way.

As Jesse thanked everyone for all of their help, she noticed Abby and Aponi off by themselves. Her sense of apprehension grew. Once they were alone, a confrontation was inescapable. Judging by Abby's expression, she knew it wasn't going to be good. She was thankful Toby was there to act as a buffer between them. The dark clouds grew. The brewing storm would pale in comparison to the one about to happen inside the weathered cabin. Jesse sighed and retreated back inside to await the inevitable.

"Abby, do you want Little Deer to take you down the mountain?" Aponi asked.

Leaving was something she hadn't considered and the question caught her off guard. She had never met anyone like Jesse. She was kind, strong, and gentle, and Abby liked the way she felt when she was around her. She couldn't imagine her life without Jesse in it.

Smiling, Abby said, "I'm going to stay to make sure Jesse gets her strength back."

"I'll be back soon. Want to come check on Jesse. And you," Aponi said.

After waving their goodbyes, Abby walked inside the cabin to find Jesse and Toby sitting at the table sipping on hot coffee. "I could use some of that myself. How are you feeling?" Abby poured herself a cup.

"Sore, but I can manage," Jesse said with a cautious smile. She liked hearing Abby's voice again. At the very least, she was grateful to speak to her again. Sitting together at the table, Toby dealt the cards for the three of them. As they played, Jesse tried to tease information out of Toby as to what had happened to him.

Jacob Carlson found Toby that night and took him to Doc Tilson, who mended his head wound. Jesse was baffled as to how Jacob came to find Toby that night. She couldn't imagine why he would have been at their house. After Toby recovered, he had an arrangement with the owner of the stables. Toby cared for the horses in return for a bunk in the tack room and two hot meals a day.

The thought of Toby living in a barn all this time hurt Jesse's aching heart even more. She blinked tears from her eyes and hoped nobody noticed in the light of the fire. The sadness, soreness, and tiredness conspired to take Jesse down for the night. She excused herself to bed.

Abby prepared some food. After getting Toby settled in at the table, she took a plate to Jesse. They finished their meal as they listened to the rain pound in the darkness. Toby climbed the ladder. It wasn't long before his snores reverberated down from the loft. Abby got up from the table and walked toward Jesse. A loud clap of thunder echoed through the cabin.

Ah, Jesse thought, *here comes the real storm.* Jesse began, her voice low and pleading, "I am so sor—"

Abby raised a quieting hand as she sat down on the bed. "So, do you like pretending to be a man?" she asked, crossing her arms over her chest.

"No! Of course I don't. I never wanted to do it in the first place. But I was scared to go into a town looking like myself. After what happened to me when I was young, I wasn't sure what to expect. Frieda and I thought it would be best to disguise myself, so I'd be safe. I was only going there to check things out. I never imagined I would meet someone like you. I didn't even know I could feel this way about someone. It just happened. I wanted to tell you so many times, but I was scared to tell you. I didn't want to lose you."

"When I found out, you know, that you're a woman, I was shocked. I honestly had no idea that you were—are a woman. It never crossed my mind. Ever!"

"I never meant…"

"I felt like a fool and I was so mad at you for lying to me all this time."

"I'm so sorry. I didn't mean… I never meant to hurt you. I really wanted to tell you."

"I have spent a lot of time thinking about you. About us. I know in my heart you would never do anything to hurt me. I still trust you with my life."

"I hate that I wasn't honest with you from the start. The whole thing just snowballed out of control and I let it. I wish I could go back to the night I met you. If I could, I would do things a lot different. I had no idea I was going to end up having feelings like this. I didn't even know I could ever feel this way about anyone."

Abby nodded, a single tear escaping down her cheek. "Jesse. That night. I knew the first time I saw you that you were different. Not like anyone I had ever met, and the more I got to know you the more I wanted to be around you."

"I wanted to be around you, too. I know it's wrong, but I can't help the way I feel about you," Jesse said, her voice breaking under the weight of her confession.

"Jesse," Abby said, taking her hand, "right or wrong, I really don't care. I don't care what you look like underneath your clothes. You are the most loving and caring person I have ever met. I do want to be with you, regardless."

"I want to be with you too, more than I have ever wanted anything. But I live here and your life is down there."

Abby shook her head. "I've realized my life is wherever you are. Up here or down there, I don't care where we end up. As long as we are together, that's what matters."

Jesse pulled Abby down into an awkward but heartfelt embrace, her heart overflowing with emotion. "It's been a long day. Will you stay here with me tonight?" Jesse asked, pulling back the blanket.

Abby crawled under the blanket next to Jesse. Both women, on their backs, looked up at the loft above them. Abby asked, "Are you attracted to men?"

Jesse reached up and rubbed her temple. "I don't think so, but I know I'm supposed to be. I can remember my mother telling me that one day I'd grow up, get married, and have kids of my own. But after the things I've seen, I'm not sure I could ever let one touch me without thinking about my sister. Maybe I should never leave Mount Perish again, and then I wouldn't have to worry about such things."

Abby turned her head and asked, "Tell me what happened that day."

"Abby, I saw things. Horrible things. Things no one should ever have to see."

"Will you tell me?"

"Are you sure you want to know? It's hard to hear."

"Yes, please. I want to know everything about you."

"I was only ten and already thought I knew it all." Jesse rolled her eyes. "I knew nothing. I was a stupid kid. I saw," Jesse cleared the lump from her throat, "everything that day. I stayed home that morning by myself and went fishing. My father and older brother, Daniel, were out hunting. Mother, Toby, and my sister, Jamie, went to Granite Falls to pick up some things we needed. Later that day when I got home, I ran into Toby out in the barn. We heard our mother and Jamie scream. Toby told me to hide in the stall with the horse. I was so scared. I buried myself in the hay."

Abby placed her hand on Jesse's arm.

"Toby ran to the house. I didn't know what was happening. I was too scared to move. It seemed like I waited in that hay for hours, but I'm sure it was only minutes. I can still smell the hay. I heard someone coming to the barn. I thought it was Toby, but I was wrong. Are you sure you want me to keep going?"

"Yes, I want to know," Abby said, reassuring her. She held onto Jesse's forearm.

"It wasn't Toby. It was Jamie, only she wasn't alone. That blond guy I killed by the waterfall was with her. I saw him throw her down, kick her, and…" Jesse swallowed hard. "He raped her. I saw it all."

Abby gasped. "Oh, Jesse, I'm so sorry." She rolled onto her side and placed her head on Jesse's chest.

Jesse wrapped her arm around Abby and continued. "After he finished with her, they left the barn and I heard Jamie scream again. I had to see what happened to her. I found a knothole in the barn wall and I saw Jamie holding Toby. His face was covered with blood. He wasn't moving. I thought he was dead. I think Jamie did, too. There were four men there that day, and three of them were standing over Toby. The other was still in the house with my mother."

Jesse swallowed another lump and fought back tears. "I didn't know it then, but I know in my heart that the man in the house was raping my mother." She exhaled a long breath, trying to keep her chin from trembling.

Abby clung to Jesse's shirt.

"I saw the blond guy take Jamie back into the house, and two of the men rode off. I don't know how long it was, but then I saw my father and Daniel. They were coming back from their hunt. I wanted to yell to them and tell them there were two men in the house but I couldn't make a sound. I tried. Nothing came out. As soon as they opened the door, the men inside shot them. I saw them fall on the porch."

Abby lifted a hand over her open mouth.

"Are you sure you want me to keep going? It gets worse."

How could it get any worse? Abby placed a comforting hand on Jesse's chest. "Please. I want to know what you went through."

"I don't know if I can. This part is almost more than I can handle."

Abby leaned up on her elbow to look into Jesse's eyes. "You don't have to go on."

Still holding onto Abby's shoulder with her right hand, Jesse used the other to clear the tears from Abby's eyes. "I want you to know everything about my life. Just give me second."

Abby placed her head on Jesse's chest again. She lightly rubbed her fingers on the soft skin of Jesse's neck.

"After they killed my father and Daniel, I kept waiting for them to leave. It seemed like they were in there forever. Of course, I just stayed in the barn like a coward."

Abby's hand stopped. "Jesse, you are no coward. For God sakes, you were a ten-year-old girl!"

"Still, it hurts me so much that I didn't do anything. I should have tried harder. Maybe I could have saved them."

"They would have killed you."

"Sometimes I wonder if that would have been better. Living with this has been so hard."

"Don't say that. I can't imagine what you went through, but I'm glad you stayed in the barn. There was nothing you could have done."

"Frieda told me the same thing."

"Well, Frieda was a smart woman."

"Yes, she was." Jesse smiled at the thought of her old mentor. The smile vanished. "Those men finally came outside."

Abby clutched Jesse's shirt in a fist, knowing what was to come would only be more horrific.

"I was so happy that they were finally leaving. I couldn't wait to run to my mother and Jamie." Jesse cleared her throat before taking a big swallow. A loud clap of thunder ricocheted through the cabin, flashing lighting brightening the room through the lone window.

Abby squeezed Jesse's shirt tighter in her fist. "You don't have to say anymore. I know your mother and Jamie were inside and they had already killed them before they walked out." A long silence hung in the air. A warm breath blew across Abby's face. Jesse's hand squeezed her shoulder.

Then, Jesse let it all out in a rush. "I didn't know it, but when they came out, they had already set the house on fire. Abby, they burned my mother and sister, alive. I heard their screams. I still hear their screams. I'll never stop hearing their screams."

Tears streamed and a body trembled, only this time it was Abby experiencing the terror.

"Are you all right? I knew I probably shouldn't have told you."

Abby leaned up on her elbow again. "I'm so glad you killed them, but a bullet was too gracious. They should have suffered more. A lot more."

Jesse wiped away Abby's tears with a thumb. "The man that raped Jamie. Well, I shot him first, but not to kill him. Abs, I shot him in, you know, down there. I told him that was for my sister. Then I killed him."

Three consecutive claps of thunder rattled the cabin, shaking dust from the ceiling.

Abby waited for the rumbling to stop. *Why tell her it was Jake and Clay Roberts?* Abby thought. *Putting names to the faces won't change anything.* "If any man deserved that it was most definitely him," Abby said. "How'd you get shot?"

"I didn't know the other one had another gun. By the time I realized it, well, we both fired at the same time. I was just lucky my shot was better than his that night."

"I'm glad they're dead. Just think how many more lives you have saved by ridding the world of them."

"Still, I have blood on my hands. I took two lives. I had no right."

"We both do, Jesse. But I sleep really good at night knowing men like them and my late husband can't hurt us or anyone else anymore."

"I guess so."

A loud snore emanated from the loft above. "Sounds like someone is sleeping good tonight," Abby said, looking up at Jesse.

"Sheesh, he's loud. I think he is shaking the cabin. Probably won't be any shingles left on the roof in the morning." Jesse smiled down at Abby.

A smile spread across Abby's face for a moment before melting. She looked longingly into Jesse's eyes. Overwhelmed with emotion after hearing about the losses Jesse had suffered, she desperately craved solace.

"What is it?" Jesse asked. "Are you all right?"

"I will be. I feel like I can't get close enough to you."

Jesse held her tighter. "That's not exactly what I had in mind. I meant, I want to be with you. Really be with you."

"You mean…"

"Yes," Abby said.

"Are you sure?"

"More sure than I've ever been."

Jesse felt her stomach flutter. "I'm not sure how. I've never been with anyone before. Like that."

"Don't worry," Abby said, getting out of bed. She began to slowly undress, staring into Jesse's eyes as she dropped her clothing on the floor beside her. Jesse's heart raced at the sight of Abby's body in the glow of the flickering firelight.

A quick flash of lightning illuminated Abby's stunning figure. The rain poured down harder and thunderclaps echoed again. If not for the sounds of the storm, Jesse would swear Abby could hear her heart beating.

Abby sat on the bed and started to unbutton Jesse's shirt. "I've never wanted anyone more than I want you," she said, confessing out loud what her heart screamed inside of her.

"I want you, too, but we can't do this. Toby is right there," Jesse whispered, pointing to the loft above.

"We'll be quiet. Besides, he's a sound sleeper. He snores so loud the fish outside can hear him, so don't worry about him hearing anything." Abby smiled as she continued unbuttoning Jesse's shirt. After helping Jesse out of the rest her clothing, being careful not to touch the poultice-covered wound on her back, Abby tossed them next to hers. Unlike so many times in the past, she was met with no resistance at all.

Jesse's body was incredible, muscular and gorgeous. Abby felt more attraction than she ever thought possible. She knew how she felt about Jesse on an emotional level, but being attracted to her physically was something she had never expected.

For the first time ever, the two lay against each other with no barriers between their bodies. Abby lowered the blanket and settled herself atop Jesse's pelvis. Another rumble of thunder shook the cabin.

Abby caressed Jesse's body, lightly, running her fingers over shoulders, arms, and stomach. She took her time. Savored every inch. "You're so beautiful," she whispered, pulling her closer. Their lips met, and their tongues followed suit, intertwined in a battle neither wanted to end.

She felt Jesse's body tremble. "Are you all right?"

"Um-hum, I'm just nervous," Jesse said, her voice uneven.

"I was nervous my first time too. Do you want me to stop?"

"No," Jesse said shyly, "it's just...I've never had anyone touch me like this."

"I'd never do anything to hurt you."

"I know you wouldn't."

Abby kissed her again; let her lips trail along Jesse's jawline, all the way to the soft skin of her neck. She nibbled lightly, a hand tracing along the contours of Jesse's toned stomach. Jesse's body twitched again. Abby looked into hesitant green eyes. "We can stop whenever you want," she murmured. "Just say so."

"All right." Jesse's voice and body quivered. She had experienced some frightening things in her life. Nothing had prepared her for this.

Abby's hand was more insistent now, moving lower. She drank Jesse up—her thirst unquenchable.

Jesse sucked in a breath as her body trembled again. The sensation was an explosion coursing through her body. She bit down so hard in an effort to keep quiet she thought her teeth might shatter. Abby smiled knowingly as Jesse shuddered next to her.

Jesse guided Abby onto her back; wrapped herself into her as she made her way to Abby's chest. She showered her with kisses from the soft curve of her neck all the way down to her navel.

Abby was the one trembling now.

Barely whispering a kiss on the small indentation, Jesse quickly made her way back to Abby's lips. Parting once more, she left Abby wanting, trailing lower across hills and valleys of heated skin. Abby laced her fingers through the fiery hair. Jesse didn't have to think about what to do. She did what felt right. She kissed the warm inner thighs that beckoned for her, before exploring deeper.

Jesse knew from Abby's sounds and movements she was pleasing her. She felt Abby's hips rise, begging for her. Jesse lay on top of her, their tongues colliding as her hand wandered between Abby's thighs. Their bodies rocked together in harmony, slowly at first, then building in speed and intensity.

With each movement, Jesse became more aroused. The sensation caused her to increase her momentum. They moved in perfect rhythm together as if they had danced this dance a thousand times. Beads of sweat trickled off their bodies from the heat of their love.

Abby dug her nails into Jesse's back. The sting only served to fuel her fire. Thunderclaps, and the drumming of the pouring rain on the old wooden roof, masked the sounds of their lovemaking. Abby arched her back as she panted in Jesse's ear. "Oh…oh my God. Oh…it feels incredible," she said, her voice breaking.

Their moans grew louder and longer until they both exploded in ecstasy.

Jesse's heart sank when she saw the tears. "Abs, I'm sorry. I didn't mean to hurt you."

"You didn't hurt me," she said, a blush to her cheeks. "It's just…well, I've never felt like this before. It was incredible. You were incredible."

Afterward, in Abby's embrace, Jesse was overwhelmed with emotions. No longer able to hold them back, she trembled as her own tears spilled over. Never in her life had she felt so connected to someone else. Her core shifted to make room for the intense love growing inside her. "Abs, I love you," she said, looking into Abby's eyes, her tone soft and timid.

Although the voice was one Abby had never heard before, she knew right away whose voice it was. Jesse had always been so tough and guarded, and it surprised Abby to see her so vulnerable. Knowing exactly how it feels to love someone so completely, Abby held her tighter as she said, "I love you too, Jessica Pratt."

The adventure continues in The Devil Behind Us,
book two of The Devil Series.

ACKNOWLEDGMENTS

I'd like to thank you, the reader, for picking up my book. I truly hope you enjoy my little story.

Thank you Paul Saylor and Amy Mullen. I couldn't have done this without you. You each hold a special place in my heart and I am forever grateful.

Thank you to Erica at Serendipity Formats for creating the beautiful book cover and formatting my manuscript.

I also want to thank some wonderful people who had a hand in helping me make this story what it is. Michael Christopher, Stephanie Dolan, Andrew Donaldson, Tosha Futrell, Sue Hurst, Kenzie Lynn, Jenn Mishler, and my mother, Linda Wilson (Thank you for being my hero). Without them, this novel wouldn't have been the same. I am forever grateful to each and every one of you.

A NOTE THE AUTHOR

Dear Reader,

Thank you for reading The Devil Between Us. I truly hope you enjoyed the story as much as I enjoyed writing it. If you're inclined, please leave a review on Amazon, Goodreads, or your favorite book website. Even if it's only a few words, I'd greatly appreciate your feedback. Thank you again for your continued interest in the incredible life story of Jessica Pratt.

You can follow me on Facebook at The Devil Between Us or on Twitter @SCWilson_Author to find out more information about any upcoming novels.

The Devil Behind Us

The Devil That Broke Us

S.C. Wilson

Made in the USA
Columbia, SC
09 January 2021